THE MISSING
MATCHMAKER

Cindy Holbrook

ZEBRA BOOKS
Kensington Publishing Corp.
http://www.kensingtonbooks.com

ZEBRA BOOKS are published by

Kensington Publishing Corp.
850 Third Avenue
New York, NY 10022

All Kensington titles, imprints and distributed lines are available at special quantity discounts for bulk purchases for sales
promotion, premiums, fund-raising, educational or institu-
tional use.

Special book excerpts or customized printings can also be
created to fit specific needs. For details, write or phone the
office of the Kensington Special Sales Manager: Kensington
Publishing Corp., 850 Third Avenue, New York, NY 10022.
Attn. Special Sales Department. Phone: 1-800-221-2647.

Zebra and the Z logo Reg. U.S. Pat. & TM Off.

First Printing: December 2001
10 9 8 7 6 5 4 3 2 1

Printed in the United States of America

"DO NOT GIVE UP ON HIM, MISS THOMPSON."

"I will not." Georgie flushed, still embarrassed that her twisted ankle required her to be in Lucas's arms—and that Adams had witnessed it.

"She most certainly will give up on me," Lucas said. "Indeed, tomorrow at ten o'clock, to be exact. We will exchange the money and save Aunt Clare. Then this imbroglio will all be over."

"Indeed it will be." Georgie nodded dutifully.

Lucas narrowed his gaze upon her. "You are bamming me. Your brain is already whirling with ideas. But two can play that game, Georgette." He strolled toward the door that Adams rushed to open. "I just might turn my matchmaking skills upon you. And I have greater experience."

"I am sure I will be most excellent at it myself."

"If you use a pistol perhaps."

"Unfair." Georgette laughed. "Very unfair."

"I think I will match you with Mr. Ferret," Lucas said as he carried her out the door and down the steps.

"And I will match you with Mrs. Frampton's daughter. She is a widow and takes after Mrs. Frampton," Georgie retorted.

Suddenly the playful banter gave her pause. A very serious and frightening pause. What was she thinking? Tomorrow at ten o'clock it would be all over. As it should be. As it must be. No matter how "unlordly" Lucas was, he was still far above her touch and she mustn't forget it.

BOOK YOUR PLACE ON OUR WEBSITE
AND MAKE THE
READING CONNECTION!

We've created a customized website just for our very special readers, where you can get the inside scoop on everything that's going on with Zebra, Pinnacle and Kensington books.

When you come online, you'll have the exciting opportunity to:

- View covers of upcoming books

- Read sample chapters

- Learn about our future publishing schedule (listed by publication month *and author*)

- Find out when your favorite authors will be visiting a city near you

- Search for and order backlist books from our online catalog

- Check out author bios and background information

- Send e-mail to your favorite authors

- Meet the Kensington staff online

- Join us in weekly chats with authors, readers and other guests

- Get writing guidelines

- AND MUCH MORE!

Visit our website at
http://www.kensingtonbooks.com

One

A resounding bang echoed through the gigantic entrance hall of the Earl of Kelsey's town house. It had not gone unheard. Twenty servants came to attention. Those who were tardy in doing so jumped as Adams, the earl's butler, clapped his hands.

"Blimey, she is two hours early." A heavy-eyed footman muttered as he entered the queue that formed to the right.

"Bless her sweet heart," Mrs. Milligan, the earl's housekeeper said as she took first position in the queue to the left. " 'Tain't right how they're treating her. She ain't a criminal."

"Silence." Adams's tone was even. He studied his staff with a gimlet gaze. "Miss Wrexton will be visiting us for the next few months, while her brother, Lord Wrexton, is in foreign lands upon a *most* important diplomatic mission. He has bestowed a great honor upon our master in placing the care of such a fine lady into the earl's hands, and therefore into our hands. While she is resident, it is imperative that we do all that we can to make her and her entourage to feel welcome."

"Threw her and her kitties overboard is what Lord Wrexton did," Mrs. Milligan spouted. "Shameful I say."

"Madame?" Adams raised his brow.

"Forgive me, Mr. Adams." Mrs. Milligan's pugnacious face showed no regret.

Another bang upon the door redirected Adams's attention. He moved toward the door, but then halted. He turned and levied a stern look upon the youngest maid. "I wish to stress, before we greet Miss Wrexton, that Lord Montieth, due to his past association with her, addresses Miss Wrexton as 'Aunt Clare.' We, however, shall not employ that unpardonable familiarity with Miss Wrexton again, shall we, Jane?"

"No, Mr. Adams." She blushed. "It slipped out just that once, it did. Aunt Clare, I means, Miss Wrexton, never minded nohow."

"Simply because Miss Wrexton does not stand upon ceremony with anyone does not give you leave to lower yourself to such impropriety. It is our duty to treat her with the respect that she does not demand. I must emphasize that we have special duties in regard to Miss Wrexton since she is arriving here without any of her own servants, Lord Wrexton deeming it necessary to take his entire staff with him to France."

"Old curmudgeon," a voice whispered.

Fortunately, it was not apparent who had spoken and Adams could therefore ignore such rank disrespect with dignity. "Lord Wrexton is a great statesmen with many duties. If he saw fit to leave Miss Wrexton without one of her own servants to support her . . ." The outraged clamor that instantly arose forced him to halt. Rebellion appeared imminent. The next loud bang at the door went unattended.

"Silence." Adams clapped his hands. He sighed. "I fear I must warn you again . . . as I have before. Lord Montieth's instructions are very clear. You shall in no manner assist Miss Wrexton in any suspicious behavior. This means you are not to assist her in any schemes, plots, or ploys. If she should come to you for assistance, you must inform me."

"We're to be the poor dear's gaoler," Mrs. Milligan claimed.

The next bang upon the door was emphatic. Adams, rather defeated, spun upon his heel and went to the door. He opened the door with the grace of many years of service. He promptly pedaled backward with shock as a blast of howls and shrieks met his ears.

Before him stood a grimy urchin. The boy was silent. It was from a stack of wicker cages that the howling arose, a displeased cat entrapped within each one of them.

"Here, gov." The urchin tossed a wadded paper directly at Adams.

"I beg your pardon?" Adams caught the missile. He spoke to thin air, in regard to the urchin that was, for the lad had taken off down the street. Only the caged cats responded to Adams with plaintive howls. The earl's staff added a chorus of exclamations.

"Remain at attention!" Adams ordered. The staff, fully recognizing the sharpness of his voice, fell back into line and silence. He unwadded the paper and read it. The color drained from his face. He staggered over to a high-back ornamental chair and fell into it, heedless of its delicate cream silk damask. The staff this time remained at attention, due more to confusion than proper obedience.

"Mr. Adams?" Jane finally ventured. "Are you all right?"

"What?" Adams murmured.

"Are you all right?" Jane asked again.

Adams did not respond.

"Lawks. He's gone off into a stare," Mrs. Milligan said. "Someone go and fetch His Lordship."

The staff looked at her, looked at Adams, and looked back at her. That was the extent of their movement.

"Jane, get his lordship." Mrs. Milligan deepened her voice with authority.

"But he will still be with his valet." Jane gasped. "Mr. Adams said we should *never* interrupt . . ."

"Get him, Jane!"

The staff bent looks of commiseration upon Jane. She finally broke from the ranks and ran.

"Now let us bring those poor kitties in here." Mrs. Milligan clapped her hands together. "I can't abide their caterwauling."

"Port." Mr. Adams said in a strangled tone.

"You want some port, Mr. Adams?" Mrs. Milligan asked, her face shocked.

"No. For the cats." Adams murmured. "A quarter of a glass each."

"Yes, Mr. Adams, you just sit there." Mrs. Milligan nodded as she trounced toward the door. The others followed her, clearly pleased to have direction. She lowered her voice. "Gone off the beam he has."

It demanded the efforts of all eighteen servants to bring in the caged cats, and that only after much spitting and scratches, on the cats' part that is. The din was dreadful. It reverberated through the great stately room. Nor did it lessen until each cat was freed. Then the felines pelted away, swift to forgive their captivity, and swifter to explore their surroundings. It became a game of chase as footman and maid dashed after a Persian who came close to toppling a Ming vase, and a calico who scratched at the damask chair, and a gray-and-white tabby who toppled a miniature of great artistry.

Into this scene, Lucas Montieth, the Earl of Kelsey, strolled. A tall man, gracefully slim rather than large-muscled, whose air of natural authority was unmitigated by his lack of cravat and coat. His coloring, of copper hair, black brows, and white skin could not help but attract attention. His contained air, however, sat at odds with the vibrancy of his features. Alarm neither crossed his finely chiseled features, nor did surprise enter his deep, sherry-colored eyes. Only, perhaps, a small glimmer of enjoyment sparked within their depths as he halted.

One black brow flared high. "A bit early for such a rout, isn't it?"

With those mild words, the entire scene changed. The cats meowed and five of them dashed at him. His servants froze for a moment and then jerked to attention.

"My lord, forgive me!" Adams sprang from his chair as if his employer's appearance had been a bucket of water dashed upon him. His face twisted with torment as he noted his lordship's dishabille. "My lord, we have disturbed you!"

"Not at all, Adams," Lucas said. "Though you did send Pendleton into strong palpitations. I left Jane and the smelling salts with him. A fine valet, Pendleton, but he does suffer extreme sensibilities." Lucas bent to run a white hand over the fur of one of the four cats swirling around his feet. "Welcome, Peaches." He petted another. "And Cream, old man, how are you?" Another meowed. "Yes, Shakespeare, I shall attend it." He stood. "I wish a bottle of port and twelve glasses." He glanced at Adams, who appeared even more mortified. "Make that thirteen glasses."

Now Mrs. Milligan appeared mortified as well. "My lord?"

"Yes, Mrs. Milligan." Lucas nodded. "These felines are lushes, every one. They have witnessed a taxing morning, however. A spot of port shall soothe them." He strolled over to Adams. "*You* may have an entire

glass of course. What has sent you into the bows, my
good man? I warned you about Aunt Clare's cats, did
I not?"

"Yes, my lord." Adams trembled and held out the
paper with a shaking hand. "But . . . it is Aunt Clare.
She has been abducted. They want five thousand
pounds for her!"

"You don't say?" Both black brows rose as Lucas
took the paper and uncreased the sheet. The entire staff
roared. Lucas lifted one hand as he lowered his gaze
to read. "Be so kind as to take count of the cats,
please."

He read the missive while his staff attempted to do
his bidding. They lost count as the cats moved about
and intermingled.

"Never mind." Lucas looked up from the missive.
He folded it. "There are only eleven I will lay odds."
His gaze roamed the room. "Sir Percy is not here."

"He is not?" Adams peered about. "My God. They
abducted him too."

A smile, warm as wine, crossed Lucas's face. "She's
bubbled you, Adams."

"My lord?" Adams exclaimed.

"I warned you, did I not?" Lucas offered Adams the
missive back, shaking his head. "Lord Wrexton must
have left her without the detail of guards I told him to
employ in sending her to me."

"Gore!" Mrs. Milligan gasped. "Cruel you are!"

"No, Mrs. Milligan. Only one step ahead of Aunt
Clare." He frowned. "Or I was, until now. Lord Wrexton must have been fooled by Aunt Clare's promise
not to draw anyone into her schemes and plots."

"My lord, I—I do not understand." Adams struggled
valiantly for dignity. "Why . . . why do you think it a
bubble?"

"You didn't read the entire message, I presume. The

note says I must take the money and go directly to Miss Georgette Thompson's house. Giving both the direction and the demand that I be there within the hour."

"Yes, my lord." Adams appeared more confused. "They wish to make an exchange, do they not?"

Lucas studied him. A whimsical look crossed his face. "I always thought you omnipotent. Yet Aunt Clare has caught you off guard."

"I beg your pardon?" Adams stiffened.

"Do not take it to heart. Aunt Clare might very well pull the wool over the Almighty's eyes, that is if she weren't so very busy asking Him for an added notion or two." Lucas's eyes did light up then. "The piece of the puzzle you are missing in this little charade is this Miss Thompson. Aunt Clare, despite all wisdom and common sense, has decided that the woman should be my perfect match."

"Has she, my lord?" Joy flared in Adams's eyes.

"Glory be!" Mrs. Milligan breathed. "She didn't forget you after all."

"No, Mrs. Milligan, she didn't. I am the last of her boys to remain unwed and she promised she would not deny me her services. No matter if I told her no." Lucas looked levelly at his butler. "Aunt Clare will catch cold at it, however. So do stop looking so inanely happy, Adams."

"Yes, my lord." Adams stiffened and dutifully frowned. "Forgive me."

"Certainly. Now be a good chap and dismiss everyone. Then attend to the cats and your port." Lucas smiled, and turning, strolled away.

"My lord?" Adams called out. "What are you going to do about Miss Wrexton?"

Lucas halted, his expression sardonic. "Nothing, of course. This is merely a ruse of hers to force me to meet Miss Thompson, since I have firmly refused to do so before this."

"What if she truly has been abducted?" Adams countered.

"Yes, my lord," Mrs. Milligan cried. "You can't leave Aunt Clare in such a fix."

Amusement lit his eyes. "Can't I?"

"My lord, Aunt Clare has none of her own servants to aid her," Adams objected. "She is an honest lady. She would not have drawn anyone else into a scheme if that is what she promised Lord Wrexton."

"Except for this Miss Thompson, I make no doubt. When it comes to her matchmaking, Aunt Clare can bend the truth to any shape that fits her plans."

"Aunt Clare has no protector but you, my lord."

Lucas walked back to Adams, his smile wry, though the shimmer of something sad passed through his eyes. "If I rode *ventre à terre* over to this Miss Thompson's house with five thousand pounds, I would only raise the poor woman's hopes and Aunt Clare's as well. That would not be kind, now would it? I will never fall in love with her. No matter how many scenes she and Aunt Clare play out."

"You are the one who caused Miss Wrexton to be on her own, my lord." Adams stared straight ahead.

"I was attempting to stave off this very thing from happening."

"Yes, my lord."

Lucas stared at his butler. "I vow, the only way to manage this is to ignore her letter."

"She could be in danger, my lord."

Lucas's gaze narrowed. "Miss Thompson's father went to his rewards but two weeks ago, Adams."

"Poor thing," Mrs. Milligan murmured.

"Exactly. She *is* poor. Her father was a mere baron." The arch of Lucas's brow was a challenge. "That is who Aunt Clare wishes to palm off on me. A platter-faced spinster, Adams. Are you truly that desperate for a mistress of the house?"

Surprise crossed Adams's face. "Aunt Clare called her platter-faced, my lord?"

"No. Indeed not." Lucas's voice was droll. "She was very careful not to mention the poor girl's looks. What she did tell me was that Miss Thompson and I held much in common and that she was a very spirited lady."

"She's fusby-faced." A footman nodded.

"Precisely. Then Aunt Clare begged of me that I would *befriend* her dear Georgette in this sad time and offer her the guidance the sweet child would need. Indeed, Aunt Clare painted a charming picture of the great platonic relationship we could share. I could be her 'mentor,' don't you know."

Adams coughed. "That does not sound sinister, my lord."

"Aunt Clare also added that Miss Thompson is a girl after her own heart. Indeed, Miss Thompson reminds her of herself. Now that should give you pause, should it not?"

"Miss Wrexton is a delightful woman, my lord." Adams frowned. "She saved your life once."

"Yes," Lucas said. "And I am grateful, but not grateful enough to marry her lost little lamb."

"Miss Wrexton only said that she thought you should be friends."

"I am many things, Adams, but not gullible. I have not misread the situation." Lucas sighed. "She was at her vaguest and did not mention the word 'love' once in the discussion. That tipped me off, old man."

"If you say so, my lord. But if you are wrong, this could be a calamity."

"I am not wrong. You have no notion what kind of

scene will await me if I am foolish enough to obey this missive."

"That I do not." Adams stood erect. "But Miss Wrexton has been placed in your charge and your charge alone. You must rescue her."

"If you weren't such a fine butler, I'd sack you this minute." Lucas sighed. "Very well, I shall go posthaste to this Miss Thompson's."

His faithful servants cheered. They immediately halted as their master offered them a quelling look.

"I might as well settle this directly. Aunt Clare is past hope, but I have no doubt that I can persuade this Miss Thompson to withdraw from her efforts. You request that I go and break this spinster's heart, then I shall do it."

"Thank you, my lord." Adams bowed. "We will await the return of you and Miss Wrexton."

"Expect me back within an hour. I doubt I will require more time then that." He spun on his heel and strode from the hall.

Adams finally eased back. "Bless Aunt Clare. If anyone can save the earl from himself, it will be Aunt Clare. We might have a mistress in this house after all."

"Martha, you may put that within the coach." Georgette waved her maid along the walk to her waiting coach, an equipage quite antiquated. Her three other servants streamed down the steps from her town house, carrying silver and pictures and various odd objects.

Her housekeeper, Mrs. Brimston, stood within the house's doorway, a dark disapproving shadow. "Miss Georgette, you cannot do this. You simply cannot. You will get yourself killed. I just know you will!"

"I most certainly shall not! I am not a naive bubblehead, I assure you." Georgette's entire staff paused in their work. She tilted up her small chin. "I am not a bubblehead at least." Still her staff paused. "I am not. I have considered it all, I assure you." Her staff settled down to a frozen stare. "It makes no difference. I am going and no one will stop me." She cast a look at her coachman, Trump, who had taken a moment to lean against the old coach and pick at his teeth. "Trump, please help Sally secure that painting atop the coach."

"Yes, mum," Trump gargled out between his fingers. He remained at his personal toilet, not moving a jot.

Georgette sighed. Zounds, but she would enjoy sacking her father's servants. Indeed, after this crisis was dealt with, she would do so within a trice. Unfortunately, she had not a moment to spare. She tossed the long black veil she wore over her shoulder. Lifting skirts of black armazine trimmed with only one serviceable row of black crepe rouleau, she marched determinedly to the coach. With a grimace, she cinched on the black leather elbow-length gloves required of a proper miss in mourning. With only two attempts she successfully clambered up to the coach-box. "You may give that to me, Sally."

"Yes, Miss Georgette." Sally, all of sixteen, hefted the large picture, one that Georgette had always thought especially ugly, upward. Georgette caught it. With precarious balance, she turned with it and worked to arrange it amongst the other booty secured. With so much already atop the coach, it was not an easy task.

"Oowee, would you look at that!" Sally said from her stance upon the ground.

"What?" Georgette glanced back. Approaching down the quiet street was a lone horseman. His mount had to be the most magnificent animal alive.

"Coor, I bet he's a prince." Sally breathed. Her gaze was wide with infatuation. Clearly it was for the man and not the horse.

Georgette was forced to own that the man was as magnificent an animal as his horse. Stunned at her thought, she snapped, "Do stop gawking, Sally. He must have taken the wrong turn and is lost." She forced herself to turn back to her project.

"I think he's coming here." Sally clapped her hands and squealed.

Georgette jumped at the pitch. She drew in a breath. "Then you can give him directions to Hyde Park. No doubt that is where he intends to go."

"Can I, Miss Georgette?" Sally cried. "Can I?"

"Only if you refrain from squealing. Now I do not wish to hear another word out of you."

"I think he really is coming here," Trump observed. "And Sally don't know the directions to Hyde Park, but I do."

"Then give them to him. Only do not pester me." Georgette gritted her teeth. Here she was dealing with matters of life and death, while they sat about ogling a passerby. She shook her head. Had she remembered everything she needed? She sincerely hoped she had. She'd been packing feverishly for three hours.

"Oowee!" Sally giggled. And giggled. And giggled.

"Stop, Sally!" Georgette ordered, studying her handiwork one last time. "I don't want another peep out of you."

"Er, Miss Georgette . . . ?"

"Or you, Trump!" Satisfied, Georgette carefully crawled backward onto the coach-box. Biting her lip, and knowing better than to ask for help, she started to climb from it.

"May I assist you, madame?" a liquid voice asked from behind.

"What?" Georgette gasped, stunned as much from the offer as to the fact that it came from an unknown source. She whirled to see the speaker. She lost her grip in astonishment. She beheld the vision of a striking face. Then she was falling. The veil of delicate black net trailing from her charcoal gray beaver hat snagged upon the box as Georgette toppled directly into the arms of the man who had caused her hasty descent.

"Very well done," that male voice drawled. "You could not have planned it better."

Georgette blinked as she stared into the amused eyes of a stranger. His arms were steel bands about her, holding her both safe and captive. His gaze was that of sherry, his hair burnished fire within the morning sun. His skin, in contrast, was alabaster. It was Sally's prince. Georgette shook her head. No, he didn't look like a prince. He looked more like . . . "A Titian."

"I beg your pardon?" He quirked an arrested brow.

"You . . . look like a Titian painting."

"And you are a Madonna." His sherry eyes lit for a moment in appraisal. "Though your eyes . . ."

"What about my eyes?" Georgette tensed.

He smiled. "They look like a she-wolf's."

"They do not! They are gray, plain, simple gray." Georgette looked at him darkly. "You may set me down."

"That did destroy the romance, didn't it?" He said with irony. He set her down. "But I have done my part. Our prerequisite dashing meeting has been effected."

"What?" Georgette swayed from the change in atmosphere.

He steadied her with two beautifully manicured hands upon her shoulders. His smile transformed his features. Yet, the sarcasm in it could not be mistaken. "I have saved you from peril, have I not?"

Georgette frowned and stepped out of his clasp. She didn't like the notion one whit. "No, only from an inconvenient fall, certainly not from peril. I should know the difference. I have never been in peril my entire life. Unless it is from boredom."

A laugh escaped the man. It chased the nasty cynicism from his features. Georgette trembled at the change. She quickly turned away from a face she feared could fascinate her all too easily. She jerked at her snagged veil in frustration. It perversely resisted. "Drat it!"

The man, his height of six feet being far more advantageous than hers of five and four, reached over and gently tugged it from its confinement. "What an . . . extensive veil you have, madame."

"It has a purpose." Georgette pulled it from his hands, and stepped away. "Now, sir, if you will excuse me. I do not know who you are . . ."

"Yes, you do, *Miss Thompson.*"

Georgette's heart leapt. "You know who I am?"

He nodded slowly. "And you know who I am. How long have you been waiting for me?"

Georgette stared. He might be a magnificent-looking man, but he was queer as Dick's hatband. As well as being as smug as a sultan in his harem. "I haven't been waiting for you, and I do not know who you are. Nor do I have time to stand about bandying words."

She saw surprise cross his face. Then that laughter entered his gaze again. A thrill passed through Georgette. Blast! She looked to Sally, who had remained silent, actually stricken like a statue in her adoration. It would never do. "Sally, bring me my father's books from the library. We shall load those as well."

Mrs. Brimstone's gasp was so loud as to be heard even from where they stood. "You cannot, Miss Georgette. You cannot."

"Yes I can, Mrs. Brimstone." Georgette said. "I have inherited them and they are mine." She caught the stranger's speculative look. "Now, Sir . . ."

"Very well. We shall pretend." He bowed. "Permit me to introduce myself. I am Lucas Montieth, the Earl of Kelsey."

"The Earl of Kelsey?" Georgette stared. "You are one of Aunt Clare's boys, are you not?"

"Yes. Precisely."

"Thank God." Georgette exclaimed, in more relief than she cared to admit. "I am glad that you are here then."

"And you were not before?" Lucas quizzed.

She flushed. "My lord, I have no time to spare. Since you know Aunt Clare, I feel I can confide in you."

"Most certainly," Lucas said. "Do open your heart to me."

Georgette stiffened. She attempted to remember what Aunt Clare had said about this particular peer. Astonishingly enough, she realized that Aunt Clare hadn't spoken much about him. Now she could see why. He was quite an officious person. "My lord, I must tell you that Aunt Clare is in grave danger. She has been abducted."

Lucas nodded, his lips twitching. "I know, dreadful is it not?"

"How do you know?" Georgette frowned. Then she gasped. "Did—did you receive a letter too?"

"Of course. Why else would I be here?"

"Gracious." Georgette attempted to think this through. Only she couldn't help watching the earl. She frowned in suspicion. "You look as if you are going to laugh."

"A thousand apologies." Then the creature did just that. He laughed.

Georgette stepped back, appalled. The man was a satyr. "How can you!"

"I am sorry." He subsided to chuckles. "I am merely enjoying your performance."

"My performance?" Rage shot through her. "Well, my lord, I am not enjoying your performance. I—I have never known someone who could be so very cold-hearted. Even if you do not care for Aunt Clare, for you to laugh at her predicament is abominable."

"No." He reached out and clasped her arm. Gone was the cynicism. Gone was any laughter. Gone was his smugness. His eyes burnt with only anger. "What is abominable is your attempt to lure me into your trap."

"Lure you?"

"Yes. Lure me."

Dazed, Georgette shook her head. "My lord, I do not understand."

"Stop your lies! I am here to tell you to give up the scheme before it even starts. I promise you, no matter what Aunt Clare has told you, I am not an easy catch. And though you are more comely than I first expected, you'll not succeed in your attempts."

Georgette gasped. Her servants did too. Georgette realized that she was dealing with a man who was dangerously unhinged. That must be why Aunt Clare never talked about him. She was a woman who never wished to say anything harsh against anyone, even a man cracked in the bone-box. She bit her lip, frightened. The day was going from bad to worse. Calm. She warned herself. Calm. "Er, very right, my lord. Now I—I understand." She said it in soothing tones. "Now you were kind enough to er . . . save me. And I—I thank you. But I—I have some very important matters to attend. As you can see I—I am preparing to leave town."

He sighed. "And just where are we supposed to be going?"

"We?" She quelled a shiver. "Er . . . *we* are not suppose to be going anywhere. Now c—could you please release me?"

"Certainly." Frowning, he did so. "Where are *you* going?"

"That is none of your business, my lord."

"You are going after Aunt Clare, aren't you?" His voice was suspicious, his gaze a rapier cut in its discernment.

"No!" Georgette yelped. Then she drew in her breath. "I—I am leaving on a different matter. You were right, I was only bamming you about Aunt Clare. But, you're fly to me and I won't try to lure you."

"You are lying, Miss Thompson," Lucas said sternly.

Georgette snapped. Anger replaced fear, solely because she was tired of the fear. "That is the second time you have unjustly accused me, my lord. I—I wish you would leave. I do not care if you are addle-brained with a top loft to let, I am not going to allow you to insult me. Or frighten me. Or stop me."

His stare was incredulous. "You think I am crazy?"

"Cooee," Sally murmured.

"Cracked!" The very sane indignation that spread across his features gave Georgette pause. "Very well. Only unhinged."

"I am not," Lucas exclaimed.

"Good." Despite herself, Georgette breathed a little easier. "Prove it by leaving me be."

His face darkened. "Miss Thompson, I believe we must talk."

"You may talk while I work, my lord." Georgette looked at her servants, who watched. "What are you all standing about for, pray tell? We have more to load into the coach."

He frowned as the servants moved to go back into the house. Georgette hastened toward the coach, determined to focus upon her preparations.

"Hold one moment." Lucas shook his head and then sighed. "Miss Thompson, it is clear we are at loggerheads. But if you are honestly going after Aunt Clare because of an abduction note, I must strongly urge you not to do so."

"Why?" Georgette glared at him.

"Because she hasn't really been abducted," Lucas said. "It is a ruse of hers and nothing more. She has set this up herself."

Georgette stared at him. She put her hands to her hips. "I thought you said you were not balmy."

"I am not." He narrowed his gaze. "You said you know that I am one of her 'boys,' right?"

"Right."

"Do you know that she has successfully found wives for all her other 'boys.' "

"Yes, she mentioned that she was able to introduce them to their prospective wives." Georgette tried to hold her patience. "What does that signify?"

"Is that all she told you?" Lucas asked.

"Yes." He looked at her narrowly. Georgette lifted her chin. "And if you dare call me a liar again, I declare I shall . . . I shall kick you!"

"I will not call you a liar. But I promise you, this is all a ruse of Aunt Clare's."

"Why would it be a ruse of hers?"

He looked her straight in the eye. "You, Miss Thompson, are supposed to be my true love. We are supposed to marry."

Georgette gaped at him. The oddest feelings welled up within her. "That's it! You are *past* balmy. You are as mad as the maddest bedlamite!"

"I am not. Aunt Clare promised us all to find us our perfect match. You are to be mine."

"No. It is you who lie." Georgette shook her head vehemently. "Aunt Clare wouldn't do that to me."

"Why not?"

"She knows better." Georgette said angrily. "She knows I am never, ever, ever, going to marry. Now if you will excuse me." She could hear the loathing in her voice. She could tell that the man had defined it as such as well. She spun away and noting a vase in Thomas's hand, she went and grabbed it from him. She marched toward the coach.

"Will you hold one moment?" Before she knew it, he had halted her in midstride, a firm hand to her elbow.

She narrowed her gaze upon that hand. "My lord, release me. If you do not, I will have Trump confine you and I shall send for the watch."

"Will you?" Lucas smiled. "I haven't boxed the watch since my salad days. It might be amusing."

Georgette clenched her teeth. "You best take me seriously, my lord."

"Now, Miss Georgette, why not listen to the man?" Trump slouched away from them. "That Aunt Clare is the zany one, if'n you ask me."

"I did not ask you." Flushing, Georgette lifted her chin and looked as fiercely at Lucas as she felt possible. "Do not force me to take stronger measures, my lord. I promise you, I can take care of myself."

"Good Lord." Lucas dropped his hand. Though it was clear he did it in exasperation rather than the fear Georgette was hoping to inspire. "I could box Aunt Clare's ears, I vow." Before she could speak, he cast her a telling look. "Do not say it, Miss Thompson."

"Very well." Georgette bit her lip. She noticed two more servants coming out of the house and was grateful for the distraction. "There you are. Those should go inside the coach."

Lucas turned to study them. "You may return those things to the house."

They halted.

"No, put them in the coach," Georgette countered.

They proceeded.

"You must cease," Lucas demanded.

The servants ceased once more.

Red-hot anger flared in Georgette. "I am ordering you to bring those things to the coach."

"And I am telling them to stop," Lucas said, his tone calm now. "You may go haring about the countryside if you wish, but only after we talk about this."

"There is no *we* about this. They are *my* servants, not yours." She glared at her servants. "If you do not do my bidding this very moment I shall sack each and every one of you."

"You are being childish, Miss Thompson," Lucas observed. "Do attempt to be reasonable."

"No," she said. She looked at her servants. "Well?"

"Aunt Clare said you were spirited. She should have said mulish, I do believe." Lucas flicked a glance at the servants. "Do not listen to her. I can hire you just as quickly as she can sack you."

"Owee. Hire me." Sally raised her hand eagerly from behind them. "Please hire me."

"Very well. They are sacked and now you may employ the entire lot." Georgette spun about, marching toward the coach-box. "You will still not deter this *mule*. You may order them all about, my lord, but you may not order me about."

"Miss Thompson . . . ?"

She glared at him. "Do not think to stop me."

He sighed. "That mule comment was quite unworthy. Forgive me?"

"You are forgiven." She climbed into the box. She bit her lip and looked about, in a quandary. Just what did a coachman do next?

"Miss Thompson . . . ?"

"What now?" She cast him a fierce look. "Will you take your servants off, my lord, and cease detaining me?"

"Most certainly," he said solemnly. "I have but this one small question."

"What is it?"

"Do you know how to drive a coach?"

Georgette lifted her chin. "I shall contrive I am sure."

"The answer being no." A wry expression crossed his features. "Very well. Before you leave, would you permit me to at least show you the ribbons?"

Georgette glared at him suspiciously. "Why would you do that?"

"I am doing penance." A slight smile tipped his lips. "You'll be no good in rescuing Aunt Clare if you over-turn your coach and break you neck." He cast a glance to the servants. "Proceed with packing this lot and then cease. This old coach will handle only so much stress."

He climbed up beside Georgette. "Now, let me show you how to hold the reigns." He took the reigns and with the smoothest voice directed her in the usage of them. Since Georgette had never even ridden a horse, let alone driven a coach, the words he threw at her were discombobulating. She didn't even notice the minutes passing, so desperate was she to learn the pointers.

She had bluffed him in her anger. Yet she could not back down. Aunt Clare's life depended upon it. Worse, she felt as if her own life depended upon it. If she didn't step out and grasp it by the horns, she doubted she ever would.

"Now, permit me to show you the use of the whip."

Georgette's eyes widened in distaste. "That too? Must I use that?"

Lucas paused a moment. "Just where are you intending to go?"

"I am going to the Boar's Head Inn which sits on the crossroads of London." She recited it by memory.

"I see. Do you have directions?"

"They drew a map."

"Of course." He shook his head. "For that distance you must learn to handle the whip as well."

"Very well. Do show me."

Lucas looked back. "Is everything within the coach?"

The group of servants stood gaping. They nodded. "Very good." He looked at Georgette. "To properly show the use of the whip I really should tool you about first. Permit me to show you. I am sure once we are out of London you shall have gained the knack."

She looked at him in suspicion. "I do not trust you."

"We shall have my new coachman, Trump, is it not, tie my horse to the coach and once you are certain of your team, I can then leave you."

She bit her lip. "Very well."

"Though I do think you should let my new coachman ride in the coach. I will lend him to you if you can convince me that this abduction is for real and Aunt Clare is in danger, *and* if I cannot convince you of the opposite."

Georgette bit her lip all the harder. She should turn him down directly. Yet a scholar had raised her and to not at least listen to the man went against the grain. She refused to admit that she would be in the suds without his direction. "Very well."

Lucas waved for Trump to do his bidding. Once it was accomplished, Lucas took the whip and flicked it with a sure hand. He started up the horses and coach. He directed Georgette's attention to all of the intricacies of driving a coach. She was completely involved with that enlightenment, until they entered into the main streets of London. She could not help but notice as the earl tipped his whip to an elegant equipage passing by, then to even more elegant gentlemen and ladies strolling upon the thoroughfare. Georgette noticed the flabbergasted expression upon their faces.

"Dear me, we are causing a stir, are we not?" She flushed.

"It is of no significance." Lucas laughed. "You see, they all know the same as you. That I am irrevocably cracked in my upper loft."

Two

Lucas eased back against the old coach's squabs. He was lodged between a musty satchel and a frightfully ugly statue. Georgette had finally conceded to let Trump drive the coach, while they adjourned to the inside, there to try and discuss more than whips, leads, and ribbons.

Granted, to gain this private audience, Lucas had been cornered into permitting her to tool the coach along a quiet stretch. Which in truth had not been too taxing. Her pride in her accomplishment was unmistakable. The team had crawled along at a snail's pace for that distance, yet she had laughed as merrily at her accomplishment as if they had been at Newmarket racing neck-or-nothing to a first-place finish.

Now, Georgette sat across from him. She hugged a large sewing box on her lap, there being little room for it anywhere else. An odd assortment of objects crowded beside her as well. He studied her smooth oval face, framed by the silkiest raven hair pulled back in a smooth chignon. Her eyes were a pale gray, circled with a darker charcoal about them, then set with long lashes. Her frame was slight, enshrouded in a black dress of some stiff fabric topped with a sooty gray spencer with sleeves gathered along her arms as if it were fashioned for arms four inches longer, or broader, than hers.

"I am glad to see that you dare trust me in enclosed quarters, Miss Thompson," Lucas said. "Have I proven sufficiently that I am not a raving lunatic?"

"Perhaps," she said.

Lucas grinned. He had surely made grounds in swaying her. "Excellent."

"I wish to hear more of your arguments in regard to this abduction." She said it most primly. "And why you think it is nothing more than Aunt Clare hoaxing us."

Lucas frowned. He hadn't won her over as much as he thought. He'd better gain the required information as fast as he could. "Why don't we exchange the letters first?"

"Very well." Georgette withdrew hers from the cuff of her capacious sleeve. She held it away until he withdrew his and then she held it out. It was apparently an exchange in which she felt the need to be wary. She took his missive. He took hers. She gasped as she studied it. "They are asking five thousand pounds from you."

"And five hundred from you." Lucas noticed. "It is clear Aunt Clare knows each of our circumstances."

"It isn't Aunt Clare." Georgette shook her head. "This isn't her writing."

"She had someone else write them." He studied her. "Aunt Clare never spoke of me to you?"

"No. She often spoke of the others. Though we have not seen each other as much of late. She told me she had taken up a few charities."

"Charities?" Lucas couldn't retain his growl. "We boys were her charities."

Her eyes widened and a giggle escaped her. "I suppose you were."

Lucas shook his head. "Only Aunt Clare would look

upon matchmaking as a charity. Though, for the other men, I own it was."

"But not for you?"

"No." He cast her a level look. "Not for me."

She chewed her full lower lip. Then she peeked at him. "What did she tell you about me?"

"Aunt Clare said you were like a daughter to her. And a girl after her own heart."

"She did?" Georgette broke out into a proud smile.

"Yes." Lucas nodded slowly. The girl had a smile that could tug at one's own lips. "And that we had much in common. Why are *you* determined not to marry?"

"I have just now gained my freedom and I shall never give it up. I want to do things, and see things, and discover things."

Her voice was vibrant with longing. Lucas smiled, remembering a time when life held just that kind of promise for him. "And, of course, if you marry you cannot have those things?"

"Of course not." She said it simply, without anger or confusion. "Men don't permit it. They may have all the adventures they wish, but they will destroy any chance for a woman to have them."

"Poppycock," Lucas returned mildly.

She stiffened, a challenge flaring in her eyes. Only then she hid it, looking away. "Why would Aunt Clare try and attempt to arrange a marriage between us? We are frightfully mismatched."

Lucas lifted a brow. "You mean, because I am insane?"

"There is that." She said it solemnly. Then the tease in her gaze gave her away. "Other than that, you . . ." She paused. "You are above my touch. I do know that much. You could marry anyone you wish."

"Not anyone," Lucas said. "Not the lady I love."

"You are in love?" Her eyes opened wide in surprise. "Then how . . . why would Aunt Clare . . . ?" She gurgled to a halt.

"Attempt to match us?" Lucas forced a calm to his voice. "Because the woman I love is married to another."

"I am so sorry." Her gaze was honestly sad.

"Isabelle wished to wed me, but her father forced her to marry another. A duke of the realm to be exact."

"I see." She sat, mulling it over. She shook her head. "No, Aunt Clare would never do that to me. She loves me too much."

"I beg your pardon?" Lucas stiffened.

Georgette looked at him directly, confusion still on her face. "She would never shackle me to a man who has already given his love away. A man like that is . . ." She halted once more.

"No, you may say it." Lucas was stunned, but he could read her thoughts as if she were shouting them. "Is damaged?"

"I didn't say that." A flush painted Georgette's cheeks. "But, you cannot deny it. To be married to a man who doesn't love you would be abysmal."

"Very polite." Lucas nodded. So much for breaking the spinster's heart. Accordingly, his natural sense of humor came to the rescue. He had thought that Aunt Clare was palming Miss Thompson off upon him. Apparently the lady thought the boot was on the other foot. "Just why are you so very against marriage? It is apparent you haven't given your love to a man as yet."

"And I hope never to." Georgette said it quite eagerly. A surprise entered her eyes. "Gracious, I had never considered it before. I do have to be grateful to my father for never forcing me to marry."

It didn't take much to know that her father must have much to do with Georgette's dislike of men. "Was he . . . very cruel?"

"No, surely not." She sighed. "The only thing he ever forced me to do was to live a very dull life."

"I see." Lucas attempted to hide his thoughts.

She looked at him. "That does sound quite ridiculous, does it not?"

"You could have had worse," Lucas said judiciously.

"Yes. But I could have had better." Her eyes lit up; indeed, her entire body did so. The energy exuding from the woman filled the entire coach. "I have a . . . a competence you know? Father left everything to me. Mr. Thurbur, his lawyer, says it is completely legal." She leaned forward, and lowered her voice. "With that I can live the way I have always dreamed I could. No restraints. I am going to be very outrageous, I assure you."

"Indeed." Lucas leaned forward, drawn by her fire despite himself. "And what wild things do you dream of doing?"

Georgette tossed her head back. "I going to go to Bath and live by the sea. In a cottage on a cliff."

Lucas froze. Her gaze was sincere. He bit his lip and nodded his head. "I see. Very wild."

"I am going to become an artist." Georgette lifted her chin and dared him to refute her. "Not in watercolors. *But oils.*"

"Far too decadent," Lucas exclaimed. He didn't wish to divert her with the information that not only was he a connoisseur of art, but a creditable artist himself.

"I am also going to read!" She said it most emphatically.

"Do you not now?"

"No. I mean I am going to read everything!"

"Indeed? Everything?" Lucas murmured. "You certainly shall be an abandoned creature."

"Heraclitus first, I believe." She peeked at him to see his reaction. "And perhaps Lord Byron next."

Lucas stifled his chuckle. "Do not look to me. I would not stop you."

"No one is going to stop me." Suddenly, she was not looking at him, but past him. "Father said the only proper thing for females to read was religious sermons."

"Good God!" A tremor of disgust ran through Lucas. He himself read extensively. Forced to read but one thing would be stifling. Rather like being entombed alive.

"I have read every one ever written." She frowned. "They change their minds quite regularly, you know, on just exactly what a proper young lady should do for the salvation of her soul." The frown turned even darker. He had teased her about she-wolf eyes before, but they were truly most fierce now. "That is, when they allow us to possess souls at all."

"You have read some very old tomes I see," Lucas said. "What did you conclude about them?"

Her mood lightened, as if she had tossed off the restraining thought. "I realized all those sermons were written by scholars like my father. Which means you cannot depend upon them too much, for the more scholarly a man is, the more he believes that few have souls but himself."

"Faith!" Lucas choked, and choked hard. Outrage and sheer amusement welled within him.

"I have shocked you, have I not?"

"No. Only I—I confess that many consider me a scholar."

"Do they?" She sighed. "Aunt Clare has been kidnapped and we must decide what to do."

Lucas shook his head. "Why such a swift change of subject?"

"What?" She had already fallen into a brown study. She glanced back at him. "Was it swift? I didn't think so. It is clear that we would be a very sad match. Aunt

Clare is not such a noddy. Therefore, it is most apparent that she has been truly abducted."

Lucas frowned. Her logic was rather strong. He himself began to doubt his stance. Could he have jumped to a conclusion? Could he accidentally have arranged for Aunt Clare's abduction? He had been so certain that she would attempt to match him and Georgette that he had done everything to cut Aunt Clare off from those who, though they could help her in her schemes, would also look to her well-being. Granted, Lord Wrexton had been in complete accordance. Yet now Lucas feared that he had merely set her up for some villain to abscond with her.

A shot rang out. The coach jerked to a bone-shattering stop. Another shot rang out. Lucas groaned when he heard the shouted order to stand and deliver.

"Good gracious!" Georgette looked to Lucas with astonishment. "What is happening?"

"If I am not mistaken, Miss Thompson, we are being held up in broad daylight."

"Are you bamming me?" Georgette gasped.

"No, I am not." Lucas narrowed his gaze. "Just where did you learn your vocabulary, Miss Thompson? Surely not from those religious sermons."

"Must we discuss that at this moment?" Georgette sat upon the edge of her seat. "I never dreamed that highwaymen could be so bold."

"Indeed," Lucas said curtly. He knew who could have dreamed such a thing, even if Georgette did not. Still, his confidence had been shaken. He had no way of knowing which way to proceed.

A deep voice demanded they exit the coach. Frowning, Lucas looked swiftly about. The coach pistol was not in its strap. "Tell me, Miss Thompson, did Aunt Clare know your stalwart coachman well?"

"Yes." She frowned. "Why?"

"Nothing. I was merely curious." He drew in his breath. There was only one way to discover if his assumptions were correct. He looked sternly to Georgette. "Please permit me to descend before you, Miss Thompson."

"If you wish." She said, her gaze intent.

Lucas opened the door and slowly stepped down from the coach. The two fierce highwaymen sitting upon their mounts sported black satin capes and masks. Aunt Clare's dream villains to the last mark. Lucas barked a laugh. "I am right."

"My lord?" Georgette gasped from behind.

Both would-be villains' horses skittered. They had difficulties settling them. Lucas turned to Georgette in amusement. She was preparing to alight from the coach. So involved was she in it all, she still carried the sewing basket, clearly forgetting its presence in her arms. Lucas opened his mouth and then shut it. *Men destroy all chances of adventure for women.* He found himself unable to do it. These brigands had been paid already by Aunt Clare. Why waste those funds for nothing? Especially as Georgette's gaze showed as much excitement as fear.

"That we must be vary careful, Miss Thompson." He held out his hand and assisted her down. He lowered his voice. "Very careful."

"Certainly," she said, her voice calm but for a slight tremor.

"Make no false move, sirrah," the highwayman first to gain control of his mount demanded. His voice rolled with a Shakespearean timber. " 'Else I shall shoot you. Your coachman has already run off, so do not look to that coward to assist you."

"I shall not, I assure you," Lucas said, turning to face the dangerously romantic villains. "What is it that you want from us?"

"Hand over all your valuables, man," the highway-man said.

"Yes." The other villain nodded. His voice was less developed and he had more of a cockney accent, which assisted his role. "Or else we'll take the lady!"

"What?" Georgette frowned. "Why ever would you take me?"

"Because . . ." The first man halted, no doubt daunted by Georgette's deep consideration. He attempted an evil look. "Yer a comely lass."

She but frowned at him more deeply, apparently not believing that his heart was filled with lascivious desire. Lucas hadn't aided Aunt Clare over the past year for naught. "Please do not argue with them, Miss Thompson. These are vicious, desperate villains. They would take you so that they could sell you into white slavery."

"Oh!" She did pale then. "Yes, I suppose they could make money that way."

"Yes. Yes, we can." The man shook his pistol and looked at Lucas. "Now hand over your valuables and money."

"And keep your chaffer shut," the other added.

"Ah, yes." Lucas grimaced. He wouldn't look very heroic now. Strangely enough, it mattered. Miss Thompson's low opinion of men and him in particular needed no more fueling. "I would gladly hand over all my valuables . . ."

"Oh dear, no." Georgette moaned. "That money is to save Aunt Clare!"

"Unfortunately," Lucas continued, "I fear all I have is a twenty-pound note upon me. You may have that, however."

"What?" Georgette gasped. "Surely you jest."

"Hey! If that is all you have, he can't . . ." The second robber clamped his mouth shut.

"I do not lie." Lucas looked squarely at the man. "I vow it as a gentleman."

"Cut the line. You're supposed to have the dibs," the first one said. He paused, and drew in a breath. "I mean, you look to be a rich lord. How come you only have a twenty-pound note?"

Lucas offered him as much of a warning look as he could. "I *meant* to be traveling with a rather great amount this morning. However, due to an oversight, I do not have it."

"You truly do not?" Georgette whispered.

"I do not," Lucas gritted. "I never intended for it to proceed this far."

"I see." Georgette frowned and clutching her sewing basket, she stepped forward. "Sirs, you may take what is in the coach. There are some most excellent paintings. Lovely china. Vases?"

"No. No." The first man held up his hand. "We aren't after setting up house, miss. We want what we can take on horseback. Like money and jewels."

"I do have some jewelry. Though the stones are not fine, and . . . and one or two are glass." Georgette's voice dwindled off.

"That's all?" The second villain stared.

"Y—yes." Georgette nodded.

Lucas lifted a brow. She was supposed to have five hundred pounds for Aunt Clare's abductors.

"That's it then!" The first robber squared his shoulders and looked at Lucas. "We are going to take the lady's jewelry. However, if you wish to save your lady's valuables"—he frowned—"and you do want to save them, don't you?"

"Oh, indeed I do." Lucas nodded, waiting to see where this might lead. Clearly the man had devised a way to return to the original script.

"Then why don't you and I fight for it. If you are brave enough?"

Amusement lit Lucas's eyes. Faith, but Aunt Clare didn't miss a trick. What woman didn't wish to have a man fight for her or her valuables? Even if they were only glass. "I am brave enough."

"Oh no. I shall give you my jewelry." Georgette gasped. "There is no need to fight . . ."

"Yes there is," Lucas said calmly. Aunt Clare would be terribly put out if he failed in this scene. "As I would have fought just for you. Or to keep the money to save Aunt Clare . . ."

The first villain nodded. "That's good, my lord. Very good."

"What is it to be?" Lucas asked. "Fisticuffs?"

"No. It is to be swords."

"Swords!" Lucas was forced to clamp his mouth shut.

"Swords?" Georgette looked confused. Then frightened. "Do you know how to fight with swords, my lord?"

"Indeed, I do." Lucas blessed Georgette's naïveté. Any woman who was worldly would have wondered at swords. Yet Aunt Clare's fantasies still harkened back to the duels of earlier years. Regardless that it would be one rare highwayman to know the noble art, much less to be sporting a rapier on his person.

"Then let us have at it." The first man lumbered down from his horse. He immediately drew from his saddlebag two excellent foils. He turned. "The first piqued will be the winner."

"Indeed." Lucas nodded solemnly. He glanced at Georgette. Then and there he decided to have a strong word with Aunt Clare. He could tell by Georgette's pale calm that she was frightened. It did not appear after all that Georgette was the type of lady who enjoyed a man actually fighting for her and her valuables.

He took the foil the highwayman offered, knowing that they must proceed. Neither of them could afford to be unmasked at this moment. He tested the foil and offered Georgette a wink. "If you thought I was good with a whip, you need to watch this, madame."

"I shall." Georgette mustered up a brave and almost roguish smile for him.

The actor performed his own flamboyant display. Nodding, the two men then engaged. Lucas found the actor proficient. He neither overly attacked Lucas, nor did he do so too weakly. Lucas enjoyed the art and soon both men were testing their knowledge with vim and vigor.

That was until Georgette's voice interrupted. Her tone was firm. "Cease, this instant."

"Do, Chauncy, please," came the other man's nervous voice.

Lucas, watching the other man carefully, nodded and they ceased. He turned to where Georgette had called. His own eyes widened and he gripped the foil convulsively. While he had been engaged in duel with the one actor, Georgette had moved. She stood close to the other actor, leveling a pistol upon him. His gaze strayed to the discarded sewing box upon the ground. And he had thought she didn't know she carried it.

"God!" the actor murmured.

"Now d—drop your sword. 'Else . . . I shall shoot," Georgette threatened.

"Do it, Chauncy," the one actor said. He glanced at the pistol. "I don't think she's acting."

"Certainly I am not." Georgette's voice was indignant. "But I refuse to have you pique the earl . . . whatever that means."

"You better do what my lady demands," Lucas murmured.

"I—I don't think she is well acquainted with fire-arms, Chauncy," the highwayman said nervously.

"Indeed I am." Georgette offered a scowl that any actor could tell was feigned. "I—I shoot all the time. Granted, not highwaymen, but I will."

"No need to do that!" Chauncy said quickly. "No need. We—only let us go in peace."

"You are robbers. That is bad," Georgette said sternly. Lucas groaned. Her prodigious ingestion of religious doctrines was showing. "Very bad."

"I am sure they will repent after this," Lucas said. "And turn to a new stage of life."

Both men were vociferous in their agreement.

Georgette considered the two for a long moment. She nodded. "Very well. However, in order for you to repent, I am going to rob you."

"What?" Chauncy exclaimed.

"Perhaps you will be more cautious about taking other people's money if it is taken from you." She rattled her pistol, making all three men jump. "Now give me all your valuables."

Lucas could only stare as the two actor highwaymen turned out their pockets and gave the contents to Georgette. Between the two of them they possessed one hundred pounds. Apparently Aunt Clare must have paid them each fifty. "Thank you, sirs. Now, please, be off. And do think about reforming."

The two actors didn't even wait for a further lecture. They departed posthaste.

Lucas shook his head. "I find it astonishing that you robbed those two men."

"I needed to do so," Georgette said solemnly. "We still must collect five thousand pounds to save Aunt Clare. Well, four thousand and nine hundred pounds."

Lucas actually felt heat rise to his face. "Do forgive my *faux pax*, I see I should have brought the money.

However, I truly did not intend to lend myself to this escapade."

"I understand." Georgette nodded. Her expression unreadable, she looked away. "Y—you may return home now."

"I beg your pardon?" Lucas didn't know if he should be insulted or amused. "I just fought for your jewelry and now you intend to send me packing? Cast me off? That, Miss Thompson, is shabby treatment . . . quite shabby. Aunt Clare would be aghast."

"No! I did not mean it to be so," Georgette said. "However, you did not wish to accompany me, and only look what happened. You might have been piqued. You may return home."

Lucas's good humor won out. Georgette was both a conundrum and a challenge. She had also brandished a pistol with full intent to save him from being wounded. No man could overlook that. He maintained his dignity. "I will have no more of this. I am not going home until you go home. Is that clear?" He watched her intently, determined to know her true feelings.

"I will not turn back until I have saved Aunt Clare," Georgette said levelly.

Lucas smiled wryly. So much for the fair damsel falling into his arms after his brave behavior. Rather she was pound-dealing. He laughed and held out his hand. "Let us make a pact. *We* shall not turn back until *we* find Aunt Clare. I shall watch your back, so to speak. How is that?"

She paused in consideration. She delivered her decision warily. "Since the objective is the same, I accept. But only if . . ."

"If what?" Lucas lifted a brow, his hand still unaccepted.

"I shall watch your back, too." Georgette nodded.

"That is it. We shall be equal partners. I would not be beholding to you one whit then."

"But of course. We certainly would not wish for any *beholding* to transpire between us." Lucas's lips twitched. "It would most certainly crimp the sense of adventure, wouldn't it?"

"Precisely." She smiled as if a deep worry had dropped away.

"Exactly." Lucas struggled with his pride. His heart might be given to another, but regardless, he was still accustomed to having women jump at any chance to further their connection with him. Miss Thompson was considering the prospect as she would a tooth being drawn. Worse, his hand was still proffered and empty. He wasn't about to draw it back. "Do let us shake upon this, Miss Thompson. I am gaining a cramp in my hand."

"Oh, yes." Flushing, she shifted the pistol to her other hand with the pound notes. She then put her one hand into his. "Until we find Aunt Clare."

"Yes." Her hand was small, smooth, and trembled in his. A shock coursed through him as a protective feeling rose within him. No matter that the fragile member had just held a pistol seconds before. Lucas forced a smile and released Georgette's hand quickly. "Are you worried you have made a pact with the devil?"

"No, of course not." Her gray gaze was dark. Clearly she lied. "Are you?"

"Of course not," Lucas returned. She was certainly a girl who adhered to tit for tat.

Her gray eyes cleared. Satisfaction welled within them. "We now have one hundred pounds more than before."

He frowned. "Yes, madame, but do not think that we are going to begin holding up others upon our travels."

"No." Her lips curved. "But we shall contrive, I am sure of it."

"By the by, is that pistol loaded?"

"Indeed it is," Georgette said. "I specifically had Trump load it."

"And then you put it in the sewing basket rather than the coach?" Lucas said. "I must make my apologies to Trump. I thought it was he who had been lax."

"No. Not in that fashion."

"Do you truly know how to shoot, Miss Thompson?"

"No." She lowered her voice. "But I didn't wish the highwaymen to know that."

"Thank you for sharing your secret with me," Lucas said dryly. "And you thought that I was the crazy one?"

"I . . ." She flushed deeply.

Suddenly Lucas tumbled to it. She'd had the sewing box on her lap the minute they entered the coach. "Miss Thompson!"

"What?" She presented him an innocent expression.

"You were holding that pistol in reserve for me, were you not?"

"Ah . . . I must go and find Trump." Georgette turned away without another word.

Lucas watched her as she trudged away, her hands full of pistol and ill-gotten money, her black skirts billowing, her long veil trailing in the dirt. She called out for her cowardly coachman in a clear and happy voice.

A severe doubt assailed Lucas. He had vowed not to become embroiled in Aunt Clare's schemes. He had been determined to break the spinster's heart within an hour. Well, more than an hour had passed. Nor was it Miss Thompson who had insisted on a partnership. Or asked for a handshake upon their agreement. He frowned.

Had he just made a pact with the devil?

"I am positive it will work," Georgette said, her voice firm with eagerness.

Lucas shook his head ruefully as the carriage drew up before the inn. As he expected, its atmosphere was quaint, charming, and romantic. Aunt Clare's favorite type of inn for a tryst. Though in this case, it was meant for an abduction and ransom. "No one will ever believe you are my grandmother, Miss Thompson."

"Yes, they will. That is why I have the veil," Georgette said with sublime confidence. Her gray eyes glowed with excitement. "I have planned it all, you see. I did not know that I would have any traveling companion. Therefore if I were accosted, I planned to be an old woman. In fact, I already know how I intend to act. I am going to act exactly like Mrs. Frampton."

"Mrs. Frampton?"

Georgette laughed. "Yes. She lives down the street from me. She knows royalty, you know? At least, that is what she says. Of course, the Regent has never visited her." She frowned. "Nor have her children. She can be fractious sometimes, but one cannot help but feel for her. If she were not so lonely, I am sure she would be far nicer."

"I have no doubt." Lucas frowned. "However, you are not going to pretend to be Mrs. Frampton. Did you not consider that many would consider an old lady an easy victim?"

Her eyes shaded with consternation. "No, I had not."

Lucas felt rather cruel. The disappearance of her enjoyment was marked. "Though I imagine if you weigh it, a young girl traveling alone would face certain other dangers that could be avoided by an old woman."

That light appeared again. "Yes. And now it will serve in protecting your reputation."

"What?" Lucas exclaimed, stunned.

"You are an earl. You have a reputation to think of. Heaven only knows what your noble peers would think if you were seen with me. I am only a baron's daughter. It would lower your consequence, I am sure."

Lucas stared at her. He was not about to explain what his peers would truly think, or that it wouldn't damage *his* reputation one whit. "Madame, I fear it is your reputation we must be consider."

"Why? I do not need a reputation. I am going to be a very free and wild woman, regardless." She laughed. "Indeed, it might offer me a mystique when I move to Bath. A woman with a history. Only think, before I had no history whatsoever."

"No. No." Lucas held up his hand. "I concede. You may be an old woman."

"I may?" Georgette smiled with delight.

"Yes, you may." Lucas laughed. He found he could not say nay to her. The girl was intrepid. He reckoned this inn was far enough from society that he need not worry. And they needed an excuse for traveling together. "However, you must be an elderly great aunt. Everyone is aware that my grandmother has gone to her rewards."

"Very well." Georgette pulled her veil down. "What is you great aunt's name?"

"Emily."

"Emily." Georgette nodded as Trump opened the door. She pulled her veil over her face. "Hello, Trump. I am the earl's Great Aunt Emily."

"What, Miss Georgette?" Trump's mouth fell open. "Go on with ye. You ain't nobody's great aunt. You've never had any relatives ter speak of. S'fact. Yer without parents now."

"I know that." The soft net of Georgette's veil puffed out from her hiss. "But just pretend that I am. That is an order."

"I don't work for you no more, Miss Georgette," Trump was brave enough to say.

"But you do work for me, Trump." Lucas alighted, attempting to keep his composure. "And while at this inn, you will treat Miss Thompson as my Great Aunt Emily."

"Yes, my lord." Trump scratched his head. "I'll try ter remember that if ye wants me ter."

"I do." Lucas held out his hand. "Come, Great Aunt Emily."

"Thank you, Sonny." Georgette offered him her hand. Lucas was both pleasantly surprised and amused as she descended from the carriage with a creaky slowness, a bent figure. She looked at Trump. "You, boy, I want every one of my trunks brought to my room."

"Gore!" Trump's mouth dropped open. Then he grinned and pointed. "Mrs. Framtpon! Yer acting the spit of Mrs. Frampton, ain't ye?"

"You noticed." Georgette's voice oozed pride. "Then I am good at it?"

Trump scratched his head. "But yer supposed to be his lordship's Aunt Emily. Not Mrs. Frampton." He looked to Lucas. "How does yer Aunt Emily act?"

Lucas could see the trap a mile off. Refusing to bat an eyelash, he said in serious tones, "Exactly the same, I assure you."

"Thank you!" Georgette crowed. "And all three of us wish for you to bring in all my trunks, Trump."

"And that is an order." Lucas hid his smile. He took Georgette's arm. "Just why must you have all the trunks with you, Miss Thompson?"

"My lord, I would not have them stolen. They have many valuables within them."

"I doubt that we would be robbed twice in one day," Lucas said dryly as he led her at a snail's pace into the inn.

"Gracious," Georgette exclaimed as they successfully cleared the threshold. "How charming."

Lucas gazed about. The inn's floor was flagstone. The walls whitewashed. Great hewn beams ran the length of the room. It was quaint. It was private. "Aunt Clare's abductor has excellent taste, doesn't he? Or perhaps she?"

"Or perhaps they." Georgette nodded, clearly missing his sarcasm.

A man stepped out from behind a rough-hewn column.

"Jupiter!" Georgette squeaked.

With good cause. Lucas lifted his brow. The man standing before them was burly, heavy-browed, dark-haired, and certainly didn't belong within the charming setting of the inn. He might have belonged in a dark alley with a club, but not in the inn.

"Forgive me, madame. I did not mean to frighten you." The man offered a semblance of a bow. His humbleness didn't match his large frame, just as he didn't match the room. "I am Burt, the proprietor."

Lucas noted Burt's obsidian gaze upon Georgette. He decided it best to redirect the man's curiosity. "Good day. I am Montieth, the Earl of Kelsey."

"Good day, my lord." The man nodded quickly, a broad smile crossing his thick lips.

"And I am his Great Aunt Emily," Georgette offered in a querulous voice. "What do you mean by sneaking up on a body like that?"

Burt stared at her. He then looked at Lucas, confusion within his gaze.

"Yes?" Lucas inquired. Actually, he thought Georgette's impersonation rather good.

"Forgive me, my lord." Burt blinked. "But your missive said you would be traveling with your niece."

"His missive?" Georgette gasped. "What missive?"

"Ah, yes. My missive." Lucas tightened his grip upon Georgette's arm in warning. He should have known.

Aunt Clare had grown accustomed to arranging all details for her quarry. She had certainly shot wild, though, when deciding to call Georgette his niece. She could not have recognized the significance. Just who was advising Aunt Clare in all this? It wasn't him. It wasn't Ruppleton and Wilson, for they were in France. It wasn't Georgette, as he had first assumed. It could be any other of her boys, but if so, they should have known better. "I changed my arrangements as you can clearly see. I am traveling with my Great Aunt Emily instead."

"Of course." He bowed. "I have your suite prepared."

"Suite?" Georgette gasped. Then she coughed and proceeded in a cantankerous tone. "That will not do, young man! We must have two rooms."

"Madame"—Burt glanced to Lucas for support—"there are two chambers within the suite."

"I mean two separate suites, you young cawker." Georgette's voice was definitely cranky.

"Indeed, Burt." Lucas grinned. "I apologize for the confusion. But Aunt Emily must have her way, you know."

"I would certainly like to fulfill her wish and your wish, my lord." Burt sounded anything but contrite. "But I don't have another suite available."

Lucas lifted a wry brow. "Indeed? You are so very busy?"

Burt didn't bat an eye. "They have all been bespoken for, my lord."

"Indeed? By one person no doubt?"

"Indeed not, my lord. By several different individuals." He puffed out his chest. "I am receiving notes from many noble names, my lord. I am unable to break my confidentiality, of course." He bowed. "Just as I would never disclose to anyone that you were traveling with your niece."

"He isn't. He's traveling with me, his great aunt. That is perfectly proper, you great looby!" Georgette's Mrs. Frampton apparently was quite the tartar. "You must make different arrangements and be quick about it. I don't have time to stand about with my achy bones."

"Forgive me." Burt's gaze narrowed upon Lucas. "I would not wish to bear the wrath of my noble clientele. Not for nothing, that is."

Lucas smiled wryly. Burt was asking for a bribe. He knew better than to think he would get far with a twenty-pound note. "Very well. We shall be forced to make do with what Burt has for us, Aunt Emily. We would not wish for him to put anyone else out."

"Of course we would," Georgette snapped. "I want my own suite."

"Let us go to our suite, Aunt Emily," Lucas said and took Georgette by the arm.

"That young chowder-head doesn't know who he is speaking to," Georgette snapped. "I know royalty, I do."

"This way, my lord." Burt bowed, his face darkening. He turned and moved ahead.

"I am a rich woman!" Georgette said loudly. "A very rich woman. I could buy an abbey if I wished. That I could. He'll be sorry he doesn't treat me right!"

"If you don't be quiet, *you* will be sorry," Lucas muttered. He leaned close and whispered into the veil, "You are overplaying it, Miss Thompson."

"What?" She fell silent for a moment. Then she whispered. "Gracious, I quite forgot myself, I fear. It is no wonder Mrs. Frampton acts the way she does. It feels rather good, I'll own."

"Well cease it this moment." Lucas shook his head. "Poor Aunt Emily. She is the mildest thing. It is her reputation you defame."

"I am sorry." Her voice was not attentive. Indeed

she lifted it up in Aunt Emily's tones. "Burt! Slow down, Sonny. Do you want to rush me to my death?"

Burt swung around. His look spoke in favor of the notion. "Madame?"

"Was there a message left for my great nevy here? Or for me. I mean, for his niece, Miss Thompson?"

"No, madame. There was not."

"Well, we . . . or Montieth here is waiting for one. Make sure he gets it when it arrives."

"That I will, madame." Burt grinned. "I'll send it right along, I will."

When he turned, Lucas let out a sigh. "That is it. We are going to kill Aunt Emily the moment we reach the suite." Lucas murmured. "Is that clear? I want the unadulterated Miss Thompson back and no one else."

"You shall, my lord, in a moment," Georgette whispered. She lifted her voice again. "And you'd best send your servants to assist my coachman in bringing in my trunks. Do you hear? The clumsy fellow might drop them t'otherwise."

"I will have Nick and Ned assist him directly, madame."

"Young rascal." Georgette humphed, very much like an old lady. "I'll lay odds they bungle it. Though they can't do less than *your* man Trump, nevy."

"Proprietor," Lucas called out loudly. "Just how much would it cost for my own separate suite?"

Burt turned back only once. He barked a laugh. "I don't have one, and it's your own choice I would say. You bought my best suite for you and your niece. Ye should have kept it that way."

"Uppity popinjay is what I say!" Georgette snapped.

Lucas sighed. He hated to admit it, but the man was right.

Three

Georgette wiggled beneath the cover and stared into the dark. She had done so for the past three hours. Excitement thrummed through her. She had determined upon her father's deathbed that she would find adventure in life. She'd no notion, however, that she would find it so quickly, and in one day at that. Truly, it was wondrous.

It might be a wicked thought so close upon her sire's demise. Yet, the Baron Thompson had rarely taken note of Georgette while he was alive. She did not feel he would be overly worried about her behavior now that he was dead. He had been a strange, cold man, his only fervency showered upon scholarly pursuits. Georgette wondered if he would have been a different father if her mother had lived past Georgette's birth.

She steered her thoughts away. How many times had she gone down that path? As a child it had been an obsessive dream. Her father would be a warm, caring father. Her mother, whom she had painted on her heart's canvas as spirited and lovely, would always keep their house full of laughter and excitement.

She shook her head. There was no use in such fantasies. She had learned that growing up. However, certain fantasies continued to seep back into her being.

Faith, after today, they were no longer seeping. She wiggled her toes in delight. They were running rampant!

With the passing of her father, she vowed that so would all the rules and restrictions in her life pass away. Shockingly, he had left Georgette his estate and funds with no demands attached. For a man who had set his fifty-seven commandments down for the young Georgette and had then left her with a governess and servants to administer them, it truly was an odd thing.

His few relatives believed that he must have mistakenly delayed making his provisions, no doubt thinking that he would not pass away so early. Georgette held a different opinion. She believed that her father, when he thought of her, thought of her as the demure child who needed no consideration or direction.

She couldn't fault him. She had been that child. For too many years she had kept her spirit and fantasies well hidden. Sharing her hopes and dreams with her father's servants had never been alluring. If he had managed to hire servants like Aunt Clare's, she would have shared her entire world with them, but her father had hired servants after his own stamp.

Her nanny Birdie had been the only one who had been different. It was she who had taught Georgette within the four walls of the nursery that Georgette could be anything her mind could imagine. However, when she was amongst adults, and particularly her father, she should be seen and not heard. Nanny Birdie's language had been a colorful palette of Cockney and colloquialisms. Once again, saved for only within the nursery and amongst friends. She always told Georgette that when she became a lady "right and proper," that then she could do whatever she wished in the outside world, but to keep "mum" until then.

Nanny Birdie had been retired of course when Georgette grew of an age when she required a governess instead. Still, Georgette had continued to visit her every year thereafter, until Nanny Birdie had passed on to her Maker. If heaven were everything that Nanny Birdie touted it to be, there would be a traveling troupe of actors performing Shakespeare and Nanny Birdie, with all her wondrous girth, would be rendering up the finest performance of Lady Macbeth ever given in heaven or earth. Nanny Birdie had held the strongest belief that the impossible dreams one dreamed upon earth were merely a good notion about what one was going to be doing in heaven.

Georgette smiled to herself. *I must be a lady now, Nanny Birdie, because I am finally going to do what I want. I am going to have great adventures.*

Only look at what she had done so far. She had chased after her dear Aunt Clare, who was captured by villains. She frowned for only one moment. It was odd that the villains had reserved a suite for her and the earl. Lord Montieth had not said a word on that head. Georgette wasn't a widgeon. She knew he thought Aunt Clare was behind it all and that she had arranged such to throw them together.

Lucas had been most polite and cool. Once Trump and the inn's footmen had delivered the trunks into the salon, he had said that he imagined she would be tired and would care for her meal in her own room before retiring. Georgette hadn't particularly cared for that. However, she had bent to his will. After all, it was most likely that it was he who was tired and wished to retire after his heroic efforts of the day.

She knew she would never forget that scene of Lord Montieth with his flashing blade and brilliant eyes as he fought the ruffian. In truth, her heart had been in her throat, watching him duel with the highwayman. And he had done so in order to save her and her valuables. She had been glad to be able to assist and hold those robbers at bay with her pistol. She owned she had only gained the courage to do so after watching Lord Montieth's bravery.

She didn't know what to think of the man. She couldn't decide if she was glad for his presence or not. From their morning encounter she knew that he was mercurial and autocratic. A man who could so ruthlessly hire away her servants in order to stop her was indeed a man to avoid. Yet, by this afternoon she couldn't help but think that he was a man who one might trust to watch one's back as he had promised to do.

Yet she knew better. He was a man, after all. Her first opinion of him was the correct one, to be sure. If she were wise, she'd not allow that other image to supplant it. She sighed. It was a pity that men were so very appealing to women. She knew it was how they lured them into marrying them, and how they then could constrict them and set commands upon them. Georgette frowned and tried not to think of the fact that the earl lay not far away in a connecting room. Granted, a complete salon lay between them, but when a lady harbored such worries, it did not seem far enough away.

A noise interrupted her stream of thoughts. She tensed, staring into the darkness. Without a window in the room it was pitch dark. She sensed, rather than saw, the connecting door open. As she heard another noise and a breath, she stopped her own.

Someone was in her room, someone who came by stealth. Her mind roiled. Could it be Lord Montieth? No, she knew little about men, but she did know already that he was not the type of man to creep about a lady's boudoir. That much trustworthiness she would concede to him.

A strong odor drifted to her nostrils. It reeked of onions and a lack of personal attention to one's toilette. Georgette didn't waist one more second in cogitation. It clearly wasn't Lord Montieth. He smelled marvelous. That Georgette remembered from this morning when he had held her.

She pooled her courage. She had left her sewing box and pistol upon the chair beside the bed. In truth, before retiring, she had first drawn out the pistol and laid it upon the bedside table. After today's escapade it had seemed a reasonable notion. She had then come to the conclusion that no civilized lady could possibly have convivial dreams while knowing a pistol lay within full sight, mere inches from her. What would the maid think of her in the morning? Concealing it within the sewing box had made her feel less uncivilized.

Now, as she crawled from the bed and crept toward the chair that held the basket that contained the pistol, Georgette regretted her decision. Indeed, at this juncture she wished she had slept with the cold steel beneath her pillow. She let out the slightest sigh as she felt the box under her fingers. Then she let out a shriek as she felt a touch. A surprised curse echoed in the room.

Screaming with full force, Georgette snatched the sewing basket up and whirled about. A satisfying *woof* sounded as it rammed into a body. Something fell to the carpet with a thunk.

"Bloody hell!" a voice wheezed.

That voice was gruff and nasty sounding. It spurred Georgette to seize the initiative. She lifted the sewing basket and struck out with all her might. A howl of pained rage greeted this decisive action. Then strong arms grabbed her close. She jerked back with such force that she and her captor tumbled to the floor. Her shoulder struck a chair as she fell. A crashing sound and a blasphemous word let her know that her attacker had disturbed the bed table.

Callused hands clamped her shoulders. "Stubble it."

Georgette did not stubble it. She vented a lusty cry, calling for Lord Montieth. After that, she boxed what she hoped was her assailant's ears. He cursed loudly enough to make her think she had succeeded. She redoubled her efforts, flailing out with her bare foot. Her captor attempted to gain a stronghold against her dervishing arms.

Eons passed before a glow illuminated the room. The earl's voice cracked through the room. "Georgette!"

"Over here!" She wheezed from beneath her attacker, who did not display well when the light was shed upon him. He was ferret-faced, squint-eyed, and scarred. His eyes harbored both malice and fear, certainly not a felicitous combination. He also wore the scratchiest, rattiest coat, from whence the suffocating odor came. The only thing good that could be said was that the man himself was far smaller than the coat he wore. "Help!"

"Apparently, I was wrong. It is happening twice in one day. Is a hero's work never done?" Lucas set his candle down upon a bureau. Georgette gained an impression of an amused expression, and more astonishing, a naked chest. Since her assailant chose that moment to attempt to strangle her, it was only an impression. The thought of dying with that teasing impression upon her mind forced Georgette to fight more fiercely. She wanted life, drat it, and this ferret was not about to take it from her!

"Release her, varlet," Lucas called out, his voice ringing with confidence. Faith, but the man took danger lightly, Georgette thought with a gurgle. So very confident was he that the ferret paused to gape at him, revealing that his possession of teeth numbered to six. "Unhand Miss Thompson or I shall call you out, sirrah!"

The man employed all six teeth in a snarl of sorts. He rolled away from Georgette and sprang up. He lunged at Lucas. Though, to Georgette's bemused observation, she wasn't positive if he charged at Lucas, or at the door behind Lucas. The question was moot, however. Lucas snatched the little man by the collar of his coat and lifted him off the carpet. "You cannot escape so easily. I wish a word with you!"

The man did not answer, but swung a fist at him. Lucas's face showed surprise. It lasted but a moment. He whirled the man about like a top and cinched the man's arm to his back.

"That isn't too, painful, I hope?" Lucas murmured.

Georgette bit her lip, gaining enough of her equilibrium to drag herself up to a sitting position. It might be spiteful, but she hoped Mr. Ferret suffered a fair amount of pain.

Lucas shook the man. "Tell me of your involvement with Aunt Clare."

"Whot?" The little man stilled. His expression became wily. Once again, that mingled with his fear, did not make for a good expression. "Er, I don't know. I needs ter think. If'n you let me go . . ."

Georgette's stomach revolted. She shot up to a stand, a wavering one to be sure, but a stand. "No, my lord, do not!"

"Your wish is my command, Miss Thompson." Lucas's tone was nothing but indulgent. He turned his gaze from the little man to her. His eyes widened.

"Hey now. Don't listen ter that old bat! She . . . she . . ." The little man gurgled as he finally looked at her. "Gawd!"

"What?" Georgette frowned, more at her lightheadedness than anything else. Lord Montieth's upper torso was as magnificent as any statue, full of strong-muscled, chiseled curves, cast in warm alabaster. She swallowed, growing dizzier by the moment. Gracious. What was happening to her? "What is the matter?"

Lucas turned his gaze away. "Your nightgown is torn, Miss Thompson."

"Gawd! Yer just a chit!" Mr. Ferret accused. "I was bumfuddled how an old lady could feel the way ye did. Now I know why!"

"Heavens!" Georgette's hand flew to the neckline of her night rail. It indeed was rent, quite rent. Burning heat rose to her cheeks. Lucas, as a gentleman, had turned his gaze away, but Mr. Ferret's beady eyes bored upon her. Clasping her neckline together, Georgette bent and picked up the sewing basket. She drew it up to her front to cover her lack of proper *décolletage* and opened it, searching for a pin. That was when she was reminded of her pistol. She had actually forgotten it in the excitement. It was of little importance now compared to the necessity of a pin. She withdrew it and laid it alongside the lid.

"Oh Gawd!" the little man cried out, his eyes widening.

"She is a domestic little thing, isn't she?" Lucas murmured with good humor.

For a moment Georgette was taxed beyond her dizzy state. She simply lacked the required hands to hold the basket, pistol, and search for a pin.

"Permit me to take the pistol, Miss Thompson," Lucas offered, his tone kind.

"Thanks, gov. Ye can't trust a petticoat with a popper," the little man muttered. He still watched her with that disgusting, rather lascivious look.

"Are you going to shoot him?" Georgette stepped toward them eagerly.

"Please stop where you are, Miss Thompson," Lucas ordered.

"Bloodthirsty wench." Mr. Ferret shivered. "What did you two do with the old gal. Off her?"

Georgette laughed, a flush of pride running through her. "Yes, I did. My lord didn't like her so I did away with her."

"Bloody hell!" Mr. Ferret swallowed.

"Watch you language in front of the lady." Lucas released the little man for a moment, moving quickly to relieve Georgette of the pistol. He leveled it upon the intruder, who actually appeared to breathe easier because of it. "You are taking too great of liberties with your role, old man. Now do cease with the histrionics and just give us the message. It is late and both Miss Thompson and I are tired."

"Yes we are." A flood of relief washed through Georgette. Lucas's cavalier manner dispelled all her fear. She would have to acquire that fashion of confidence if she was to be a successful adventurer, she decided as she delved into the sewing box and found her pin. She turned away from the two men and dealt as swiftly as she could with her gaping neckline. She didn't wish to miss anything.

"Message? Er, yes. Message." Mr. Ferret shifted, and shifted again. He sighed. "Blimey, gov, your mort has gotten me so rattled, I can't think anything up. I don't know any message."

"Then why are you here?" Lucas asked. "What is your purpose?"

"What?" Georgette spun about in astonishment. Mr. Ferret's look was the same as hers. She was surprised that Lucas was so slow-witted. "He wished to rob me, my lord. That is quite obvious."

"I wouldn't put it so strongly now. Leastwise, not while he has that barking iron." Mr. Ferret's gaze flicked to the pistol nervously. "Let's say I was going ter barrow some blunt."

"No, you came to steal it," Georgette said firmly.

"Very well. I came to steal it."

Lucas shook his head. "Not two in one day. It is all too repetitive."

"It *is* shocking!" Georgette nodded.

He cast a dire frown upon Mr. Ferret. "Are you positive you had the correct instructions?"

Mr. Ferret jumped. "I didn't receive any instructions. Swear to God I didn't."

"Forgive me, but I had expected something more creative this time," Lucas persisted.

The bewildered Mr. Ferret looked to Georgette. "Is he cracked in the nob?"

Georgette laughed. "I suspect that he is."

Mr. Ferret paled, and hissed through his few teeth, creating quite a whistle. "Why don't ye take the popper back, missy? Between the two of you, I guess I'd rather have you holding it."

Lucas's brow shot up. He looked to Georgette, who attempted to maintain a straight face. It was he who broke into laughter. "Very well, have it your way. You came to steal from Miss Thompson. There's nothing for it. Turn out your pockets, man."

"Oh yes." Georgette brightened.

"What?" Mr. Ferret gasped.

"Turn about is fair play, old chap," Lucas drawled. His eyes twinkled as he winked at Georgette. "And unless you wish a lecture on reform from Miss Thompson you'd best do so posthaste."

"She's one to talk about reform," Mr. Ferret muttered. "I ain't killed no old lady. And I don't go about with barking irons hidden in my basket. I don't hold with those nasty things. That I don't."

"I believe he is stalling, Miss Thompson." Lucas's eyes glinted.

"I do too." Georgette smiled.

Mr. Ferret paled. "I don't have any of the ready. That's why I was going to rob the old lady. I'd heard that she was rich as a nabob."

"Oh dear." Georgette flushed.

Lucas looked at her solemnly. "Let that be a lesson to you, Miss Thompson, not to puff off your own consequence. Gossip like that travels."

Georgette decided to ignore Lucas. "I'll lay odds you have the ready. Those highwaymen said they had nothing this afternoon, and they did."

"You—you held up highwaymen? Gore." Mr. Ferret gasped, his eyes wide. "I've never met a more wicked pair like you two in all me born days."

"I am beginning to believe that you have more in your pockets than I first imagined. This should be interesting." Lucas smiled. "He must have more than fifty pounds, Miss Thompson."

"I do hope so," Georgette said.

"Clean out your pockets, my good man."

"Very well." The man reached into his coat pocket. He didn't bring out any money; instead he drew out the oddest item.

"What is that?" Georgette stared in fascination as he threw it to the carpet. For some reason, it looked sinister.

"They are called brass knuckles, Miss Thompson." Lucas's voice was calm. He just as calmly drew back the hammer of the pistol. Georgette jumped. A completely different man appeared before her eyes. A cool, dangerously cool, man. His sherry-colored eyes turned more to the color of a deep garnet. "What else do you have? Unburden yourself."

"Now don't get nervous, gov." Mr. Ferret lifted his hands high.

"I am not," Lucas drawled. Georgette thought he was the only one in the room who wasn't. "Do proceed cautiously. I am slightly deranged as you noted."

"All right." Mr. Ferret reached into the pocket and withdrew a thin little knife.

Faintness overtook Georgette. "He's got a knife!"

"That is a stiletto, to be precise, Miss Thompson," Lucas observed.

"Oh." Georgette stared at it, her blood chilling. It still looked like a knife to her.

"I never use it much." Mr. Ferret shrugged. Then a hope filled his eyes. "Listen, gov, you look like a man who knows business. I'll give you all that I got! If'n you will just let me keep the knife me da gave ter me." He delved into his coat pockets and began tossing out its contents. And tossing. A rain of knives and strange weaponry fell to the carpet.

The silence in the room was thick.

"I am glad you don't hold with pistols like you do knives," Lucas finally drawled. "Is that all?"

"I should hope so." Georgette swallowed.

"Is it?" Lucas repeated.

"All right." Mr. Ferret bent and dug a knife out of his boot. He tossed it to the floor. "That is all. On me mother's grave, it is!"

Georgette's eyes crossed in her effort to study the clutter of weapons. "Which one is your father's knife?"

"It's over there?" Mr. Ferret grimaced. "I dropped it when ye hit me."

"Oh." Georgette's stomach capsized. Unaccountably, she began to tremble. She was perfectly all right, she reminded herself. She was! She hadn't been killed. Only if she hadn't surprised him, and if Lord Montieth hadn't arrived—she refused to think about that. She hadn't once fainted in her life and she wasn't going to do so now. "I see."

"You are very heavily armed, are you not?" Lucas said.

Mr. Ferret shrugged. "I ain't a big bloke like you. I got ter have protection."

"Clearly." Lucas nodded. "I regret that I will not return your father's knife, or any of the others for that matter. We are going down to see the innkeeper, whom I expect shall send for the authorities."

"Here now. Why d—do you want to do that for?' I ain't stole nothing. Fact is, you stole from me!"

"I have no doubt that the authorities will know of something you have done."

"Please, gov," Mr. Ferret pleaded. "Don't turn me in. Don't take me ter Burt. Have some mercy."

"I am sorry. Now do let us proceed." Lucas moved toward the bureau to take up the candle. "We should leave Miss Thompson to her rest."

"What?" Georgette gasped. Fear struck her with its own wallop. She didn't wish to be alone. She couldn't be alone! Acting quickly, she sprung to the bureau and snatched up the candle before Lucas. "No, no. I will hold the candle for you. Do proceed, my lord."

Since Mr. Ferret had started for the door already, Lucas couldn't hesitate. He followed, saying over his shoulder. "You may give me the candle, Miss Thompson."

"That is quite all right, my lord." Georgette controlled a shiver. She had reached a surfeit of excitement for the day. "I am . . . watching your back for you!"

"That is very kind of you, Miss Thompson," Lucas

said. "But I must point out to you that you are not precisely dressed for this endeavor."

"Neither are you," Georgette retorted as they entered the darkened hall. Not a wall sconce was lit within it. It only strengthened Georgette's position.

"She's got you there, gov." Mr. Ferret barked a laugh and then gasped. "Gawd, that might be me last laugh."

"Not if Miss Thompson has her way," Lucas said dryly.

The flickering shadows on the walls only played upon Georgette's jangling nerves. "Everyone is asleep. No one will see me."

"The innkeeper will see you in due course, Miss Thompson," Lucas said sternly. "That I cannot applaud."

"Burt is a randy old goat at that," Mr. Ferret admitted. "I wouldn't be giving him no ideas, miss. We all can turn around if ye wish?"

"No!" Georgette said. "I shall leave. Since it is clear you do not wish for my company. I shall return to my room." It was a brave speech. Georgette's head recognized the sense in it. Her feet did not. They continued pacing behind the two men.

A silent moment passed.

"Miss Thompson?" Lucas asked.

"Yes?" Georgette said.

"So that *is* you behind us then?" Lucas said. "I thought you had left."

Mr. Ferret chuckled. "You were right, gov. She tickles one's ribs, she does."

"There is no need to be so rude," Georgette said with dignity. "I *am* going. Here, you may take the candle, my lord."

"Certainly, Miss Thompson." Lucas slowed and turned to do just that.

Mr. Ferret, regardless of the dim light, clearly saw

his chance. Spinning about, he chopped at Lucas's pistol hand, driving it down. The pistol spent its bullet into the floor. Georgette squeaked. Lucas growled. Before he could maneuver, Mr. Ferret shoved at him. The little man must have been truly driven by fear, for he rocked Lucas back, directly into Georgette. The candle that Georgette had intended to offer flew from her hand as Lucas's large frame knocked into her.

"Sweet Mary's night rail!" Georgette cried out. She bent, jerked at the hem of her nightgown and doused the fire.

"Miss Thompson?" Lucas asked.

"Yes. Ouch! Yes?" She stood up and was almost run over by Lucas. Warm arms enveloped her to steady her. She reached out for support and clasped a naked shoulder.

"Gracious!" Georgette froze.

"Not Sweet Mary's night rail?" Lucas laughed.

"Er . . . no." This was a night for Georgette's limbs to ignore her head. She wanted to tear her hands from the warm flesh beneath them, but they wouldn't budge. Worse, they even wished to explore the muscle beneath their fingertips more extensively.

"Are you all right?" Lucas asked. "Is your hand burned?"

"Yes." In fact both her hands burned in curiosity. Georgette then she shook her head. "No. I mean no."

"I am glad to hear that." Lucas's voice had lowered.

"Forgive me," Georgette whispered.

There was a pause. "For what?"

Georgette blushed. "We—we lost Mr. Ferret."

"So we did." Lucas's voice sounded strangled. "That is a fine name for him by the way."

"It is all my fault." Georgette said.

"Of course it isn't. The man was wily." Lucas's voice was polite.

"It was my fault and we both know it." She sighed. "I so wanted to keep my end of the bargain and watch your back."

"I appreciate that, Miss Thompson."

"Very well, I *was* frightened," Georgette said, as if he had accused her. "I didn't want to be left alone."

"I had a suspicion of that too." Lucas chuckled.

"I feel dreadful about it." Georgette said, feeling anything but dreadful at the moment. Warm tingles enveloped her body, while her heart danced a fast pace. Without a doubt, she was experiencing another new adventure. Never had she been touched by a man, let alone held against a naked chest.

"Don't. It is only natural to feel the way you do."

"Is it?" It did feel oddly natural.

"You were absolutely intrepid, Miss Thompson, but there is only so much excitement one can tolerate in one day." He released her promptly, his voice sounding unexplainably rough in the dark. "I believe we should return now."

Georgette blinked, feeling quite bereaved in truth. "Oh yes."

"Why in the blazes are there no sconces lit?" Gracious, he was already a good two feet away from her by the sound of his voice.

"I wondered that myself." Georgette stood still, totally disoriented.

"I have a notion that Mr. Ferret, as you so aptly named him, performed the task of extinguishing them beforehand."

Deciding to follow Lucas, she stepped forward. "But then how can he see the way himself?"

"The only way he could is if he is very conversant with the rooms within the inn. There are some innkeepers who actually employ thieves to rob their own customers, Miss Thompson."

"Jumping Jehoshaphat. Ooff!" Georgette ran directly into Lucas, this time his back, by the feel of it. A shiver coursed through her. His back was smooth and expansive. Embarrassment coursed through her. "Watching his back" took on a new meaning.

"Miss. Thompson!" Lucas growled, his voice sharp.

"Sorry." Georgette skittered back. She hit the wall. "Ouch!"

"Miss Thompson?" Lucas's concerned question hit her one second before he did.

"Ouch!" Georgette cried as he stepped on her bare toe and all but overran her.

"Ooff!" Lucas grabbed hold of her instinctively. "Forgive me!"

"My lord?" Georgette gasped at what he had grabbed hold of.

"Yes. Hm. Forgive me." He only shifted his arm lower to her waist. "Once again, a thousand pardons."

"No. I—I quite understand." Georgette couldn't catch her breath. "You may release me now."

"No. I am thinking first, Miss Thompson." Lucas's voice held an odd note.

"Thinking?" Her heart was beginning to flutter at his comprehensive hold. She didn't seem to have even one thought in her own head. "About what?" Then she flushed. "Er, no. Do continue . . . thinking that is."

"We are not going to proceed very well this way, Miss Thompson."

"Indeed not, my lord." Georgette was determined to focus. "We cannot proceed if we do not move."

"I know." He chuckled. "But we cannot proceed if we keep running into each other this way either. It is far too enlightening, I fear."

"Enlightening?"

"I quite agree with Mr. Ferret." Lucas's tone was amused. "You in no manner feel like an old lady."

"What?" Georgette gasped.

"Therefore," Lucas continued, "I propose we take hold of each other's hands. It being the most appropriate choice of contact at the moment."

Georgette's shock dissipated. She chuckled. "I believe you are correct, my lord."

"And permit me to lead. I intend to proceed along the wall."

"That is a good notion." She let him clasp her hand and he did indeed lead her. A wild thought occurred to her. That was after she cast out a multitude of improper wild thoughts first. "My lord? What if we enter the wrong room?"

"I highly doubt there is a single soul in any of these rooms. The innkeeper said they were reserved, but I misdoubt anyone actually has appeared."

"But one of them might. What then?"

"Then, my dear Miss Thompson, it is quite simple. We ask them for flint and candle."

Four

"I apologize, my lord," Burt, the innkeeper, slurred. His face was black with rage. "I shall hunt this thief down and kill him. For you, of course."

"No need to do that. Just turn him in to the authorities. That is all I ask." Lucas, now fully dressed, was far less bloodthirsty than he had been before for some reason.

"No one is going to burgle in my inn without me knowing it," Burt spouted. He was the worse for drink to be sure. He leaned heavily upon the desk, an open bottle before him. He grimaced in obvious pain.

"Are you all right?" Lucas frowned.

Burt groaned. "It . . . I suffer from . . . gout, my lord. That is all."

"I see." Lucas refrained from mentioning that spirits might not be the best medicine for gout. He felt a slight compunction. "Perhaps I should search for the thief myself." If Burt found Mr. Ferret in the mood he was in, he might very well do what he boasted and kill the poor fellow.

"No!" Burt roared. He flushed. "I shall send my staff to search for him. Why do you not return to your room? I am sorry for the disturbance." He looked more like himself. "In fact, I'll drop your shot. I run a good inn here. I do not . . ."

"It is of no significance." Lucas waved his hand. He decided he preferred Burt drunk and roaring, rather than toadying. After a few more polite comments Lucas turned away from the desk.

He walked back to the suite. In truth, he hurried back. He might have lost Mr. Ferret because of Miss Thompson's actions, yet fear had driven her, which by rights it should have. He still didn't like to relive the moment when Mr. Ferret had cleaned out his pockets. He had only asked the man to do so for a show to Georgette. When the little man had started dropping his weapons, he realized that the robbery was entirely real. Aunt Clare didn't dream up scenes with brass knuckles and stilettos. He could only imagine how frightened Miss Thompson was at this moment, being left alone. Time would not have permitted her to dress properly and accompany him. She had been very pale within the dim light of the candle when he had left her.

He arrived at the suite in record time. He rapped upon the door. "Miss Thompson?"

"Is that you, my lord?" Georgette's voice sounded cautious.

He could not blame her. In fact, he needed to consider matters long and hard. Lucas didn't like the feel of things one whit. "Yes, Miss Thompson."

The door opened. Georgette stood within the framework. "Did you catch Mr. Ferret?"

For a moment Lucas could not speak. Georgette had donned a robe of a soft periwinkle blue velvet. It had been created to be quite presentable with its broad kerchief collar of satin-worked linen and mitt sleeves. However, it had deep pockets tipped with pale yellow braided ribbons. Those pockets bulged, dragging at the

robe's neckline, down past her nightgown's hap-
hazardly pinned neckline, which was still revealing.
Lucas might have said something except for the fact
that Georgette held a knife in her hands. He couldn't
help the laughter rising within him. Once again, if he
were to be the hero, his heroine was not greeting him
correctly. "Forgive me, Miss Thompson. Whatever lib-
erty I might have taken before was purely accidental.
Do not render the cut *direct* to me for it."

"What?" Her long black hair shimmered like satin
within the glow of candlelight. Her gray eyes were
dark and now, very mortified. "Oh no. I am sure I
took as many liberties . . . accidentally that is."

"Of course." Lucas could have kicked himself. How
could he have mentioned the matter? Once again he
could feel her small warm hands upon his skin. "Indeed, what transpired was entirely accidental. It was
the lack of light."

A smile, as intriguing as the glimmer in her gray
eyes, curved her lips. "There will be enough light now,
my lord." She stepped back and waved for him to enter
the salon of the suite. She clinked and clanked with
each step.

Lucas was about to ask her just why she sounded
like pots and pans, but astonishment took the words
from his mouth. The salon was aglow in a myriad of
lights. Candles set upon every possible level and position. "My God."

"I—I thought a little light might be pleasant." She
grinned. Then she grimaced. "Very well, it made me
feel far less frightened."

"To be sure." Lucas entered, gazing about in awe.
Here he had dashed back, worried for the poor, frightened Miss Thompson. He should have known better.
She had sufficiently addressed the issue by setting the
room ablaze, a prefect curtailment to both fears and

thieves. He shook his head. "Where did you find so many candles?"

"They were in my trunks." Georgette said. "I know they are frightfully expensive, but . . . but I could not be comfortable until your return. Light always makes one feel better, doesn't it?"

He still couldn't fathom it. "You had that many candles in the trunk?" His eyes widened as they lit on a silver tray upon a table by the settee. Upon it was a bottle. "And wine?" He glanced up. A jaded warning clamored within him. A thrill of pure satisfaction accompanied it. No doubt because he was about to be proven correct in his initial assessment. Aunt Clare and Miss Georgette Thompson *were* in cahoots. "Miss Thompson, are you trying to seduce me?"

Her eyes widened, even as she frowned. "My lord?"

He nodded toward the wine bottle. "Was that in your trunk, Miss Thompson?"

"Yes." She worried her lower lip. "I was unsure as to how to open it. But . . . I thought that perhaps you might enjoy a glass. Aunt Clare told me that a gentleman always requires a good wine."

"For what?" Lucas narrowed his gaze.

"I don't know. But she says it is the best way to pull her brother Bendford down from the bows."

"Miss Wrexton, I am not in the boughs."

"I know." She shifted feet. She clanked. "But I . . . I thought it might be all right if I . . . I experienced a glass. Not a lot." She blurted out fast. "Aunt Clare explained that too much for a lady will make her feel frightfully ill the next morning. But she does give her cats a quarter of a glass without harm."

"Certainly, Miss Thompson." Lucas strolled over to the table. The silver glowed in the light. She at least had found the proper tools. There were two goblets of crystal set upon the table. "Miss Thompson, why did

you bring wine and silver along, if you were rushing
to save Aunt Clare?"

She would not meet his gaze. "I brought it in order
that I might trade it for Aunt Clare if possible."

"What?" Lucas exclaimed.

"I am hoping that I have brought enough to equal
five hundred pounds in trade."

"That is why you brought it?" Lucas cleared his
throat. "You truly thought you might pawn wine and
silver to the abductors?"

"I did not know what else to do." She shifted upon
her feet. "There is more. Everything in the coach."

Lucas felt the oddest sense of disappointment. There
was no doubt about it. Georgette was being honest.
She had not thought of seducing him. Worse, he truly
had wronged her. "My God. I just thought . . ." He
paused. "I'm not sure. I just thought you were a
woman who overreacted and over packed."

"You read the note. It said I must set out within
four hours of receiving it. I thought that the most important thing. At present I still do not have access to
any of the ready. It has not been transferred to me."
Georgette lifted her chin. "But I promise you, this all
belongs to me now."

Lucas stared at her. Aunt Clare had given him no
time in regard to raising the money because she knew
he had access to it. She had given Georgette four
hours, and clearly the girl had not wasted a moment
of that time. She had stripped her house because she
loved Aunt Clare. He had almost refused to even answer the note. He picked up the bottle. "I would say
that you deserve more than a quarter of a glass today,
Miss Thompson." He opened the bottle and poured the
wine into the glasses. "Indeed, I believe you deserve
a whole glass." He picked it up and offered it to her.

"Thank you, my lord." Georgette took the glass

from him and sat down with another clank. She sipped daintily from the goblet. Then her gray eyes lit from within. "Now that's the dandy."

"Er, yes." Lucas poured himself a glass and sat in a chair. He took an exploratory sip before he asked. "Miss Thompson, may I be so bold as to inquire why you clink when you move?"

"I have Mr. Ferret's weapons." She smiled. "They make one feel . . ."

"I know. Better. Like the light."

"Exactly." She sipped from the wine. Lucas's eyes widened in amusement as she let out a sigh and wiggled her bare toes.

That innocent but very telling action turned something within Lucas. His blood warmed. "You didn't bring slippers?"

"No. I forgot to in my haste." She studied him. "Would you teach me how to use Mr. Ferret's weapons?"

"Good God, no," Lucas exclaimed before he could stop himself. He said less vehemently, "I don't think I would even know how to use those weapons myself. His collection goes beyond the normal for self-preservation."

"I see. Perhaps then you could show me how to shoot a pistol."

"No," Lucas said firmly. Georgette's toes wiggled again as she took another sip of wine. What else would wiggle if she drank . . . He frowned. "Definitely only one glass for you, Miss Thompson."

"What?" She clearly was very much enchanted with the wine.

Lucas knew better than to say his real thoughts. He spoke his second thought instead. "A lady with as much weaponry upon her should have but one glass, Miss Thompson."

She laughed. "Certainly, my lord. I would not wish to become tap-hackled."

"Indeed." Lucas sipped his wine. "Now, I believe, would be a good time for you to explain to me why you employ such a vocabulary as you do."

Georgette leaned back against the settee's cushions. Her smile was as delighted as the rest of her surely was. "You do not like it?"

"I do not mind. Only it seems very much at odds with your rearing."

"Precisely." She sipped from her wine.

Lucas attempted not to look at her toes this time. "Why precisely?"

"I may not be interesting," Georgette said, "but at least my language might be."

"Miss Thompson." Lucas frowned. "You are interesting with or without your lively vocabulary."

"Thank you." Her cheeks flushed to a wonderful rose.

She truly was a very beautiful girl. Her looks were so very out of the ordinary, that anger rose within Lucas. It was ridiculous for her to think so very little of herself. "You are not common, Miss Thompson. Or dull. Or any of that rot."

She looked at her wineglass. "Words can be an adventure in themselves sometimes. And no matter the restrictions in one's life, just speaking particular words can tickle one's fancy."

"Yes, Miss Thompson." Lucas sighed. "You do not wish me to compliment you, I see."

"Oh no." She looked at him quickly. "I quite like it. Only, I'm not accustomed to it. And . . . it makes me feel rather odd."

Now Lucas flushed; at least, inside he did. She may not wish to have anything to do with a man, but he could only imagine what kind of woman she would become with some true love and attention. "I am sure it is only the wine."

"Perhaps." She stifled a yawn. "Strange, I am growing sleepy."

"Then why do you not go to sleep, Miss Thompson?" That would be the best advice for both of them.

"I prefer to be here." She took another sip.

"Then sleep here." Lucas drank from his own wine. "I am not sleepy and shall keep watch over you, if that is your concern."

"It was. Just a little, you know." She looked at him with dilated eyes. Her body clearly wished for rest, despite what her formidable mind wanted. "Why should I be so sleepy? It—it has been such a very exciting day. That alone should keep me awake."

"I don't doubt that we shall have another exciting day tomorrow," Lucas said dryly. Between Aunt Clare's antics and the real-world antics that fate preferred of late, Lucas never doubted it. "I promise you, I shall wake you if anything exciting transpires, Miss Thompson."

"Thank you. You are so very kind." Georgette set her glass of wine down upon the table. She sighed slightly and then capsized with a clatter to the settee cushion. "Which is . . ." She squirmed to a better position, her eyes already closed. "Is . . ."

"Is what, Miss Thompson?" Lucas asked.

"Hmm?" she breathed.

"You said I am very kind, which is . . . what? Miss Thompson?" Lucas received no answer. She was finally out. Lucas studied the sleeping girl. Perhaps Aunt Clare was right. Not in Georgette being his true love, for that she could never be. Only one woman was that.

Isabelle's image immediately filled his mind's eye and heart. Golden-haired, with violet blue eyes, she moved with a superb grace. She was the Botticelli's

Birth of Venus come to life. And she knew a man's soul like no other woman. She could tease and flirt with one until nothing mattered in life but her.

Lucas drank the last swallow of his wine in a gulp. That would be that. As Georgette had said, he couldn't become tap-hackled. There was a thief out there stripped of his favorite weaponry, there was a drunken and very angry landlord out searching for said thief, and there was a sleeping . . . a sound filled the room, very slight but obvious . . . make that a snoring woman, whom he had promised to watch over. Georgette murmured and curled up with a shiver.

Sighing, Lucas rose and walked quietly from the salon and to his room. He stripped it of its blanket. He could very well become a mentor to Miss Georgette Thompson. The charming platonic relationship Aunt Clare had painted didn't seem so far-fetched after all. He smiled as he carried the blanket back to the salon. He moved quietly to her and covered her with the blanket.

"A surprise." Georgette jumped and sat up quickly. The clanking followed.

Lucas stepped back. "I beg your pardon?"

Georgette looked at him. Her eyes were open but he knew she wasn't truly awake. "It is a surprise that you are so very kind. That is what I meant to say."

"I take that as a great compliment, Miss Thompson." Lucas smiled. She shook her head and a sleepy pout appeared. "I have offended you?"

"I don't like being called Miss Thompson."

"A thousand apologies." Lucas sat down upon the settee beside her. "I do not wish to be overly familiar, Miss Thompson, but . . ."

"I know. But *Miss Thompson* makes me feel very like a . . . a governess."

"No, I was going to ask you to give me all your

weapons," Lucas said. "You might hurt yourself sleeping upon them."

"They *are* uncomfortable." Georgette sighed. She dove into her pocket and struggled to pull out a knife. "I am supposed to be an adventurous woman now." It caught in her folds. "Not a *Miss Thompson.*" Her voice was singularly cool and haughty.

"I do not say it that way, Miss Thompson." Lucas chuckled.

"Yes you do." Georgette sniffed. *"Miss Thompson."* She drew out her hand from her pocket. "Drat. They are not that uncomfortable. I will sleep on them." Georgette started to lie back on the settee.

"No, Miss Thompson!" Lucas reached for her shoulders and held her up. "Permit me."

"Hmm?" Georgette sighed and her eyes closed. "Though I don't like Georgette either. It, too, is formal, don't you think?"

"Perhaps." Lucas reached into her right pocket and drew out knife and stiletto and brass knuckles. Then he shifted the limp lady against him and reached into her left pocket. The softest sent of violets teased his nostrils. Silken hair brushed his cheek. He determinedly drew out weapons even he didn't recognize. Georgette rendered no objection, easily sleeping through it all. "There." He gently pushed her away and propped her against the cushion. He shook his head. "After that rather intimate procedure, I believe you are right. Why stand upon ceremony?"

"Hm, what?"

Lucas stood. "You may now lie down and go to sleep, Georgette."

"Thank you." She dutifully fell to the settee and curled up. A sublime smile crossed her lips. "I like that better."

"Yes?" Lucas began to cover her with the blanket

but halted. Her toes peeked out from the hem of her nightgown and robe. They wiggled in pleasure. Smiling, he was unable to resist. He said it again. "Georgette?" They wiggled again. And that warmth coursed through him again. "Er, yes. Go to sleep." He quickly dropped the blanket over her and her speaking toes. He strode back to his chair and sat. "I suppose you could call me Lucas then."

"No." Georgette sighed. "You are 'my lord.' "

Lucas frowned in displeasure. Then he sighed. What was the purpose of pulling caps with a sleeping woman? He stood. Knowing what he needed, he walked over to one of Georgette's various trunks. He found a very dry book on the history of Rome and carried it back to his chair. Sitting down, he began reading. He had sleepily read half of the beginning when he heard a noise at the salon door.

Frowning, he rose and paced quietly over to the door. A scrap of paper had been slipped beneath the door. He smiled. Finally. Aunt Clare's next missive. He hoped it requested them to leave this inn as fast as possible. He had worried that Aunt Clare would wish to keep them kicking about this romantic little inn far too long.

He bent down and picked up the note. He opened it. It was in the same handwriting as the other two notes had been. However, it contained severe differences from the others. The differences were that the line "bring the money" had been scratched out. Above it, in a different ink, ten thousand pounds had been scribbled. The ransom had gone up.

The next revision appeared where the note requested they go to a "Glendon Folly." That, too, had been scored out. Above it was written "The Hangman, Lundun."

Lucas's frown deepened. The handy map Aunt Clare

customarily provided had been also scratched through. Indeed, the note took a very rude turn. Next to it the missive read, "Find it your bloody self."

Lucas clenched his teeth. He walked slowly over to his chair and sat down, deep in meditation. That was when he flipped the sheaf of paper over. Another addition had been made. "Bring ten thousand more if you want the damn cat too."

"Blast and damn!" Lucas muttered.

"What?" Georgette murmured in her sleep.

"Nothing, Georgette." Lucas stifled his groan. Aunt Clare had gone and done it. She had succeeded in being truly abducted. His gaze strayed to the sleeping Georgette. What was he to do with her? Matters had just become dangerous, too dangerous for a young miss to be involved.

He sighed. He would leave her here. She wouldn't know about the note nor have a lead to where he was going. He stood. That was what he would do. Once he had saved Aunt Clare he would return for Georgette. He tread quietly away from the settee toward his room.

"Lucas?" Georgette asked.

Lucas froze. He actually bit back a curse. He couldn't believe the pleasure that went through him upon hearing his name used by Georgette. Unfortunately it had been uttered in trust. He felt quite the cad. "Yes, Georgette?"

"You swore."

"No, Georgette, I didn't." He returned to his chair.

"Oh." She sighed, eyes still closed. "I thought you did."

"Very well, I did."

"Why?"

Lucas paused. She was not truly conscious. He could tell her anything he wished. Yet he, fool that he was, had shaken hands and made a pact with Georgette. He was caught between chivalry and nobility. And Georgette's unconscious trust. "I am afraid you were right."

"Right?" Even that didn't make her open her eyes.

"Aunt Clare has been kidnapped."

"Of course." She breathed. "We must save her."

"Yes, we must. We shall have a very exciting day tomorrow," Lucas said, surrendering completely. "Just as I promised."

"Sir Percy?" Aunt Clare called and poked her head into the taproom of the Hangman. She halted with a gasp. It appeared to be a very large room and it was excessively crowded. Men and certain ladies sat at unvarnished tables, or milled about. It astonished Aunt Clare. It was indeed teatime, but she had not expected a thief's den to be so very full for the time-honored custom. She attempted to look past the throng of rough characters. She raised her voice. "Sir Percy, dear!"

She gained attention at that, but not one feline response was amongst it. Clare glanced back. She truly should not have gone off without the boys to accompany her, but her fear of what trouble dear Sir Percy might get into in such a place drove her onward. He'd been gone for three hours. Picking up her skirts, she cautiously entered the taproom.

She stopped at the first table she came upon. A weasel-like little man sat at it alone. He offered her a glare, nothing more. "Pardon me, sir, have you perchance seen Sir Percy? He's an orange marmalade cat."

"Have I seen him?" He lifted a hand from the table. A long red scratch ran along it.

"Oh my, so you have." Aunt Clare sighed. "I do apologize for him. He quite loses his decorum once he is back within this atmosphere. Could you please tell me where he went?"

"He'll be at the bar with François. Only fitting. Both of them are devils."

"The bar! Tsk. Tsk. Thank you, sir." Aunt Clare didn't wait a second more. She begged her pardon through the crowd until she saw the bar.

"Naughty. So very naughty." Aunt Clare shook her head. Sir Percy was at the moment stalking along the length of the bar, his scarred tail a flag. He came upon a glass and partook of it.

Unfortunately, the glass had been attached to the hand of a large brutish man. He must be François and he did look like the devil. He looked even worse when Sir Percy spat whatever his drink was upon him. "What?" He turned and seeing Sir Percy, roared, "You bloody cat, stay out of me Blue Ruin."

"Gracious," Aunt Clare breathed. "Not gin!"

The large man unclenched his glass and attempted to clench Sir Percy instead. He received a snarl and a grand swipe of sharp claws. Cursing, he jerked his hand back. "I'll teach you, you bugger." In a flash, wounded hand or not, he pulled out a knife from his vest pocket.

"Oh, dear no!" Aunt Clare dashed up to the man. "François! Stop!"

The man ignored her completely, and swung at Sir Percy. Sir Percy merely sprang up, landing with a swipe to the man's wrist as he knifed at the empty air where the cat had been. François howled.

"No, oh no!" Aunt Clare grabbed hold of his arm. "Do stop."

"Heh!" François growled and attempted to shake Aunt Clare off. She clung to him like the proverbial limpet. "Leave off. Do you want me to kill you or the bloody cat, old woman?"

"I'd prefer neither . . ." Aunt Clare gasped, "to be honest."

"You heard her, Tobias." A soft voice said from behind them. Its accent was French. "If you do not honor Madame's wish, it shall be you who dies, *fripouille.*"

"Bloody hell, François." Tobias rumbled. "It ain't right."

"François?" Aunt Clare blinked. She stared at the dark devil before her. "Aren't you François?"

"No." Tobias said. He actually flushed red and the men snickered.

"I, madame, am François," the voice with the French accent said.

"Oh dear." She dropped the dark man's arm and turned. Her heart stopped. The man who stood before her was patrician thin. A mane of white hair halloed his face, and eyes, as dark blue as her own were light, smiled at her. He wore a shirt of pristine white, a fall of lace at each cuff. "I—I thought he was François. Do forgive me."

"Well you should apologize, *Mademoiselle,*" François said. "To dare to attach my name to that great clod is very close to unforgivable." The men about them laughed. He offered her a courtly leg. "But for you, *mon ange,* I shall forgive you anything."

"Thank you." Blushing, Clare curtsied demurely.

"Go on with yer, François," Tobias howled. "Look at yer fancy courtin'."

"You shall leave my bar, Tobias, this very moment." François did not look at the man, his gaze still warm upon Aunt Clare. Aunt Clare stared at him. Light rose within her. "I told you that no one was to touch Monsieur Percy, did I not, Tobias?"

"But the bloody cat spat me Blue Ruin upon me."

"He dislikes Blue Ruin excessively," Aunt Clare

murmured. The stunning knowledge exploded within her.

"Yes. *Mot juste.* So he should. He is a cat with excellent sense . . . and taste." François nodded. "But I fear he has enjoyed the ale far too much. It has made him rather mean." He finally turned his gaze toward Tobias. "Whereas Tobias here has no excuse, I regret to say. He is mean without a potion. You may leave now, Tobias, while I still am too enchanted with the lovely lady to consider your offense. Yes?"

"I'm going." Tobias shoved away from the bar. Looking neither left nor right at the watching crowd, he departed.

"Mademoiselle, permit me to lead you to a table." François offered her his arm.

"Oh my, yes. Thank you." Tears formed in Aunt Clare's eyes as she took his arm. She could not speak as he drew her to the corner of the taproom and she permitted him to draw out a chair for her. She sat, ignoring the tiers of lawn and appliqued satin of her jonquil gown caught under a leg of her chair. She but gazed upon him as he then sat across from her. Finally, alas. The moment she had been waiting for all her life. "It is you."

"Yes, *ma chérie?*" The man lifted a white brow, though his dark blue eyes showed the depths of the widest ocean within them.

Sir Percy at that moment sprang up to the table. She glanced at her beloved feline. "Sir Percy, you dear cat. You have found him for me."

"I thought I had found you for *him*" François laughed. His gaze darkened. "Are you recovered, *ma chérie?*"

"I—I do not know." Aunt Clare drew in a deep breath. "Are you?"

"Of course." He smiled. "But never shall you step in front of a knife again, do you understand?"

"Oh no. I shall not." Aunt Clare flushed. "At least, I shall try very hard not to do so. I merely did not think. I did not wish for him to hurt Sir Percy."

He nodded. "Or, Monsieur Percy to hurt him."

"Yes." Aunt Clare sighed. She didn't need to explain such to her true love. He understood. She smiled at him. "And I do thank you for engaging in such a duel for me."

"*Je vous assure,* it was nothing." He waved his hand. "It is not as if we had pistols."

"No. That is why it was ever so much more amazing." She studied him, the man she had been waiting for all her life. She frowned slightly. "That one man said you are a devil. Are you?"

He did not flinch. "My life has not always been good, *mon ange.*"

"I suspected that. That is no doubt why it took you so very long to find me." She shook her head. "No doubt you were out doing things that kept you away from me."

He neither laughed nor looked at her as if she were a widgeon. "I will not deny it."

"What do you do?" Clare asked in bemusment.

"A bit of this and that," François murmured. He waved to the room. "I barkeep at the moment, mademoiselle. But only for the moment. Tomorrow it will be something different. And the day after that, yet another thing."

"A very talented man." Clare sighed. "I knew you would be so."

"Some employ the term here-and-therian, *ma chérie.*" His blue eyes twinkled.

"Oh no. I cannot believe that." Clare smiled. "I assure you. I did nothing but the ordinary thing for the greater part of my life and it was excessively dull."

"Of the ordinary things, *mon ange,* do you perhaps mean virtue and propriety and those things that make you the very lady I see before me?"

"Yes," Clare said.

"I then am grateful for your dull existence." A sad smile marred his handsome features. "Alas, we speak as long-lost friends. We do so but in passing, I fear. I am not a good man for you to know. But I would cherish the memory of your name if you would give it to me."

Aunt Clare's eyes widened. "Gracious, we are in need of a proper introduction, are we not?"

"No." He smiled warmly. "I believe I liked our own introduction far better. Proper introductions are . . ."

"For strangers." Aunt Clare nodded.

"Yes, *mon ange.*"

She flushed. "My name is Clare. Clare W—" Her name was drowned out as a roar arose in the room. "Gracious!"

Chairs toppled, men cursed and sprang up, pulling out various kinds of weapons.

The cause was two men who had entered the tap-room confines, both with pistols drawn.

The first, a tall, lanky fellow, his sandy hair tousled with a cowlick shooting upward and to the left, gurgled at the prompt attention. His right cheek was scratched severely. He possessed brown cocker spaniel eyes, which bulged in desperation as he yelped. "Aunt Clare!

"You here, Aunt Clare?" the second boy called. He was the spitting image of the first lad, except his cowlick sent his shock of sandy hair shooting up to the right. He also vaunted a black eye as well as the scratches.

"I'm over here, boys!" Clare stood up and waved at them.

"They belong to you, *ma belle?*" François rose, frowning.

"Yes, they do." Clare nodded. "They are not up to snuff, I fear."

"Mon Dieu! Everyone return to your drinks," François ordered. Everyone turned to glare at him. He shrugged. "They are the friends of Mademoiselle, *oui,* therefore my friends as well."

"Aunt Clare." The first goggled, charging forward with pistol waving. Or actually, flopping in different directions, causing many to duck. "You shouldn't be here."

"Neither should you be," François said. "Please hand over your pistol before you hurt yourself."

"Aunt Clare?" The second drew in with a puff. "You should not have escaped like that. That was bad. Very bad."

"Give me your pistol too," François ordered.

Both stood and gaped at him. The first frowned. "Who is he?"

"I am François. Who are you?"

"This is Nick and Ned, dear," Clare said.

Disbelief and displeasure crossed his face. "These are your nephews, *ma chérie?*"

"Oh no. Not at all. Whatever gave you that notion?" Clare asked. Her eyes widened. "Oh, I understand. No, everyone calls me Aunt Clare."

"But you," Nick said with what looked like a fledgling glower.

"Yes," Ned said. "You call her 'ma sherry.' She is Aunt Clare."

"It is all right, boys," Clare said quickly. "He is the barkeep here and has been dreadfully kind. He saved me from a very big and angry man."

"What?" Nick yelped.

"What?" Ned howled.

She pursed her lips. "And you really should give François your pistols. You are being rather . . . rude, I fear."

"Oh, er, yes." Nick flushed deeply. He dutifully handed the pistol to François. "Was frightened for you."

"That was kind of you." Aunt Clare smiled warmly at them.

"This is a bad place." Nick puffed out his chest.

"Yes." Ned looked solemn. "You're a lady. You shouldn't be here."

"Men come here." Nick nodded.

"For a spot of comfort," Ned said.

"Something to wet their whistle," Nick said. "Warm their cockles."

"Yes. I know." Aunt Clare nodded. "And help clear their thoughts?"

"You're a knowing one." Nick nodded.

"Jolly sort." Ned beamed.

"But not for ladies." Nick grabbed hold of her arm.

"Most improper." Ned snatched up her other arm. "Tea. Lemonade. That clears ladies' heads. Now come with us."

"Certainly, dears." Aunt Clare sighed. She looked to François. "I must go with the boys."

François performed a wonderful bow that made Aunt Clare weak. *"Au revoir, ma chérie."*

"When shall I see you again?" Aunt Clare asked.

"Can't." Nick shook his head vehemently. "He's a barkeep. You can't come here. Just explained that."

"Then it is good-bye forever, Mademoiselle," François said, his eyes glittering. "You two escort *mon ange* away from here. Yes? Do not wait another moment."

Nick and Ned nodded and dragged Aunt Clare away from her true love. Aunt Clare looked back at him. He smiled reassuringly and then nodded to her, still holding Nick's and Ned's pistols.

Five

"Is the lady safe?" François asked the two lads who sat in a haze of Blue Ruin. It had taken but two glasses to put them in such a state. They had returned for their pistols as he had intended. They had also readily accepted his offer for a drink. After the first, they had decided, without his suggestion, to have another. They had apparently locked on to the lovely Clare's notion that men drank to clear their heads.

"Think so." Nick nodded.

"For the n—nonce," Ned said.

"That is good," François said. "Forgive me, but I must tell you that you should take better care of *ma chérie*. She is a very trusting lady."

"Ma who?" Ned asked.

"That is Aunt Clare," Nick whispered. He frowned. "We try to take care of her, but she's a quick one. Gave us the slip. Escaped on us in a winking!"

Ned frowned. "If Burt had found out we lost Aunt Clare he would have killed us."

"Who is Burt . . . ?" François asked.

"Burt is our stepbrother." Nick shook his head vehemently. "Not really our brother you understand. He has bad blood."

"Very bad." Ned nodded his head just as fervently. "He is a rum'un. A dirty dish. A scaly fish . . ."

"I believe I understand." François frowned all the more. "And this Burt is involved with *mon ange?*"

"Yes." Ned nodded. "And we got to do the job right or else."

"We mustn't queer the lay." Nick said. "And if we bumfuddle this . . ."

"He will have our liver . . ." Ned said.

"And feed it to the birds," Nick entailed.

"And our hides . . ." Ned said.

François lifted a brow. "Will he feed that to the birds too?"

"No." Nick sighed heavily.

"He will make gloves from them." Ned sighed as well.

"Did he give you that bruise?" François asked.

"No." Ned smiled with pride. "Aunt Clare did. The scratches are from Sir Percy."

Ned nodded. "Sir Percy is a Trojan."

"A bruising fighter . . ." Nick nodded.

"Like Burt?" François asked dryly.

"No. Sir Percy is a right'un," Nick clarified. "We like him."

"Burt isn't," Ned clarified even further. "We don't like him."

"Sir Percy protects Aunt Clare," Nick then said.

"Yes." Ned broke into a huge grin. "Burt shot himself in the foot 'cause of Sir Percy."

"Monsieur Percy is a good cat to be sure," François agreed solemnly. He promptly poured the lads another glass. "It sounds as if you two have much upon your minds. Whatever is this thing you must do right?"

"Must make a plan." Nick nodded.

"Have to think," Ned said.

"I shall leave you two to do just that." François

stepped back two feet. He pretended to turn his attention to the rest of the taproom. Then he truly did focus his attention as he divined a new addition to the taproom. He was always aware of a person's entrance into a room. In his line of work it made the difference of living to retirement or not.

Indeed, there was a new addition to the taproom and he could well understand the change in the atmosphere. It was a lovely girl, dressed in mourning. François' brows rose. Another invasion of an upper-class lady into his den? He did not believe in coincidence. He stepped back to Nick and Ned and lowered his voice. "Gentlemen. Do you know anything about that young lady who has entered?"

Nick turned drunkenly upon his stool. He squinted and then shook his head. "Never seen her. She's pr-pretty."

"V—v—very pretty." Ned nodded. A befuddled look of concern crossed his features. "Sh—should she be here?"

"Don't know," Nick said. "Wouldn't think so."

"Hm." François sighed.

The miss looked about the room with innocent and fearless eyes. She then just as fearlessly and unwisely stepped over to the table where Tobias now sat. François had directed all away from the bar except his two marks.

"Excuse me, sir," the girl said. "I wonder if you could perchance help me?"

"Heh?" Tobias's eyes glazed over and he sprang up. "Certainly, love."

François sighed. He didn't want another encounter with Tobias. Yet the burly man lacked any kind of technique with even the Hangman's regular light-skirts. He could not expect him to perform well with a true lady.

Tobias snaked out his long arm and pulled the lady to his chest. "I'll pay. I'll pay well."

That was true. François frowned in consideration.

"Not good," Nick murmured. "Shouldn't hug a lady without asking. Ma said so."

"No!" The petite lady was shoving at his chest, very obviously also holding her breath. "I need no money. Well, I do, but that is of no significance."

Tobias's eyes lit as if heaven had come down to him. "Ye want old Tobias without pay?"

"I beg your pardon?" She gasped and batted ineffectually at him. "Sir, I fear one of us is confused. I only wished to know if you have seen an orange marmalade cat."

"What!" Nick and Ned yelped in unison.

"You said you didn't know her," François accused.

Tobias rumbled deep in his chest. "Yer here to make a game of me, ain't ye?"

"Gracious no!" The girl said. Then her eyes lighted. "Oh, I see. You *have* met Sir Percy, haven't you? Did he scratch you badly?"

Tobias growled. "Who sent you, wench?"

François strode hastily from around the bar. He stopped in midstep, however, as a man entered the taproom at the same juncture. Although he was a stranger, his air of nobility and power was not lost on François.

"Miss Thompson, did I not warn you not to wander away?" The man said it in the most amused tone as he strolled forward. His sherry-colored eyes, however, held a cool look that warned any man of sense that he was not in such a convivial mood as all that.

"Yoick!" Ned gasped.

"Know *him!*" Nick cried. "Montieth. Hide!"

Both tumbled from their stools with a crash.

"Mon Dieu!" François rolled his eyes heavenward.

The nobleman glanced their way at the commotion.

François stepped in front of the two lads. He waved and smiled in a friendly fashion. "Monsieur, would you care for a drink?"

"Thank you, but no." The man returned an even steelier look to Tobias.

"Just stay where you are," François murmured.

"Must." Ned wheezed. "Am dizzy. Very dizzy."

"Feel sick." Nick gulped. "Very sick."

So much for the Blue Ruin aiding their thinking faculties or anything else. François shrugged and returned to his study of the nobleman.

"Sorry, old man," the man said to Tobias. "But I didn't send 'the wench,' I assure you. She merely escaped me."

François frowned. Another woman escaping a capture. Impossible!

The nobleman shrugged. "She left me with a mound of trunks to attend. You know how that goes?"

François smiled and nodded. Of course Tobias didn't. "No, I don't. If'n you lost her, then I founds her."

"Lucas. He has seen Sir Percy. Isn't that bang up to the nines?" the girl exclaimed, still attempting to struggle from Tobias's hold.

"Yes." The man narrowed his gaze upon Tobias. "What would be more delightful, however, would be for this person to release you."

Tobias glared at Lucas. He'd been drinking and had had a hard day of it. Perhaps if François had not already exacerbated him by ordering him about twice already, things would have gone better. "I said I've found her and I'm goin' ter keep her."

"What?" Miss Thompson blinked at Tobias in astonishment. "You didn't *find* me. I approached you and merely asked you a question. Now you may be so kind as to release me."

"I'll pays you well," Tobias said in a stubborn tone. He unwisely glared at Lucas. "But I ain't giving you up."

"You most certainly are," Miss Thompson said, her voice firm. She lifted the heel of her shoe and kicked him with what clearly was all her might. Her face twisted with pain. "Drat! And double drat."

Her eyes widened in alarm as Tobias only grunted. "That wasn't nice, missy."

"Neither is this." Lucas strode forward. With lightning speed he delivered a swift blow to Tobias's jaw.

It served its purpose quite nicely. Tobias's arms fell loose about the girl and he toppled over.

"Saint Mary's night rail!" Miss Thompson stared in awe at the fallen man.

"Yes." Lucas grabbed hold of her arm. "Now it is time to leave, Miss Thompson. You have invaded these characters' domain long enough."

"But . . ." Miss Thompson pointed at the fallen man. "What shall we do about him?"

"I'll take care of him." François waved. "Do not concern yourself."

"Heed him, Miss Thompson." Lucas dragged her toward the door. "I doubt he will be pleased to see either of us when he awakes."

"I had not considered that." Miss Thompson was jerked out of the taproom. "I think I ought to be Great Aunt Emily after this" drifted back to all those who chose to still listen and hadn't turned back to their drinks. "I told you I shouldn't be myself."

François chose to listen. It made no sense to him so he turned back to Nick and Ned and narrowed his gaze upon them. "Who is this Lucas Montieth and Miss Thompson?"

"He's . . ." Nick swallowed.

"She's . . ." Ned burped.

"Yes?" François said. "Speak!"

Nick stiffened. He shook his head. "They are supposed to pay ten thousand pounds for Aunt Clare."

"We're supposed to make them do it." Ned looked decidedly green.

"Aunt Clare is your hostage?" François stared. "That man is to be your mark?"

Nick nodded, fear stamping his features. "Y—yes."

François flung his hands up. "Impossible!"

"Don't want to do it." Ned struggled up and sat quickly upon his stool.

"But, Burt . . ." Ned climbed up his stool instead.

"Is an imbecile if he sent you two to do such a job," François said.

"I agree," Nick said.

"Told him we weren't handy at crime." Ned sighed and rolled onto his stool.

"But Burt couldn't leave," Nick said. "Had a shot foot."

"Had other important work to do," Nick said as if a shot foot wouldn't detain Burt. "Very important he said."

"You cannot . . ." François halted. What did it matter? These two were pigeons for the plucking. And as for the man, Burt, François knew that he did not like the fellow. It would be a pleasure to pluck the absent man's feathers clean off him. He studied the two castaway boys. "Are you two the only ones in this caper?"

"No. Little Ike, the Boot is," Nick said.

"He's watching Aunt Clare now," Ned said.

François narrowed his eyes. Little Ike was a worm, a worm who always crawled away safely from dead witnesses. The Burt was not such a fool as he had thought. Obviously these lads were to be the front if things went awry. Worse, the sweet Clare had taken the two under her wing. It was the innocent covering the innocent. "I see."

"We want to make a plan, but not with him," Nick said. "He frightens us. Calls us names. Everyone does. But his are worse. He said we had to do the deed. He would back us up."

François' brain whirled. He would be quit of this place within the next day if all went well. He had his own job to tend to. Reason told him that he should let nothing interfere with it. It was far too important to him. Yet, he could not resist. He could easily pull two jobs off at once with some slight maneuvering.

"And so he shall." François nodded. "This will be a piece of cake. You two can manage it with your hands tied behind your back."

"What?" Nick gulped. "Did you see what that Montieth just did to Tobias?"

"Floored him." Ned offered his diagnosis. "Leveled him. One blow. Handy with his fives . . ."

"Yes. Yes. A bruiser too," François interrupted quickly. "But do you think him as dangerous as your Burt?"

"No," Nick and Ned said in unison.

"Of course he isn't," François said. "He is a nobleman. An impatient one. *Vraiment?* Ten thousand pounds won't mean much to him. He will pay it to keep his aunt safe. As well as his lady, this Miss Thompson." François thought quickly. "Your brother . . ."

"Stepbrother!" squeaked Nick.

"No relation." Ned gasped.

"Yes. Stepbrother." He smiled. "Was right. It will be like falling off a log. There shall be no trouble."

He stepped away and came back with paper and ink. He set them before the lads. "You will write the ransom note."

"Y—yes." Nick reached for it so very slowly that François found himself clenching his teeth. François was not a man who clenched his teeth often.

"I shall write it then." François reached over and took it up. He penned the missive.

"What does it say?" Nick frowned.

"Montieth must meet you in the courtyard in the back of the inn, underneath the large oak tree at ten o'clock in the morning." He looked at them sternly. "It must be ten o'clock. No earlier. No later. Neither nine o'clock nor eleven o'clock, *n'est ce pas?* Neither a half of the hour or a half after the hour!"

"Yes. Nine o'clock," Nick repeated.

"Ten o'clock." François frowned.

"Not eleven o'clock." Ned beamed.

"Nine o'clock." Nick shook his head.

"No. Ten o'clock." He underscored the time. "You will give Aunt Clare to this Montieth and he will give you ten thousand pounds." He paused in consideration. A gentle, amused smile crossed his lips.

"And another ten thousand for Sir Percy," Nick said. "Almost forgot."

François stared. "Pardon?"

"Burt was going to kill Sir Percy. He was angry at him," Nick said.

"But Aunt Clare said that he was valuable and would bring another ten thousand pounds."

"She is magnificent." François' lips twitched. He added the sentence that another ten thousand pounds was required for Sir Percy. Then he considered. The twitch in his lips turned into a smile. "Yes. I believe I shall be kind. Very kind."

"What are you writing?" Nick asked.

"I am adding the demand that he must come by himself. He must not bring the Miss Thompson with him." François nodded as much to himself as them.

"Yes. Money he will not fight over. The Miss Thompson he will kill for."

"No!" Nick gurgled.

"Oh no." Ned moaned.

"Non. Do not fear. If you give the Lucas *ma chérie,* all will be well." François paused yet again. He wondered if his lordship would bring in the constables. He smiled and wrote at the end, "There will be blood if the constables are anywhere near this inn." Which was quite true. The constables stayed away from the Hangman's Inn and its inhabitants, and its inhabitants tried their very best to stay away from the constables. Occasionally some were caught and the Hangman took on another overtone. He looked sternly at the two fellows. "You will get this note to Montieth tonight. Slip it quietly beneath his door and leave. All will go well tomorrow. Yes?"

"Y—yes?" Nick stammered.

"Yes?" Ned turned a pale blue as well as green.

"Have one swallow of your gin for courage, men. Then go about this business," François advised them, though his glance strayed. Fast Thumbs Willy had just entered the taproom. "I must leave you gentlemen now. But do not wait. The longer you wait the more things can go awry. You might lose the lovely Aunt Clare again. That would be bad." He nodded to Fast Thumbs Willy. He looked sternly at the lads. "Now, you must remember not to ever say I assisted you in this. *N'est ce pas?"*

"We must be mum." Nick nodded.

"Or you will shut our traps for us." Ned nodded.

"Yes. You understand that well. *Au revoir.* " François smiled and bowed. Signaling to Fast Thumbs Willie to follow him, he left the taproom.

"Why?" Nick frowned blearily, staring after the barkeep.

"Why what?" Ned belched.

"Why is he helping us?" Nick asked.

"I think he . . ." Ned stopped. His eyes lighted with astonishment. "I th—think he's mawkish for Aunt Clare."

Nick's eyes widened. "That must be it. Doesn't like us. Pl—plain as a p—pikestaff. He's a knowing one. Must be he loves Aunt Clare."

"Sad," Ned said. "She can't ever see him again."

"Yes." Nick brightened. "But we've got a plan." He picked up the paper and put it into his pocket. Then he grabbed up his drink. "Now we have a swallow for courage. He said we could."

"That's the ticket." Ned grabbed his drink. "A swallow for courage."

They both gulped from their glasses.

"Now we go," Nick said.

"Now we go," Ned said.

They stared at each other.

"Just one more swallow for more courage," Nick said.

"Just one more," Ned agreed.

"I—I will wait for you here," Georgette stammered, staring out the coach's window at the most impressive and intimidating town house she had ever seen, not that she had seen that many houses of the *ton*.

"What?" Lucas's brow lifted. "You have been complaining ever since the note arrived about being left out of the adventure."

She frowned, glad for a distraction. "I still do not see why the note demands that you do not bring me."

"I do not know." Lucas shook his head and smiled. "Since it is a completely different handwriting yet again, I can only surmise that we have yet another abductor involved. This one, however, I am forever grateful to."

"Well I am not." Georgette lifted her chin. "I think it very rude of whoever it is to leave me out of it."

"Come, we mustn't tarry," Lucas said as Trump opened the door. "We will barely make it back in time for ten o'clock."

"I will . . ."

"Georgette," Lucas said gently. "You have fought off highwaymen and thieves; never say that you are frightened to enter my house."

"I am not." What else could Georgette say? After all, it was idiotic to be so nervous over such a simple thing. Still, her heart raced for no good reason. Still, his house was frightfully grand.

"Forgive me." Lucas alighted and turned to offer her his hand. "Of course you aren't."

"Of course I'm not," she repeated and permitted to him assist her to alight. As she leaned from the door, the short train of her sable-trimmed charcoal carriage dress became tangled about her feet and she rather tumbled from the old coach. She righted herself, but at the expense of her left ankle. "Drat!" Georgette sucked in her breath at the sharp pain.

"Are you all right?" Lucas frowned.

"Of course I am." Georgette placed a slight weight upon it. It was not too bad, or too good. Lucas stepped ahead. Georgette hobbled behind.

Lucas stopped. "You are not all right."

"Yes I am." Georgette hobbled another step, attempting to ignore the five marble steps leading up to his house. "See."

"Oh, yes, I see. Unfortunately, we do not have all night." Lucas came back and lifted her into his arms.

"My lord!" Georgette exclaimed as he then strode up steps, halting before the carved entrance doors.

"Yes?" Lucas lifted a brow.

Georgette opened her mouth to object. However, she couldn't find it in herself. Indeed, she wasn't certain she could even find the breath within herself. If she was nervous before, now she was in high fidgets. "Th—thank you."

Lucas's eyes warmed with amusement. "Finally, you thank me."

"I . . ." Georgette couldn't speak. She stared at him.

Lucas cleared his throat. "Could you please knock upon the door."

"Oh, yes." Georgette leaned over and took up the golden knocker, employing it soundly. "But will there be someone to answer the door, do you think?"

"A footman will be waiting up," Lucas said.

The door opened almost instantly.

"My lord!" the man before them exclaimed. "Thank heaven!"

"Actually, my butler is waiting up," Lucas said dryly. "Hello, Adams."

"You . . . you . . ." Adams gaped, his gaze going from Lucas to Georgette, then back to Lucas.

"Yes, Adams. This is Miss Georgette Thompson." Lucas chuckled. "Aunt Clare succeeded in her plan beyond her wildest imagination."

"What?" Adams gabbled one more minute. Then he broke into a broad smile and opened the door wide, stepping back swiftly. "Welcome, welcome, my lady."

"My lady?" Georgette asked.

He bowed. "We will be honored to serve you."

"You'll only be serving her for a minute, Adams." Lucas carried her into the entrance hall. "We will not be staying long. I have only come for the money."

Adams blinked. "You are leaving on your honeymoon then?"

"What?" Lucas turned back to him.

"What!" yelped Georgette.

Adams paused. "You are wed, are you not?"

"Wed?" Lucas roared. "No!"

"Zounds!" Georgette gasped. "Never!"

"But . . ." Bewilderment crossed Adams's face, that with closer inspection showed to be weary and sleep-marked. "You are carrying her. I thought you . . ."

"I—I only hurt my foot." Georgette attempted to wriggle from Lucas's arms. "I didn't . . ."

"Do desist, Georgette." Lucas laughed. "Look what you have done, Adams. She'll gladly jump from my arms now you have frightened her so much." He strode over and set her down in a chair.

"Forgive me, my lord," Adams said. "But you said that Aunt Clare had succeeded."

"I only meant she had succeeded in getting herself abducted." He straightened. "For real."

"Never say so." Adams cried. "I—I . . ."

"Miss Thompson can attempt to explain." Lucas nodded. "I must go and find twenty thousand pounds."

Adams gasped. "But the note said five thousand!"

"You are two notes behind, old man." Lucas smiled. "I am returning the favor in saving Aunt Clare, Adams. After this, I assume the debt to be paid in full." He cast a minatory look upon his butler. "No other act will be required, is that clear?"

Georgette knew something passed between them, for Adams colored up. "Yes, my lord. Certainly."

Lucas turned a wry look upon Georgette. "Forgive me. I must leave you in the generally capable hands of Adams for a few minutes. Do not let him frighten you."

"No." Georgette forced a smile. "I—I shall not."

She watched Lucas go. Silence reigned for a moment. Embarrassed, Georgette turned her gaze upon her surroundings. "Jumping Jehoshaphat."

"Madame?" Adams raised his brow.

"Nothing." Georgette flushed.

He then smiled, rather blearily. "It is quite beautiful, isn't it?"

"Yes." Georgette gulped. "Certainly awing."

Adams frowned. "You do not like it, Miss Thompson?"

"Oh yes." Georgette grimaced. "Only, up until now it was easy to forget Lucas was . . . I mean is, a peer of the realm."

Adams's expression clearly looked torn. A smile finally won out over the frown. "Have you, Miss Thompson?"

"I knew he was . . . I mean, is above my touch. But not this much."

"No, he is not above your touch." Adams walked over to her, his gaze sincere. "My lord is the most 'unlordish' gentleman, I assure you. And one can grow accustomed to anything, including wealth and power."

"I . . ." Georgette's eyes widened. She clamped her mouth shut as many things tumbled into place. "Lucas isn't dicked in the nob, after all."

"I beg your pardon?" Adams stiffened. He shook his head. "No, Miss Thompson. For a while he was . . . was tormented. But he is not now."

Georgette studied him in astonishment. "I beg your pardon. What do you mean he was tormented?"

Adams studied her in return. He turned his gaze away. "Nothing. Forgive me. I spoke out of turn."

"You might as well tell me." Georgette smiled kindly. "Otherwise I will simply ask him."

"No, Miss Thompson." Adams frowned. "That you would not do."

Georgette lifted her chin in challenge. Then she sighed. "Very well, I wouldn't."

Adams bowed. "Thank you, Miss Thompson. Now

I will tell you. My lord had fallen in love with a lady who married another."

"Yes." Georgette nodded. "Her father forced her to do so."

"He told you that?" Adams's brow rose. Then shook his head. "My lord took it very hard. He . . . drank heavily. The night that Aunt Clare abducted him, he had been in his cups. He was alone in the library. He had commanded that none of us were to enter and he had even locked the door. He went to stir the fire but in his inebriated state, he stumbled and fell, striking his head. If Aunt Clare had not entered by the window at that precise moment to abduct him, I fear the earl would have bled to death."

"That is why he said he is returning the favor by saving Aunt Clare," Georgette murmured, her heart wrenching at the story.

He smiled. "She has been a godsend. This past year he has been better. He has helped her with her schemes in matchmaking all the other gentlemen. It has given him something to draw him out of his melancholy. However, he still refuses to go out in society. He does not go to his clubs. He never engages in any of the sports that he enjoyed before. Worse, he will not paint."

"He paints?" Georgette exclaimed.

"Yes, Miss Thompson. Most beautifully."

She swallowed. "In . . . in oils?"

"But of course, Miss Thompson." Adams's lips twisted in humor. "As if Lord Montieth would do watercolors."

"Of course not." Georgette was torn between envy and hurt. Why had he not told her that he painted?

"He has a vibrant and masterful stroke, if I do say so myself. And a singular way with lighting." He frowned. "Perhaps I should not tell you all of this.

However, I and the staff have been most worried about him. He has become a recluse."

Georgette's eyes widened. "Like my father."

"I beg your pardon?" Adams frowned.

"Nothing," Georgette said. Where her heart had been wrenched before, now it felt as if it were bleeding. She clenched her hands, her fingernails digging into her palms. In a way she had already read Lucas's story and knew its ending. But not for Lucas, she thought angrily. Not for Lucas. Enlightenment struck. "Aunt Clare did write those first notes. She did try to be the matchmaker. I understand now."

Adams flushed. "Miss Thompson, you could never find a better man to wed than the earl."

"If I wished to marry." Georgette murmured deep in concentration.

Adams swallowed. "Do you not wish to marry?"

"No, she doesn't, Adams." Lucas approached them, carrying a large brown satchel. He lifted a quizzing brow. "Has my butler been attempting to pawn me off to you?"

"No." Georgette flushed. "Not exactly 'pawn.' "

"He would give me to you for keeps, wouldn't he?" Lucas offered the satchel to Adams. "If you will take this, Adams, I will pick up my 'nonbride' and be on my way."

Georgette flushed as he knelt beside her. "I imagine I can walk now."

"No. You walk at a snail's pace." He lifted her in his arms easily. "Which would give Adams far too much time to extol to you my sterling virtues until you became delirious with your desire to wed me."

Georgette flushed. "Why didn't you tell me you paint?"

Lucas raised a brow. "I do not know." He flashed a grin. "I believe at the time I didn't wish to look like the wild and adventuresome male that I am. I didn't wish you to be filled with too much envy."

"That was very nice of you." She bit her lip. "Adams is right, you know. You will be a catch for some lady."

"Adams, what have you said to her? Up until now she has considered me both a bedlamite and completely unmarriageable. Now look what you have done."

"Forgive me, my lord." Adams held the satchel close.

"It is something you should consider," Georgette said.

"Miss Thompson . . ." Lucas offered her a threatening look.

"Yes, my lord?" She said it in a haughty tone.

He caught her drift and smiled. "Very well. Georgette . . ."

She smiled in return. "Yes, Lucas . . . ?"

"You are a baggage."

"I know, but you should still marry."

"After you, Miss Thompson." Lucas nodded.

"No. I am serious," Georgette objected.

His gaze narrowed. "I do not like the look upon your face. If you are thinking of joining forces with Aunt Clare . . ."

"I hadn't yet thought of that," Georgette said. "But I will now."

"Adams, give Georgette the satchel. I am taking both bag and baggage to the coach."

"Certainly, my lord." Adams stepped forward and Georgette took the satchel. "Do not give up on him, Miss Thompson."

"I will not." Georgette flushed.

"She most certainly will give up on me," Lucas said. "Indeed, tomorrow at ten o'clock to be exact. We will exchange the money and save Aunt Clare. Then this imbroglio will all be over."

"Indeed it will be." Georgette nodded dutifully.

Lucas narrowed his gaze upon her. "You are bamming me. Your brain is already whirling with ideas. But two can play that game, Georgette." He strolled toward the door that Adams rushed to open. "I just might turn my matchmaking skills upon you. And I have greater experience in that department."

"I am sure I will be most excellent at it myself."

"If you use a pistol perhaps."

"Unfair." Georgette laughed. "Very unfair."

"I think I will match you with Mr. Ferret . . ." Lucas said as he carried her out the door and down the steps.

"And I will match you with Mrs. Frampton's daughter. She is a widow and takes after Mrs. Frampton," Georgette retorted.

At that moment, she caught the expression on Adams's face over Lucas's shoulder. It held an extremely satisfied look. It gave her pause. A very serious and frightening pause. What was she thinking? Tomorrow at ten o'clock it would be all over. As it should be. As it must be. No matter how "unlordish" Lucas was, he was still far above her touch and she mustn't forget it.

Six

"Are you sure of the time you wrote for dear Lucas to arrive?" Aunt Clare fretted as she and the boys wandered through an unattended courtyard that sprouted very dead bushes. Both Nick and Ned were pale and blinked in the gray morning mist as if it were the brightest of days. They clearly had shot the cat the night before. She knew how very forgetful gentlemen became after a night of imbibing.

"Thought he—we wrote nine o'clock," Nick said.

"Nine o'clock." Ned nodded. "Remember that. But can't remember if we are to be there at half of nine . . ."

"Or at half after . . ."

"Oh, it surely must be a half hour of," Aunt Clare said firmly. "It is always better to be early than late. In that fashion you can prepare yourself before anyone arrives."

"That's what Little Ike said." Ned sighed. "Glad he went before us to make sure there weren't any constables about. And that your Lucas didn't pull any fast ones on us."

"Lucas wouldn't pull a fast one on you." Aunt Clare strove for a positive note.

"Meow." Sir Percy paused before them. His hair rose and his ears went back.

"What is it, dear?" Aunt Clare asked.

Sir Percy burred and darted through the brown scenery.

"Oh my. Something is afoot." Aunt Clare picked up her skirts and dashed after him. Nick and Ned cried out and followed. She halted when she came to a huge tree. Two men stood swaying, both having a stranglehold upon the other. Sir Percy sprang at one of them.

"François!" Aunt Clare gasped.

"Mon ange?" François, his face twisted with pain, glanced her way. " 'Morning *ma chérie.* You are . . . early."

"Gracious. The boys confused the time."

"Little Ike?" Nick gaped as he crashed through the bushes to a stop.

"What?" Ned slammed into him from behind.

"Help me!" Little Ike howled as Sir Percy sunk four paws of claws into him.

The two boys, blurry-eyed, stumbled forward obediently. Only to stop again, clearly befuddled.

"What shall we do?" Nick scratched his head.

"Kill him," Little Ike clenched out.

"Kill him?" Nick yelped. He paused. A relieved look crossed his face. "Can't. I forgot my pistol."

"Me too." Ned nodded eagerly. "Forgot it."

"Kill him!" Little Ike choked out more weakly. "Use hands."

"Hands?" Nick flushed. "Er, not handy with them."

Ned nodded. "Am all thumbs."

"Enough," François gritted. With great strength he broke free of Little Ike. Regret crossed his face. "You should not see this *ma chérie.*"

"No, no. Please proceed," Aunt Clare said quickly into the midsecond pause. "Drub him well, dearest."

"Merci." François reached back and delivered a stunning blow to Little Ike. Little Ike jerked and toppled back. Sir Percy barely sprung free as he hit the ground.

François, his face dark, strode over to Clare. He performed a perfect leg. "Forgive me, mademoiselle, for such an ungentlemanly display in front of you."

"Oh no." Clare blushed. "I quite understand. That was a wonderful . . . er . . . whiskey canter?"

"Grassed him," Nick said with awe.

"He's handy with his fives," Ned observed.

Nick frowned then. "But why?"

"Yes." Ned's eyes widened. "Why?"

François did not take his gaze from Clare. He smiled and held out his hand. She put hers in his. He bent and brushed it with his lips. "You are very brave, *mon petit chou."* He then clasped both of her hands up. "I wish for you to cover your ears, my dear."

"I will. If you truly wish for me to do so."

"I truly do." Eyes warm, he assisted her in putting her hands to her ears.

"Thank you." Aunt Clare flushed. She couldn't help herself. She loosened her palms just a tad.

"Do not listen." François shook a gentle finger to her. He whirled about and strode over to the boys. "What did I tell you two?"

"Don't know," Nick confessed.

"Forgot." Ned blushed.

"You two are cabbage heads. I told you to come at ten o'clock. Not nine o'clock! Your Little Ike almost surprised me. If he had killed me, then what?"

Nick swallowed. "You would be dead?"

"Yes," François said. "And then you two would have brought *mon ange* here. And that Lucas would have come with the money. And Little Ike, hiding behind that bush"—he pointed—"would have killed *ma chérie,* and perhaps the earl. Little Ike is an assassin."

"What!" Nick yelped.

"No!" Ned exclaimed.

"Your Burt does not want *ma chérie* to live to tell the tale, *n'est çe pas?"*

Clare clamped her hands tightly over her ears. François was right. She didn't particularly wish to hear this.

François threw up his hands. "You have ruined my plans."

"Your plans?" Nick asked.

"Thought they were our plans," Ned said in cross-eyed confusion.

"What plans, dear?" Aunt Clare asked, before she realized that François most likely didn't wish for her to read their lips either.

"Ma chérie?" François turned, his expression reproachful.

"Forgive me, dear. Eavesdropping is one of my favorite follies." Aunt Clare dropped her hands. Which was fortunate, for at that moment the loudest birdcall drifted to them through the trees. She smiled. "Why. How lovely." She blinked. "It sounds somewhat like an owl. It mustn't know it is morning yet."

Sir Percy's meow was cynical.

"I cannot stay now to meet Montieth and his money." François shrugged. He reached into his vest pocket and withdrew a pistol. *"Ma chérie* is going with me. I will not leave her to you imbeciles."

"You are abducting me?" Aunt Clare breathed.

"Forgive me. But yes."

"Oh, I forgive you," Aunt Clare said happily.

He looked at Nick and Ned, his eyes narrowed upon them. "I will suggest this to you. Try and remember it. When Little Ike awakes, tell him I stole Aunt Clare

from you. You do not know where I went. You might
live. And do not be caught by Montieth! 'Else . . ."

"We'll be in the suds," Nick said.

"In the suds already," Ned said.

"Use whatever brains you have," François said
curtly. He sighed. *"Non.* Instead, try and think how
your Burt would act and do that."

The owl or whatever bird squawked frightfully loud
this time.

"We must go." François grabbed up Clare's hand.
"Come *ma chérie.*"

Aunt Clare followed, for at the moment there was
naught else to do. Sir Percy sprang behind them. She
called back to Nick and Ned, who stood looking after
them with alarmed expressions. *"Au revoir,* dears."

"Au revoir!" Nick said.

"No." Ned frowned. "Burt wouldn't do that. We are
supposed to do what Burt would do."

"Make that farewell, sweet Clare." François chuckled. "For good, yes?"

"Oh dear." The thought of Nick and Ned trying to
act like Burt rather frightened her. However, she refrained from comment. She knew better than to try
and discuss certain matters with gentlemen when they
were intent upon other things, like abducting a lady.

"A carriage awaits us," François said as they dashed
from the courtyard onto a side alley.

"How nice," Aunt Clare said.

He slowed and cautioned her to do the same. The
carriage did indeed await them. However, a man and
constable guarded it. "On the other hand, it is such a
fine morning, perhaps we should take a stroll instead."

"That is just as delightful." Aunt Clare beamed at
him.

At that moment, the man looked up. He shook a
finger in their direction. "There he is. Stop that thief!"

"Or perhaps a brisk walk?" François lengthened his stride.

"Halt, in the name of the Crown!" the constable shouted.

"Or perhaps a good run, dear?" Aunt Clare lifted up her skirts. Her petticoats flashing, she darted past him.

A laugh burst from François as his strong step sounded behind her. "I am in love! *Mon Dieu*. I am in love!"

They turned down yet another street. The streets were now actually passing through a better neighborhood. Clare blew out a relieved breath as François finally slowed to a walk. A stitch in her side nagged her.

"Are you all right, *ma belle?*" François asked, his concern apparent. He took her by the elbow with quite proper regard.

"I do believe I am." Clare smiled. She glanced behind her. Only to see Sir Percy follow at a cat prowl, not one whit taxed. "Do you think we have lost them?"

"Yes." François said it solemnly.

"Is that not good?" Clare asked, confused.

"It is." François smiled. "But now we must find you a hack. And you, my fair Clare, must leave me and go to the safety of your own."

"What?" Clare blinked at him. "Y—you are returning me? I—I thought you were abducting me."

He halted and took up her hand. His brilliant eyes grew warm. "I would be charmed to do so. And, in another time and place, I would abduct you and never give you up."

"Truly?" Clare's heart summersaulted in a manner she had never experienced before now. At her age, surely this flip-flopping of the heart should have been considered unhealthy. Yet the energy it exuded throughout her only proved to her that such exercise could only be beneficial to that organ.

A twinkled entered his eyes. "You are a minx, *mon petit chou.*"

Clare flushed and giggled. Men had called her many things. Unfortunately they were things like zany, widgeon, and buffle-headed. In her heyday, perhaps, men had said such as what François had just said. Yet they had never meant it and therefore it had never meant anything to her. Never before had it been the truth. Now it was. For Clare felt adventurous and courageous. "François."

"There is a hack. I shall call it for you." François stepped away to wave one down.

"Are you sure you do not wish to ransom me?" Clare asked quickly. "Lucas will pay far more than twenty thousand pounds I am sure."

François' hand fell. "Will he?" He frowned. He shook his head resolutely. *"Non.* I cannot."

Fortunately that hack driver read his last gesture and passed them.

"You cannot?" Clare sighed. "Very well. I understand."

"I do not think you do." He walked over to her. "I have a certain job in progress. I cannot afford to be distracted from it. Even for you, my lady."

"Gracious, what do you intend to steal that is more than twenty thousand pounds!"

An arrested expression crossed François' face. He shook his head. *"Non.* Do not ask me, for I shall not tell you."

"Very well. Only think how lovely it would be if you kept me with you until after your *heist,* is that the correct word, dear?"

He nodded, his lips twitching. "Yes."

The notion blossomed within Clare's mind, wrought with all manner of romance. Of course, in the end, François must reform and stop his thieving, but she wouldn't tell him yet. Men didn't take to change readily. *"Then* you can continue with my abduction and demand a ransom from Lucas."

He laughed. "Madame, either this Lucas Montieth loves you very much, or you dislike him very much to offer his money to me as you do."

"Oh no, I love Lucas very much. And he loves me I believe. Though he does think I am that thorn they always talk about." She sighed. "But I cannot permit him to throw his life away pining for a woman who is not his true love. He should have his true love. And surely it is more important than all his money."

François studied her a moment. "If he is a wise man, yes, he will choose the love. But the money will help the love, *n'est ce pas?* He is a fool if he has the money but will not choose the love as well. Some of us do not have that privilege. And if you are the thorn, you are surely the thorn of a rose, *chér amie."* Then he shook his head. "But it cannot be me to take his money. I fear I do not have the time. If the boys had remembered the correct time matters would be different."

She gasped. "Oh dear, the boys ruined your heist?"

"Non. It is not as tragic as all that." He shook his head ruefully. "I think my own self-confidence foiled me. Do not let it concern you. I shall remedy the setback."

"Oh dear, I cannot detain you." Clare looked swiftly about. Another hack passed. She raised her hand with determination. "Hello! Excuse me."

It slowed for her. Straightening her spine, she stepped toward the hack.

"Non!" François exclaimed. "You cannot go!"

Clare turned around. "I cannot?"

He stepped up to her and clasped her arm at the same time as he waved the driver on. His voice lowered. "We are still being watched. See that man over there, he is one of them. I do not wish for him to follow you or me."

"Certainly." Clare steeled herself. That she would have even a few more minutes with her love was wonderful, but her muscles were less ecstatic. "Shall we run then?"

"*Non.* Not this time." François smiled. "What we shall do is act as if we do not see them. We shall slowly walk here." He pulled her into a doorway of a pub. He peered around the corner and frowned. "And now we shall go in here off the street."

"What an excellent notion," Clare said approvingly.

"Guard for us, Monsieur Percy," François said to Sir Percy. Sir Percy sat down and stared at him. "I would have the lady's attention all to myself." Sir Percy meowed and licked his paw.

"Gracious, but he does like you," Aunt Clare said as he opened the door and then drew her into the pub.

"I would that this was the grandest palace, with servants to bring every course that you could wish," François said, his voice wry. "Alas, it is not."

"May I try the ale?" Aunt Clare said in excitement as she peered about the pub. "I assure you, I shall enjoy this far better. Elegant dinners always set me on the fidgets. This will be far more cozy."

François smiled and drew out a chair for her. She sat, gazing about with interest. François also sat and waved for the man to come to their table. François ordered the ale. The waiter left and Clare smiled at her love. "I have never tried ale, you know?"

François studied her. "Now, *mon ange.* You must tell

me, how you became involved with the nasty Burt and those two boys."

Clare flushed. "I—well, as Garth, my nephew, would say, I bungled it."

"Bungled it?"

"Yes. I was under the impression that the Boarshead Hostelry was a reputable establishment." She frowned. "I do not think that nasty Burt was the owner when Mathew frequented it."

"Who is Mathew?" François asked.

"He is the Earl of Raleigh. He is one of my boys. There are six of them. Lucas is the last on the list."

He frowned. "Are all your boys so . . . prominent?"

"Oh yes," Aunt Clare said. "Dear Julia would never have accepted them as fiancés if they had not been. She is quite particular, you see."

"No. I do not see." He raised his hand. "Perhaps if you tell me only the part where you became involved with the nasty Burt?"

The man brought them the ale.

"Thank you." Clare immediately reached for the ale. She tasted it and made a face. "Gracious. It is rather odd tasting."

François sighed. *"Non.* My curiosity will torment me. You said your dear Julia would not have accepted them as fiancés? Do you mean whoever this Julia is . . ."

"She is my niece."

"Your niece. But did she have six fiancés?"

"Yes."

"Ma chérie." His lips tightened. "Is she not what you English call a jilt?"

"Oh no. I assure you she wasn't. Though the *ton* considered her such. But Julia never jilted any one of the boys. I abducted them before she could do so."

"What?" François exclaimed.

"She was in love with Garth . . ."

"Your nephew." François nodded, intent upon her.

"Yes." Aunt Clare beamed at him. He listened to her, actually listened to her. "And Garth was in love with Julia. They had loved each other since they were children, only they didn't realize it. They thought they disliked each other, you see. Then Bendford . . ."

"Bendford?"

"He is my brother."

François stiffened. *"Ma chérie,* what is your name?"

"Clare Wrexton."

"I see." François nodded. "Proceed, *ma belle."*

"Bendford . . ." Clare stopped. She cocked her head. "What is the matter, my dear?"

François raised a brow. "Nothing. What do you mean?"

"Do you know my brother?" Her own perspicuity astonished her. Being attuned to that which transpired about her was not Clare's long suit, and she would be the first to admit it. Being attuned to François was easy. He did not care for her brother; that was clear.

"Who does not know of the Lord Wrexton, the powerful and prominent statesmen?" He shrugged, more as if to shake something from his shoulder than in question. "Do proceed with the story. But, please, for my sake, do use their full names as you speak."

"Very well. I shall try." Clare drew in her breath. "Bendford, my brother, had decided to try and force Julia, my niece, into marriage. He said he would disinherit her if she didn't marry. So Julia became engaged." Clare sighed. "I—I simply could not see her marry someone she didn't love. Ruppleton and Wilson, who are my butler and chef, felt the same. So we abducted Charles, who is the Marquise of Hambledon. And then Julia became engaged to Sir Giles Mancroft. So we abducted him. Then Julia became engaged to

Lord Baresford, Lord Redmond, Viscount Dunn, and the Earl of Raleigh."

"Mon Dieu." François' eyes widened in awe. "You must be as good a thief as I am. I thought myself a nonpareil."

"I own it was quite a **scramble** to abduct all four men in such a short period of time. I can only say that we were . . . were inspired." She shook her head, musing. "I find it very astonishing how once one is pressed, then the notions will appear. Just like that, and not a moment before." She frowned. "Of course, we overshot ourselves then, and abducted Lucas as well."

"Overshot?"

"He was not one of Julia's fiancés. She had intended for him to be one, but he had been out of town that day. However, Ruppleton, Wilson, and I decided we might as well abduct him while we were still . . ."

"Inspired?"

"Yes." Clare flooded with warmth. "I often look back and cannot help but reminisce with fondness. Taking that fist step and abducting dear Charles changed my life."

"As well as that of all the others, I have no doubt," François said with amusement.

"Oh yes. For dear Julia married Garth. Which was only right and good. But after coming to know all the boys as I did, I knew that I needed to make restitution for taking her away from them. I promised to find each of them a wife. Which I have. All except for Lucas." She sipped from her ale. She looked at François. "I do believe I have taken the second most important step I ever made in my life."

"Which is?"

"I have been doing everything these past weeks by myself. Before, I have always had someone to help me in my plans. Ruppleton and Wilson at first. And then each of the boys assisted me with the next one. However, things worked out this time where I could not employ their help." Clare flushed. "Indeed, Bendford took all of my servants with him to France and made me promise to not be up to any of my tricks while he was away. So did Lucas. I—I promised Bendford that I would not draw anyone into my schemes." She sipped from her ale again. "Which I knew I couldn't. Even though they would help me, and Matthew vowed I must permit him to assist me, I did not do so this time. Bendford would never forgive them, you see."

"I think that is not the true reason." François lifted a brow. "You can be honest with me, *ma belle*."

"Oh dear, you are right." Clare sighed. "Very well, to be honest, though I never planned this, it was the precise moment I was waiting for, but I never had the fortitude to attempt before."

"Yes?"

"Indeed. I realized it one night upon the seas, when the smugglers were chasing me . . ."

"Smugglers?"

"It was quite accidental. But I remember that the night was beautiful, and the experience of being upon a fast sailing ship delightful. I realized then that I would never have gone sailing without someone abducting me and forcing me to go upon a boat. And I thought then what a pity that was. I should have been having adventures because of my own efforts and not because of a mistake."

"Shameful." François shook his head, though his eyes were bright with enjoyment. "And now, rather than to ask you why smugglers were chasing you, I shall ask you the more pertinent question, how did you get this Burt to abduct you?"

"I sent a letter to Lucas and Georgette that I had

been abducted and that they together must come to the Boar's Head with the money."

"Why did you do that?"

"Lucas refused to meet Georgette. And I knew I could not tell dear Georgette that Lucas is her true love. She doesn't *like* men at this moment. I saw no use in telling her that she would come to love one to boot." She shook her head. "If you set her back up, she will go directly in the opposite direction of what she should." She pursed her lips. "I do hope Lucas will learn that very quickly. For Georgette is such a dear that this one small failing should not matter too much, don't you think?"

"I would not know," François said. "I only wish to hear how you became involved with this Burt."

"Oh, dear. I digress, do I not?" She peeked at him. She drew in a deep breath. "I must confess that I—I do that often I fear."

"Then I shall keep you to the purpose." François smiled. "Many consider it a failing of mine. I am never distracted from what I wish to achieve."

"How delightful." Clare sighed.

"Yes." François nodded. "Now. You sent a ransom note to Lucas and Georgette, and then what did you do? Fling yourself into the arms of the Burt?"

"I fear it was something like that." Aunt Clare flushed. "I had Lucas and Georgette go to this Burt's inn. My note told them they must await my instructions there. Well, when I met with Burt and asked him to help me in my ploy, explaining to him that I normally wouldn't ask it of him, but that . . ."

"That you were alone." François groaned.

"He decided to actually abduct me. And he sent me to the Hangman Inn with Nick and Ned, rather than to the delightful little folly I intended to have Lucas and Georgette travel to."

His lips twitched. *"Mon Dieu.* I am not sure who is more ruthless. This Burt or you."

"Oh dear, do you think so?" Clare sighed. "I thought they would enjoy it."

"If they were already in love, yes. But you say this Lucas and Georgette do not wish to fall in love."

"True." She bit her lip. "And now they are at the Hangman. Which is the most depressing place. Not at all romantic. However shall they fall in love now?"

"No, the Hangman is not romantic." He said quite curtly. A sternness entered his gaze. "Yet now I must return you to safety before I myself return to the Hangman."

He stood and withdrew a coin and laid it upon the table.

"Oh, yes." Clare stood, bewildered at his abrupt movement. She followed him out of the pub, onto the street.

His gaze turned sad. "Now, *mon ange.* It is time for us to say good-bye."

Clare looked away from him. She gasped then. She looked back at him. "Do look over there. Isn't that the man who is chasing you?"

François glanced to where she pointed. He frowned. *"Non.* I do not see him."

"Oh." Clare's shoulders sagged. "I—I must have been mistaken."

"We cannot take a chance." François' voice was firm. "We must go someplace that is very busy with people. Somewhere different." His gaze flared. *"Ma chère,* I know the place."

"You are Georgie. Now walk like Georgie," Georgette admonished herself. She peered around the court-yard. A shiver ran down her spine for no good reason

that she could perceive. She was alone, after all. There
was no one to even notice if she walked in an effemi-
nate manner.

Still a portion of her mind nagged at her. Worse, it
might very well be the logical portion. This might not
have been such a clever notion as she had first thought.
Granted, when Lucas had all but imprisoned her within
the room and told her to stay while he, the man, could
go out to discover clues, it had seemed a brilliant idea.
His objection for her even peeking her nose out of the
room had been that it was not safe for a woman.

Georgette could not sit back a moment longer. This
morning at ten o'clock it had not been all over. Lucas
said he had gone to the correct tree, at the correct time,
but no one had appeared. It galled Georgette that Lucas
relayed all of this to her. She should have been able
to see it all for herself. Perhaps Lucas had missed
something.

To rub salt in the wound, Lucas had ordered her to
stay in the room, while he went out to discover all that
he could. Georgette had been able to stand pacing the
small cell for a mere half hour before she had hit upon
her scheme.

She assuaged her guilt by telling herself that she
had overcome Lucas's main objection. It might very
well be dangerous for a lady. But she wasn't a lady
now. She was Georgie. She even liked the name better.
She had thought of George first. Yet George still
seemed too formal.

It had been simple really. When she had embarked
upon this adventure she had thought of every possible
costume and identity she might need to employ. She
had sent Sally to garner what she could from their
friends and neighbors. Sally had thought her cracked
to borrow an old livery from Mrs. Frampton (or actually from her cook, Mrs. Weaver). Sally wouldn't be

laughing now if she could see how Georgette's fore-
thought had paid off.

The livery she wore was very outdated, festooned
with buttons, cording, and lace, and most impor-
tantly . . . padding. It hid her slight curves well, she
thought. She worried that she hadn't cut her hair
evenly, though, but it lay like a smooth black cap,
touching at her jawline. The livery also had a very
large hat that she set atop her head at a rakish angle.

In truth it felt wondrous and very liberating, that
was until this very second. Georgette's freshly cropped
hairs rose at the back of her neck. A twig snapped.
Bushes rustled. Georgette whirled about. "Hello?"

She saw nothing. Silence met her. Yet she knew
someone was there in the overgrowth.

A chill tangled with a thrill and they both raced
along her spine. "Have you come to make the exchange?"

"How . . . how did you know?" Hoarse, the speaker
clearly struggled with English. "Wh—who are you?"

Georgette paused, thinking hard. With proper hos-
pitality she employed the French she knew. "I am the
earl's er . . . servant? Yes, his . . . his page?"

"What?" The voice rasped.

"Pardon, I—I do not speak French well," Georgette
stammered. She then spoke quickly in hopes of pressing her advantage. "He was here this morning as you
had requested. Where were you?"

"It was me who warned him away!" he returned in
French.

"Did you? He did not tell me." Georgette frowned.
She couldn't understand his French much better than
his English. She simply must persevere. "Not—not
that he would have to. I—I am only his page."

"He is safe now?"

"Yes." Gracious, there was a difference between the

French she had learned and the actual speaking of it. "He wants to make the exchange still."

"I am here now. Bring him. He must hurry." The voice sounded desperate. "There is much danger."

Georgette nodded. "I shall bring him immediately. Wait here."

Georgette turned and ran. Lucas had mentioned that he intended to go to the taproom first. She hastened there, only coming to a sharp standstill upon the threshold. She drew in a deep breath. "You are Georgie. Remember that."

She attempted a manly gait and entered the room. She thought she had done well, going unnoticed. That was until she came to stand beside Lucas. She lowered her voice and said, "Pardon me, my lord."

Lucas turned. His eyes widened marginally. The dark cloud that descended upon his face let her know that it was not going to go unnoticed by him. "Yes . . . ?"

"Georgie!" Georgette squeaked.

"Yes, Georgie?" Lucas asked smoothly. "What do you want?"

She drew in her breath. The men he had been talking to on either side of him were watching her closely. She tried a bow. It was very awkward. "I—your humble servant needs speak to you in private."

"You mean my disobedient servant, do you not?" Lucas's brow rose in disdain. Georgette flushed, but before she could open her mouth, he raised his hand. "No. I do not wish another word from you." He turned to the two gentlemen. "If you will excuse me. Good help is so very hard to find, don't you know?"

The men stared at him and then hooted with laughter.

"Oi always say that, gov!" The one man chuckled. "Me with my 'undred servants."

"I'd whip the lad meself." The other man grinned.

"It is an excellent notion," Lucas said with narrowed eyes. He nodded his head. "Let us go, Georgie. I shall borrow Trump's whip I believe."

"What?" Georgette gasped as he strolled past her. He continued to walk away from her. The two men laughed all the more. Flushing, she scurried after Lucas as he left the taproom. "Lucas . . ."

"Your lordship to you, *boy*," Lucas said curtly, rudely refusing to stop as he surged ahead in long strides.

"Your lordship!" Georgette puffed as she was forced into a run. "Could you perhaps slow down? I—I cannot keep up with you."

"Don't snivel, Georgie," Lucas threw over his shoulder. "Do be a man about it."

"But I need to tell you what I have discovered."

"No you do not," Lucas said curtly. "At this moment I do not care a rap what you discovered. How I regret we live in enlightened days. 'Else I could take a whip to you . . ."

"For my disobedience?" Georgette snapped, sudden anger rising in her.

"Your disobedience. And your stupidity," Lucas said coolly as he reached her room's door. He unlocked it and waved for her to enter.

She balked. She didn't know which stopped her more. Her anger. Or her fear. "I was not stupid."

"Get in the room, Georgie," Lucas said through clenched teeth.

"Very well. But don't think you can . . ." She gurgled to a halt at his dark look.

"What?"

"You dare not lift a finger to me, my lord. I'll not have it."

"Get in, Georgie."

"Very well." Georgette entered the room. Lucas followed behind her and slammed the door shut. She spun as he locked it.

He glanced up. His sherry eyes flared with a wicked light. "Are you frightened of me?"

"No." Georgette lifted her chin.

"You should be." He straightened. "Just like you should be frightened of stepping outside these walls."

"Well, I'm not." She only wished she weren't. "You are angry merely because I didn't listen to you. But I took precautions. I know it is dangerous for a lady. I saw that. But I am not a lady now. I am a boy."

"You are not a boy," Lucas gritted. "Anyone can tell that you are a woman."

"No they can't," Georgette retorted. "I will have you know . . ." She halted as she noted his gaze stray past her. "That the man I met . . ." Lucas walked by her. Her voice trailed to a halt. She swallowed hard as he came to stand over her cut-off tresses which she had left upon the floor in her haste.

Lucas looked at her, regret in his eyes. "Your hair was beautiful. You should never have cut it."

She shrugged, feeling regretful, too. How ridiculous. "What do I care how I look?"

"No, of course not." His tone was sardonic.

That tone only fueled Georgette's ire. "I—I like how I look now."

"Do you?" His face darkened.

"It is wonderful to be Georgie."

"Is it?"

"Yes. In fact, I wish I truly were a boy," Georgette spouted off. The unfairness of it all welled up within her. "I could have all the adventures I wished. I hate being a girl."

"Do you?" His voice was very low.

"Yes. I do." Georgette pursed her lips in disdain. "I cannot think of one good reason for being a woman."

Lucas brows shot up. "Do not be ridiculous."

"Very well." Georgette crossed her arms and glared at him. "Give me *one* good reason and I'll bet you are wrong."

"I accept." Lucas strode over to her. He reached his hand out and entwined it in her short hair.

"What?" Georgette's arms fell.

Lucas drew her to him with just the pressure of his hand to her head. His lips descended, firm and demanding upon hers. The most wonderful sensation shot through Georgette. It made her dizzy and she reached out to hold on to Lucas. He made to pull back, but Georgette, intrigued, followed with her lips. A sound, somewhat like a growl, came from Lucas. He pulled her completely into his arms and deepened his kiss. She moaned as his hands molded her slight frame to his length. Such was her unstable emotions that she felt as if they were one, the strength of his large body hers, completely hers.

"God!" Lucas jerked his lips away from Georgette. He dropped his arms from her and stepped back.

Georgette shivered as if cold. She was, severed from the wonderful completion of Lucas's arms about her. "Why did you do that?"

He shook his head, his own gaze stunned. "I believe I wished to prove to you that there was a good reason for you to be a woman."

"What?" Georgette walked unsteadily over to the closest piece of furniture, which was the rough bed. She fell in a heap upon it, her legs giving out.

"If you were a boy, I would never kiss you, would I?"

"That is true." Georgette drew in a deep breath.

"I was wrong," Lucas said quickly.

"Oh no." Georgette flushed. "You were right. Most definitely right. It *is* a good reason to be a woman. Th—the best I have s—seen to date."

Lucas stared at her. He barked a laugh. Shaking his head, he ran a swift hand though his hair. Georgette flushed. She of a sudden could understand his reaction to her cutting her hair. If he cut his, she would miss the fire of it. "Why? Why must you be so contrary, Miss Thompson?"

"What?" Georgette blinked.

"Now is the time when you are supposed to rip up at me about how you hate men. Or how I'd better not dare touch you again." His gaze was rueful. "Or how I'd lost the bet and gave you the worst reason imaginable for being a woman."

"Oh." Georgette paused. Only one thought entered her mind. "Then . . . you didn't care for . . ."

"No! What I mean is that I . . ." He halted. "Miss Thompson, such cannot pass between the two of us. It was dishonorable for me to kiss you. I—I simply wished for you to know the better things which may pass between a man and a woman. Of course, it should be within marriage."

Georgette was gaining her equilibrium. And reality. "Oh, yes. Yes, of course. I—I do understand. And it shall not happen again, I am sure. We are not going to ever be married." She stood up quickly, and drew in a breath. "But—but I do wish to thank you for, the—the enlightenment."

"It was my pleasure." Lucas bowed, his gaze amused.

"Was it?" Georgette asked. A sin it may be, but she wanted to know. Needed to know that the wonderful moment she had experienced had been shared by Lucas, not just something he had given.

He frowned. "Miss Thompson . . ."

"I only wished . . ."

"Georgette . . ." he said more gently.

"What would it hurt for you to tell me . . . ?"

He laughed, his gaze exasperated. "Georgie. I do not wish to sound . . . condescending, but we must not speak on this again. It can only lead to trouble, I promise you. It would be like opening Pandora's box."

"Very well." Georgette nodded. She didn't see any need to say that it was already wide open and its lid flapping in the breeze for her.

"I—I shall leave you now," Lucas said.

"Oh my yes," Georgie exclaimed, memory shoving its way through her tingling emotions. "And do hurry."

Lucas frowned. "I beg your pardon?"

"There is a man in the courtyard by the big tree. He is wishing to see you."

"What?"

"That is what I was trying to tell you. He missed the exchange this morning, but wants you to meet him directly. You do speak French, don't you?"

"Of course."

"Thank heaven. Mine was not very good, though I think we scraped by." Georgie worried her lip. She could still feel Lucas's kiss upon it. "He says he will only talk to you."

"Yes, Georgie," was all Lucas said.

She sighed in pleasure.

"Why did you sigh like that?" Lucas asked rather cautiously.

"I do like that name far better." She looked at him, trying to regain her focus. "Do you think I can be Georgie from now on?"

"You may keep the name." Lucas smiled. "Just not the clothes."

She flushed. "You haven't liked one of my roles yet."

"That is true." He smiled. "Perhaps I simply like you as yourself far better."

"Do you?" Inane happiness filled her.

A confused looked entered Lucas's eyes. He shook his head. "I am going this very minute, Georgie. When I return, I expect for you to be dressed in a dress. And if it is an ugly one, it will be all the better."

"Why?" Georgie studied him. "Who am I supposed to be?"

"A brokenhearted spinster antidote?" he said, his tone wry.

"I beg your pardon?" Georgie gasped.

"No. I suppose that is one role you will never play." He bowed. "Just do what you can. I am going."

And he did just that, leaving Georgie to return to the bed and fall upon it. Wild emotions, confusing sensations, and nebulous thoughts whirled in her mind. Gracious, but Pandora's box held a dreadful lot.

Seven

"My page said you wished to speak to me," Lucas said quietly. The man who hid in the shadows was thin and undernourished. Fear clung to him.

"Thank God he found you," the man whispered. "I cannot stay long. I—I have failed."

"Yes," Lucas said. "This morning was quite a disappointment."

The man started back as if he thought Lucas a demon. He trembled. "Forgive me. This may very well be my life."

"Merely tell me the plans without further ado," Lucas said. Why had he kissed Georgie? He had had a reason in the beginning. But he felt as if he had fallen into a trap. Only it wasn't Georgie who had set it. His own male desires had done that.

Desperation twisted the small man's features. "I do not know any more about the Silver Serpent than before."

"Silver Serpent?" Lucas's brow shot up. At last, he had some form of a name for Aunt Clare's kidnapper. Yet what kind of man went about calling himself the Silver Serpent? "Then what am I to do?"

"McGregor will meet you at Leatherman's farm."

"Where is Leatherman's farm?" Lucas asked. "And why this delay?"

"Things, things have gone badly." He frowned. "You do not know where Leatherman's farm is?"

The sudden confusion and suspicion in the man's face set Lucas's alarms ringing. He must pay more attention. No matter the insanity of it all, Aunt Clare's welfare must not be endangered. "I would not wish to make a wrong turn out of overconfidence. I am sure time is of the essence in regard to this."

"Yes. Yes." The little man sighed. "Forgive me."

Lucas studied the little man. He knew better than to push his advantage. "Do give me the directions."

The little man proceeded in volatile French. Lucas had no difficulty following his speech. He only had difficulty accepting the directions. He looked at the little man. "It will take five days for me to reach the farm, at least."

"Yes." The little man looked at him solemnly. "You will go though? You—you will not desert us?"

"What other choice do I have?" Lucas said. He would be on the road with Georgie for five days. Of a sudden, it was a daunting prospect. Lucas shook his head and turned to leave. He then paused. "What did you really think of my page?"

The man stared at him and then shrugged. "He seemed a good lad. Do you think he is not loyal?"

"No. *He* is loyal. That much I do know." Lucas nodded and left in deep contemplation. He proceeded to the taproom, where he asked for a brandy and received Blue Ruin instead from a boy behind the bar. He almost desired another as one of the men asked after his page and if Lucas had given the disobedient rascal a good whipping. Lucas clenched his teeth. He was most certainly not going to tell the gentlemen what he *had* given the "boy."

Lucas finished his tankard, having his answer. The world was blind, that or complete blockheads. He left the taproom. He paused. The hairs at the nape of his neck rose. He spun quickly. No one was there. He turned and proceeded. When he reached the room he paused, squared his shoulders, and knocked. Georgie opened the door.

She wore a drab gray dress. She had tied a faded black ribbon through her short hair. Her face was expectant. "Well? Do you like this better?"

"I do, but you must change again."

"Why?"

"You are going to turn back into Georgie. The boy that is. Not the girl."

"Am I? How famous." She blinked. "Why?"

"Because we are leaving directly."

"Where are we going?"

"After the Silver Serpent," Lucas said, his tone droll.

"The Silver Serpent?" Georgie repeated. Her gray eyes brightened. "Is that who has Aunt Clare?"

"So it seems."

"How very intriguing."

"I knew you would think so." Lucas sighed. "Personally, if I am ever permitted to get my hands upon the Silver Serpent, I vow I shall put a bullet through him. Now hurry. I will go and ready Trump."

"Yes." Georgie closed the door.

With the click of the latch, Lucas also heard a clatter. Tensing, he strode swiftly toward the sound that came at the turn of the hall into another. Two sandy-haired lads stood gaping at him. A pistol lay at their feet.

Lucas immediately took the fighting stance. "What do you want?"

"S—sorry," the first boy gurgled. "I—I dropped it."

"Didn't mean to." The second blushed a bright red.

"We . . . just weren't watching where we were going," the first said.

"We sh—shall be going n—now," the second said.

They turned directly, knocked into each other, bounced off each other, and then stumbled down the hall, leaving the pistol on the floor.

Lucas drew in a deep, exasperated breath. He walked over and picked it up. He checked it and found it was not even loaded. He frowned. Everything about this had a bad feel to it. He was excessively tired of pistols, loaded or not. Now what were those two lads about?

He shook his head and pocketed the pistol. It didn't really matter. If those two boys were running from him, rather toward him, he'd accept it readily. He had as much on his plate as he could manage at the moment. After all, Georgie would be stepping out soon, wearing those breeches that made her far too feminine in his eyes, while in the eyes of the rest of the world she appeared a mere lad. If that wasn't a curse, he didn't know what was.

"Oh my, what a famous place." Clare stood in the middle of the ever-changing, lively crowd of the market. Street urchins rubbed elbows with matrons and the sellers cried out their wares to all alike.

"Yes." François smiled, his gaze moving across the colorful scene like a butter knife across butter. He still gently held her elbow. "Quite famous."

"Do look at that lady's hat. And that gentleman over there. He has quite ten fobs upon him." Clare's eyes widened. "What does a man need with that many? Bendford has only three, and he only wears one at a time."

"Indeed." François' tone was dry. His eyes lit. He

drew her toward a flower booth. *"Ma chérie.* Do study the flowers, yes? I wish to leave you only a moment."

She looked about quickly. "Is he here?"

"I—I am not certain. Only remain here." François shook his finger at her. "Do not move from here."

She smiled most sunnily. "No, I shall not."

"Does the lady like my blooms?" the flower lady asked.

"What?" Clare asked as François slipped away. She blinked and gazed at the lady's flowers in order to give her an honest reply. She drew in a deep breath. "Oh, yes. I do very much."

"Which will you buy?" the lady asked swiftly, her eyes lighting with excitement.

"Oh dear, I cannot buy any," Clare said. "I—I do not have my reticule with me. That nasty Burt took it from me you see."

"What?" the flower lady asked.

"Mon ange," François said from behind her.

"Oh my!" Clare spun. "You are back so soon."

"With a present, *ma belle."* His lips twitching into a smile, he held out his hand. Upon it was a gold watch fob. "Now your esteemed brother can have another one. Tell him he must wear two at a time, yes?"

Clare gasped in astonishment. "Why, however did you get that?" Then she blushed. "Oh dear, you mean you stole it from that man."

"He had far too many, did he not?" He said solemnly.

"Perhaps, but . . . oh dear. Thank you very much, François. But . . ." She flushed. "I did not mean for you to steal if for me."

"Then I did not steal it. I merely acquired it." François smiled rather sadly now. "I know that your Robin Hood took from the rich to give to the poor, but me, I am French. Taking from the rich to give to the one I love is good enough, *non?*"

Clare struggled with the concept. "I appreciate it very much. I—I do truly. After all, you faced danger for me."

"Danger?" François' brow rose.

"You could have been caught."

"Non." He laughed a truly delighted laugh. "That was child's play. Never would I be caught at it. That is not danger, *ma belle,* I assure you."

Clare still could not take the watch fob. "Yes, but . . ."

François closed his hand. He shook his head. *"Ma chérie.* You are the danger to me."

"What?" Clare gasped and looked at him. "No, I would never wish to hurt you."

"I had forgotten such principles or such conscience." His tone was musing. "It is dangerous for you to awaken even one small ethic in me, for that can very well kill me. For me to succeed, I must be er . . . nerveless. Even ruthless."

Clare stared at him. She thought upon it. She nodded her head. "I understand. At least, I think I understand." She drew in a deep breath. "I . . . forgive me, I never would wish to belittle your occupation . . ."

"No." He smiled. "Though it is clear you do not like it."

"I own that I prefer you as a barkeep."

"But that does not make much money." He sighed. "Alas, neither occupation would do for the sister of the great Lord Wrexton."

"I accept the fob," Clare said quickly. She reached out her hand.

"No, *ma belle.*" François shook his head. "I did this to be amusing. Now, I see that it is not. Your brother

will not wear a stolen watch fob from me after all."
He frowned. "Remain here one more moment."

Before she could speak, he departed through the
crowd. She watched him go. She watched him come
close to the man with the many fobs. She watched him
bump into the man. She watched him step away. Magi-
cally, the fob he had offered to her was back on the
man. The two held some converse. The man actually
smiled and laughed. Then François returned to her, his
step light.

"There. It is gone away for the moment." He smiled
and offered her that wondrous leg of his. "Now, we
shall do it correctly. I am a gentleman courting his fair
lady." He withdrew a purse and stepped up to the
flower lady. "I would buy this dear lady many flowers,
oui."

Clare couldn't help herself. She peeked into his
open purse. It was heavy with coins and notes.
"But . . . but you are wealthy."

"I am good at what I do, *ma chère.*" He smiled.
"Now, do choose your flowers."

"Oh yes." Clare promptly chose the bright daisies.
François added a few roses. The flower woman, beam-
ing, gave them to her after François offered her some
coins.

Then they wandered the market for the next hour.
François kept watch no doubt as they did so. Clare
could not. She could only enjoy being with her true
love. Despite everything, he could laugh, pointing out
the odd person, or humorous scene, as there was always one when there were many people.

She gladly accepted any trinket he chose to buy for
her from his purse. Except soon she was laden down.
Even as her heart could not turn away from a nagging
problem. What was she to do about the two lads? She

finally sighed. "What should I do about Nick and Ned?"

François stopped in his stead. He frowned, and he looked away from her, his gaze upon the now-setting sun. "You shall do nothing, *mon petit chou.*"

"Oh but I must," Clare said. "I do fear that that nasty Burt will be unkind to them because they failed to get the money."

"Non. It is their own fault. They are dolts, *ma belle,"* François said sternly. "They must pay the consequences for their stupidity."

"But why? They are quite innocent."

"They would have gotten you killed. That is unacceptable. Any man would have known that Burt would not let you live. You know too much about him."

"But Nick and Ned aren't men. They are only boys."

"No." He sighed and nodded at the reddening sky. "The day is gone, *ma chérie.* Now, now we must pretend no longer."

"Pretend?" Clare asked, confused. "Pretend what?"

He shook his head. "Surely I had the right to steal this day with you."

"You did not steal this day," Clare said. "I have wished to spend it with you." She flushed. "Indeed, I—I must make a confession."

"A confession?" He laughed. "What could you ever confess, my sweet Clare?"

"I fear I lied about seeing that man outside of the pub." She bit her lip. "I simply didn't wish you to take me home yet."

"Did you?" François grinned. "Then I shall make the confession that neither did I see the man before the hack stopped."

"What?" Clare blinked. Then she understood and laughed. "Oh, how lovely. I do not feel so very wicked now."

"But I do. For I did steal this day to be with you. I should not have. But now we must accept reality. I must and will take you to safety. And then I must leave you."

"Must you?" Clare said.

"Was there ever such a story?" he said softly.

"What story?"

"It might even be sadder than Romeo and Juliet."

"What do you mean?" Clare's heart jumped in fear.

"A thief and a lady wellborn? Sister to the great Lord Wrexton at that." He shook his head. "And at our age, *ma chère?* Even Shakespeare did not think to write such a story. Romeo and Juliet were young, and then could be so foolish. *Oui?* But we, we are of such an age. It could never be accepted."

"But of course it could be accepted," Clare said. "I think *Romeo and Juliet* should never have ended the way it did. They were young and had all their lives ahead of them. If they had only waited to see the next turn of life, everything would have worked out quite nicely I am sure." She drew in her breath. "But . . . but we are not young. Life will not give us so many more turns. It expects us to be grown and not throw our best chances away as we did when we were young."

"No, my Juliet. I shall not let you make this mistake. I will have you be safe again. You must return to the world you know. You must never be tainted by my world, *ma chère.* I have saved you from possible death . . . now I fear, I must save you from me."

"I'd rather be saved from a life without love. Do not misunderstand me. I have enjoyed my life. But now that I have met you . . . no, do not ask me to live without you. Or return to my dull existence with my brother."

He lifted her hand. "But it is an existence, *mon*

ange. Now let us go. You will permit me to escort you to your establishment."

"Very well." Clare's eyes burned with threatening tears. She would think of something; she was certain. Still, her heart trembled in fright nevertheless. What happened if she lost François? What happened if she never saw him again?

"That is my lady." François smiled and nodded. He lifted her hand and kissed it. Clare leaned forward. Where kisses to her hand had been wondrous before, now it was not enough. When François straightened, she was but a few inches away from him. She gazed up at him, her eyes filled with her wish.

He swallowed. *"Ma chérie?"*

"Yes," Clare said breathlessly.

"Would you . . . ?"

"Yes?"

"Would you permit me to steal a kiss from you?"

She smiled. Yes, he was so very noble, to make it appear to be his notion and not hers. "Yes. I would."

Slowly, he lowered his lips and placed a soft kiss upon her lips. He drew back. Clare trembled and blushed all at the same time. Her dreams came together with that moment.

"Thank you," she said, emotions welling within her.

"Non, thank you," he said softly. He spun smartly on his heel and strode away from her.

Clare blinked. She couldn't move, so very overcome was she.

Then she didn't need to move. He spun around again and paced back to her. His face showed complete astonishment. "What am I thinking? I am not a man of honor. I am not supposed to be noble, am I?"

"No. You are not," Clare said with excitement.

"I am French," he said in an aggrieved tone. "Not this paltry Robin Hood."

"That is true."

He laughed. "Nor can I trust you not to run circles about them all. They have not taken proper care of you to date."

"No, they haven't," Clare said dutifully.

"You are coming with me," François said firmly. "Your brother has had you all his life. I may not be worthy of you. But I shall have you with me for a few days more. That is not too much to ask, is it?"

"No. It isn't." Aunt Clare smiled. It was far too little to ask in her opinion. She sighed then in pleasure.

"What are you thinking, *mon ange?*" François narrowed his gaze.

She smiled. "Only that I don't have to think of something now."

He laughed and nodded. "I feared as much."

She flushed. "I am not Juliet, my dear. I never did understand why she didn't run away with Romeo that very first night, you know?"

"You frighten me, *ma chérie.*"

She peeked at him. She giggled. "No, I do not."

He took her hand and placed it into the crook of his arm. *"Non.* But you should, this I know."

"What are we going to do?" Nick asked as he sat glumly upon the stool. He gripped a glass of gin. "First we lost Aunt Clare. Now we lost the earl and Miss Thompson."

"It's not right." Ned sighed. "Who is the Silver Serpent and how did *he* get Aunt Clare?"

"Must have stole her from the barkeep." Nick sighed. "The earl don't like him either. Wants to put a bullet through him."

"Like Burt is going to put a bullet through us," Ned said.

"If we are lucky." Nick sighed.

"Nick and Ned dear?" A sweet voice said from behind.

"What?" Nick asked, turning.

"What?" Ned turned.

Aunt Clare and François stood behind them.

Nick frowned. "Aunt Clare, you aren't supposed to be here. It's a bad place."

Ned's eyes widened. "No. It's a good place. She is here. She came back!"

"Blimey!" Nick blinked. "She did."

"Yes I did." Clare smiled proudly upon them. "So did François. He is going to help us, dears. He is going to make certain the exchange goes off safely between you and Lucas."

"You will?" Nick asked. "What a Trojan!"

"Zounds." Ned smiled. "You're a right one."

"Yes, aren't I?" François' expression was quite arrested, as if unprepared for this great munificence. He cast a quizzing look toward Clare. "Why am I going to do that, *ma belle?*"

"I don't know." Clare smiled. "But I do think that will be part of the plan. I haven't been able to think of the rest yet." She looked at the boys. "François is a thief, dears."

"What?" Nick yelped. "Thought you were a barkeep."

"I do that in my spare moments," François said. "It relaxes me after a hard night of thieving."

"That's bad," Ned said, wide-eyed.

François shrugged. "It is a living. Me, I do not abduct ladies for profit." He turned warm eyes toward Aunt Clare. "I have made the exception for *mon ange* only."

"Oh, my dear. How sweet." Aunt Clare clapped her

hands together. "I was hoping you would say the boys could keep the money."

"What?" François blinked. Then he thought, clearly reviewing his words. He shook his head. *"Ma chérie,* you are too wily for me."

"No." She blushed. "But they should have the money to give to Burt."

"Non." François gaze darkened. "We will have a better plan than that. Not a pence will that villain Burt receive. 'Else my name is not François."

"Oh yes. That is a far better plan." Aunt Clare beamed at the boys. "The boys can keep the money."

"We'd be nabobs." Nick brightened.

"Might buy our own inn." Ned gasped.

"I think that would be famous," Aunt Clare said.

"No." Nick's face fell.

"Don't want our own inn?" Ned's lips tugged down.

"Would want our own inn," Nick said. "But forgot. We lost them."

"Oh." Ned blushed. "Did forget. Have a bad head."

"Lost who?" Aunt Clare asked.

"The earl and Miss Thompson," Nick said.

"They bolted." Ned nodded.

"What?" François frowned. "What do you mean they bolted?"

"Hey!" Nick exclaimed. "You *are* a thief. You stole Aunt Clare back!"

"Did you put a bullet through the Silver Serpent?" Ned frowned.

"What!" François exclaimed. He narrowed his gaze. "What do you know of the Silver Serpent?"

"That he stole Aunt Clare from you." Nick smiled. "Like you did from us."

"Impossible!" François muttered.

"Yes, dears, I have been with François all morning

long." Aunt Clare frowned. "No one else has stolen me, I promise you."

Ned frowned. "Then why did the earl and lady go after the Silver Serpent?"

"Mon Dieu. That is a good question." François sat down upon the stool. He waved to the lad behind the bar. "Bring me a drink. Any drink."

"Who is the Silver Serpent?" Clare asked.

François gazed at her solemnly. "How should I know, *ma chère?"*

"Don't know either," Nick said. "But he's got the earl up in the boughs."

"And he's got a strange name." Ned nodded.

"But . . ." Clare gasped and closed her mouth quickly. "Oh dear, what an imbroglio. What should we do?"

François peered at her. Then a smile crossed his features. "We must follow them, *ma chère.* It is the only thing to do."

Aunt Clare paused a moment. Then she, too, smiled. "My, it will be a new adventure. How delightful."

"Will it?" Nick asked, his voice hesitant.

"Must we?" Ned asked more to the point.

"Yes, we must," François said firmly. " You must have Montieth to get the money. Nor can you remain here. Your Burt will be sure to arrive soon."

"Forgot that." Nick turned green.

"Forgot that." Ned turned blue.

"Non. We shall be gone before that," François said with confidence. Indeed, he waved his hand like a magician. "We will disappear, *oui."*

"Would like that." Nick sighed.

François paused. "Pardon. What happened with Little Ike? How did you escape him this morning."

"We didn't," Nick said. A sheepish expression

slipped across his face. "You said we were supposed to think like Burt."

"Yes." François nodded. "I did. So how did you act like Burt?"

"We tied Little Ike up," Ned said.

"While he was unconscious," Nick said.

"Should have killed him," Ned said solemnly.

"But wasn't sure we had time." Nick nodded.

"Didn't have the stomach," Ned said.

"That was the truth." Nick frowned at him. "Burt would have lied to them."

"Oh." Ned sighed. "You are right."

"That is all right, dearest," Aunt Clare said. "We are here now. You don't have to think like Burt anymore."

"Good." Nick said. "Don't like it."

"Not a jot," Ned said.

"You tied him up and then what did you do?" François persisted.

"We dragged him to our room," Nick said. "Didn't want Montieth to find him."

"Hid him beneath the bed," Ned said. "Didn't want to scare the maid."

"If there is one here." Nick frowned in consideration. "Ramshackle inn. Don't think there is one."

François stared at them. He broke out into laughter. *"Mon Dieu.* But there is hope for you yet. There is hope."

Eight

"I amaze myself," Lucas said. "I cannot believe I am doing this."

"You amaze me too," Georgette said quite truthfully. She really couldn't believe it herself. Yet there they stood, within an open field, an assortment of odd vases and objects set upon a fence a distance away. Lucas held a gleaming pistol, the handling of which he was about to instruct her on. Only a day ago she had asked him again and he had put her off. "In truth, I thought you were merely gammoning me when you said you would teach me to shoot."

"I was," Lucas said in an easy voice.

"What made you change your mind?" Georgette asked.

He shrugged. "I did not know how heartily dull it is to watch someone else reading."

Georgette flushed. She had rather lost herself in her book today. "I fear I have not been a very good companion."

"Yes," Lucas said, quizzing her. Yet the warmth within his eyes was unmistakable. "I have had plenty of time to consider many things. My first conclusion was that it might be safer for both of us if I teach you the basics. I would dislike it very much if you were to hit me when you were trying to shoot the Silver Serpent."

"I agree," Georgette said, her heart leaping in excitement.

"And my second conclusion supported my first. If you have begun your intent of reading everything in the world, I will be sunk for any intelligible communication for the rest of this journey."

"I wouldn't have read much more. They are my father's books," Georgette said, smiling in relief.

He was unbending toward her. For the two days they had been upon the road, he had been the contained, autocratic nobleman. She had been constrained herself. They both talked about the mystery of where they were going. Why would Clare's abductor play such games?

Georgette had almost started to hope that Lucas was correct, and that Clare was directing her own abduction and merely offering them a form of sport. Lucas had changed his opinion on that score, however. He admitted the Silver Serpent as a name for a villain was certainly something Clare would dream up, but everything else about this roguery proved that this was not Aunt Clare's man.

Such was merely part of Georgette's constraint. The other was the memory of Lucas's kiss. Perhaps if he had not been so stern and cool, she could pretend to forget the kiss. Surely, his return to the offhanded, rather benevolent fashion that he employed with her was a signal that everything was once again all right. She could forget the kiss. She bit her lip. The odds of doing just that were low.

"Now pay attention," Lucas said calmly. He lifted the pistol, and Georgette paid very close attention. Unfortunately, it was to the width of Lucas's shoulders and his obvious strength as he took aim. She jumped at the report of the pistol. A hideous yellow vase exploded directly.

Another sound came, a cry from the coach that was a distance away. Trump had taken craven cover within it when he had heard that Georgette was to hold a pistol.

Lucas laughed and called out, "It is all right, Trump. I was shooting. Not Georgie." He received no reply. Lucas's lips twitched. *"Now* it is her turn." A low moan came from the coach. Lucas sighed. "Your coachman lacks backbone, Georgie."

"He is not my coachman anymore. He is yours. You hired him away." Georgette grinned. "May I try it?"

"Certainly." Lucas offered her more instruction and then placed the pistol in her hands. He took a stance behind her, for safety no doubt, she thought wryly. Determined to prove herself, Georgette aped Lucas's position, lifted the pistol with one hand, and squinting at her mark, fired.

Not a single object moved. Not the red dish she was aiming at or the particularly ugly green cup beside it. Instead, her arm flew up and was well nigh jerked from her shoulder. She toppled back, fortunately into strong arms that wrapped about her.

"Oh!" Georgette swallowed as her ears rang and her arm throbbed.

"Jumping Jehoshaphat?" Lucas's voice was calm, his arms holding her close.

"Er . . ." Georgette's heart beat against her rib cage. She dropped the pistol without thought.

"Saint Mary's night rail?" he teased.

"Yes." Georgette sighed deeply.

"That wasn't bad for your first attempt," Lucas said. Georgette chuckled. "Palaverer. That was dreadful."

"You need a few more pointers, yes?"

Georgette pressed her lips together firmly. Nothing

would make her confess that she didn't want to try one more time. She had just discovered something she disliked heartily. No wonder Mr. Ferret preferred his knives. "Do I?"

"Hallo!" a voice called out from behind them. "Montieth, is that you?"

"Blast." Lucas's arms fell from about her. He spun. Disorientated, Georgette turned as well. Her eyes widened. Two riders approached them from across the open field, the man waving.

"Who are they?" Georgette whispered.

"In all the world, why must it be them?" Lucas muttered. He cast her a warning look. "Remember you are a boy, Georgie."

"Certainly." However Georgette soon discovered that she couldn't remember anything as the two drew up before them. The man, a blond Adonis, rode a black stallion. The lady, raven-haired, with flashing dark eyes, rode a magnificent bay.

"Hello, Fairmont." Lucas's voice was cool. His face didn't move a muscle. "And, Lady Chalmers. It is a pleasure to see you."

"Lucas." The lady's voice was deep and mellow. Her dark eyes, however, were bright and hot, and not upon Georgie. "What a surprise to discover you here."

"I was about to say the same." Lucas bowed.

"We are visiting Ogglethorp." Fairmont laughed. "I'll lay odds you didn't know that his country seat lies here."

"I certainly didn't," Lucas said.

"It has been frightfully dull." Lady Chalmers pursed her lips into a pout. "All he offers is fishing and hunting. He keeps country hours too."

"How disobliging of him," Lucas murmured. Now the man and woman looked at Georgette. She attempted not to blush. For once, she worried that her masquerade would be seen through. They both appeared to be the most sophisticated and knowing people she had ever met. "This is Georgie. I am escorting him home. For a friend."

"Really?" Lady Chalmers purred, her eyes narrowing.

Fairmont laughed. "He's been sent down, has he?"

"He's a rare terror," Lucas said drolly.

Fairmont studied Georgie. "Which school do you attend, Georgie?"

"It is a very private one," Lucas said. "You wouldn't know it."

"Surely." Lady Chalmers drawled. "Their taste in attire is rather outlandish, isn't it?"

"What?" Georgie exclaimed. Being unmasked would have been one thing, but to be insulted upon her dress was another.

"Who is your friend, by the by?" Fairmont grinned. "Do we know her?"

"No you wouldn't," Lucas said, his tone repressive. "She is the daughter of an obscure baron who has just passed on to his rewards."

"An orphan?" Fairmont asked. "Lucas, you devil."

"I might know the name," Lady Chalmers said.

"You will soon, Lady Chalmers." Lucas laughed. "Aunt Clare has decided to lend her her patronage."

"What ho. Sits the wind in that corner?" Fairmont laughed. "Beware, old man."

"I am." Lucas smiled coolly. "However, Miss Thompson is in need of assistance at this moment."

"Is she as zany as Aunt Clare?" Lady Chalmers purred.

"More so," Georgette said.

"If you will pardon us, I have found young Georgie is not proficient with the pistol and I thought to rectify that lack."

"You are a fortunate lad, to have Lucas teaching you." Lady's Chalmers's gaze was upon Lucas. "I know I would enjoy it if he taught me. Anything, anything at all."

Georgette nodded, far too busy biting her tongue. A cynical look crossed Fairmont's face. Lucas remained aloof. She could not imagine, as famously beautiful as the woman was, that either could be so calm. Fairmont surely should be jealous. And Lucas surely should be affected by the obvious lure. Georgette knew that she was affected, but in a waspish way.

"Thank you, Lady Chalmers." Lucas bowed.

"We shall leave, but only upon one condition." Lady Chalmers smiled.

"What is that, my lady?" Lucas raised a brow.

"That you come and see me once you are back in town. I miss you, Lucas. Just because you and Isabelle are no longer friends, it should not mean we should not be. She has broken both our hearts."

"Sarah, Sarah, you do tread where brave men would fear to tread. And Montieth has a pistol at that." Lord Fairmont chuckled. He cast Lucas a commiserating look. "Do give us some time to cover ground before you resume." His gaze was sapient. "Georgie does shoot wild."

Georgette stiffened at the remark. Though the man's instincts were good. She wouldn't mind shooting a little wild and unseating the gorgeous Lady Chalmers. For that she would gladly pick up that nasty pistol. It was a dreadful thought, she owned, but it persisted as the two made their farewells and rode away.

"Thank God you are dressed as a boy," Lucas said, his gaze still narrow upon the disappearing couple.

"Yes," Georgette said without enthusiasm. "The lady is quite beautiful, is she not?"

"What?" Lucas raised a brow.

Georgette swallowed hard. "The lady is quite beautiful. She is your friend?"

"No. She was Isabelle's friend. Bosom bow in fact. Isabelle was always too innocent to realize that Lady Chalmers was a faithless friend. Only when Isabelle married did she realize that Lady Chalmers meant her harm. In fact, Lady Chalmers put it about the *ton* that Isabelle had stolen the duke from her by design. Very few believed her of course."

"I see." Georgette's chest tightened.

"I am still friends with Isabelle." Lucas's lips twisted. "Lady Chalmers would never understand that. It would be unworthy of me, however, to remain in Isabelle's company, considering how I feel about her."

"Yes." Georgette couldn't resist. She might have been dressed as a boy, but she was female after all. "Is Isabelle as beautiful as Lady Chalmers?"

"Far more beautiful," Lucas said softly. He seemed to shake himself. He offered her a stern look. "The one you must beware of, and who is far more dangerous than Lady Chalmers, is Fairmont. He is a rake of the first order."

"Truly?"

He shook his head. "I was sure he would know you immediately as a woman."

"Yes." Georgette brightened. "He's not as knowing as he seems, is he?"

"But if he ever meets you as a woman," Lucas said. "beware of him. Lady Chalmers is feckless, with a vicious tongue. She can ruin a young girl's reputation with her gossip. While Fairmont does not only ruin a lady's reputation, but will take her virtue with a lie and a laugh."

Georgette's eyes widened. "He *is* wicked."

"Very." Lucas's jaw clenched. "I must apologize. Your notion to dress as Georgie was inspired,"

"Wasn't it?" Georgette attempted to keep the sarcasm from her voice. At the moment she felt like a complete widgeon, a very unfeminine widgeon at that. She would never be able to compete with the fair Lady Chalmers, but dressed in boy's clothes she had put herself even further beyond that hope.

A small voice did ask through her anger why she would ever wish to compete with Lady Chalmers, but it was a very small voice. Georgette easily brushed it away with the solid reasoning that no girl would enjoy being eyed as a nonexistent being. "I am glad I need never meet them again."

"Ah yes. You shall retire after this to that cottage by the sea?"

"Yes, I will." Georgie lifted her chin.

"Where you shall become heartily bored within the first month. And insane from ennui within the second. However, let us return to the business at hand." Lucas smiled. "Do pick up your pistol."

"Yes, of course." Georgette steeled herself and picked up the weapon.

"Now." Lucas stepped behind her. He put his arms about her, but this time also placed his hands to her wrists. "Keep your focus." Lucas's voice was rather grim.

Georgette nodded, a smile creeping to her lips. Georgie she might be, but it was she who had Lucas's arms about her at the moment. She narrowed her gaze upon a squat blue pot, her thoughts returning to Lady Chalmers and the way she looked as if she wished to devour Lucas.

"Aim," Lucas murmured.

"Yes." Lady Chalmers would *not* be on the list of those ladies Georgette would match Lucas with.

"Fire."

She'd make certain of that! Georgie pulled the trigger with that pleasurable thought. The blue pot exploded. Her mouth dropped open. "I did it."

"Good work," Lucas said. "If Fairmont or any man of his ilk ever comes about you, you have my permission to shoot him just the same as you did that pot."

"What?" Georgette blinked. Just why was Lucas concerned about that man? Then she smiled. At least he was not thinking overly much about Lady Chalmers. She shook herself. "I was thinking of the Silver Serpent myself."

"Were you?" Lucas's voice lightened.

"Here now!" a voice shouted. "What are you doing in my field?"

Both turned. A man upon a horse leveled an archaic-looking firearm upon them.

"A thousand apologies," Lucas said. "We had stopped, in order that I might instruct my young charge here in the art of shooting."

"Don't try to hoodwink me," The farmer cried. "You came to poach; that's what you're doing."

"With a Manton?" Lucas's brow shot up.

"Where is there an animal to poach?" Georgette asked, peering about in surprise.

These two very reasonable questions did not have their desired effect. It only enraged the farmer. He rattled his firearm and struggled to cock it. "Cheeky halfing, you ought to be ashamed of yourself."

"Forgive me, sir," Georgette exclaimed.

"We . . ." Lucas began.

"Hoity-toity muckle!"

"That must be me," Lucas murmured, his face confused.

"I'll show you, you trespassing jackanapes . . ."

"That's both of us." Georgette gulped.

The farmer finally managed to draw the hammer back.

"Yes," Lucas said. "Run, Georgie."

Georgette didn't need the suggestion. She turned and sprinted toward the coach. She shivered as she heard a click from the firearm, though no explosion followed. Lucas paced behind her, shielding her from the farmer. She reached the coach and swung wide the door. Two large hands grabbed her about the waist and tossed her into the opening.

"Ouch!" Unfortunately she landed upon the already cowering Trump.

"Blast!" Lucas cried as he dove in, unerringly on top of her and Trump.

Trump's howl was muffled.

"Fiend seize it." Lucas lifted himself from the mass and climbed to the cushion. "Trump, old man, get us out of here."

"I cannot move, my lord," Trump gurgled.

"Very well." Lucas reached over and hauled Georgette off the coachman. He tucked her upon his lap within a second. "Now you may move."

"I still cannot move." The fear in Trump's revealed face was so apparent that Georgette believed him.

"That farmer will never succeed in shooting. His piece is rusty and jammed."

"I still cannot move."

"Very well. But if I have to drive, I am going to give you back to Georgie to employ."

"No! I'll go." Trump's look of fear deepened. He scrabbled up and sprang toward the door and out it.

"Well I like that!" Georgette exclaimed indignantly.

"It must be all your trunks. That will teach you to travel light." A loud blast sounded and a ball plunked into the door.

"The old fellow shot it off after all." Lucas lifted a brow.

Trump's howl arose and the coach jerked into motion. Georgette broke into laughter, even as Trump drove so wildly that she and Lucas, well entwined within each other's arms, bounced and swayed.

"Remind me . . ." Lucas said as they slid to the left. "The next time . . ."

"Yes?" Georgette gasped as they slid then to the right.

"No more pistols." They bounced forward.

"Y—yes." Georgette's voice acquired a vibrato.

"I'll teach you . . ." They slammed back against the squabs.

"What?" Georgette gasped.

"Painting." Lucas laughed.

"Will you?" A thrill of excitement passed through Georgette, pure and unadulterated. "Oh, Lucas!" Before she knew it, Georgette kissed him. The gratitude in it dissipated as the kiss lengthened, and deepened. No small feat as she and Lucas slid back and forth. It mattered not to Georgette, since her world was rocking anyway.

The motion of the coach slowed. Georgette's world still rocked. Deep sensations, strange and new, coursed through her. So strong and frightening were they that Georgette pushed away from Lucas, gasping.

He sat very still, his sherry gaze filled with a fire as he watched her.

"I—I am sorry." Georgette shivered. "I planned not even to think about kissing you, let alone doing so. I know I shouldn't."

"No." A slow smile crossed his face. "It was I who taught you such, after all. You merely are a brilliant pupil."

"Then you aren't angry?"

His eyes widened. He chuckled. "No, Georgie, very far from it."

"That is good." She breathed in relief.

"Not exactly." His face was wry, his voice taut. "Now do move to the other seat, Georgie."

"Oh yes." Flushing, she scrabbled off his lap and sat on the opposite squab. No doubt he was afraid she would kiss him again.

"I believe this mode of travel is one of the finest." Clare drew in a deep breath of morning air. She held an old tin cup of tea as she sat before the fire in a small clearing. Large trees surrounded it.

François shook his head. "You are a wonder, *ma chérie*. Most ladies would faint to think they must travel by cart."

"I think the tinker's life is famous." Clare glanced to Sir Percy. "Do you not think so, dear?"

"Meow." Sir Percy sounded cranky. His eyes were at half mast and he lay sprawled, as if bored to flinders.

"Now, now." Clare frowned. "I fear you have become quite spoilt. Which is a shame. François has made certain that we have enjoyed amusing and refreshing stops upon our journey."

"I am glad you approve." François chuckled. "Never think to make a living as a tinker, *mon ange*. We have traded the best of our pans for the meanest of crockery."

"But that dear lady wanted and needed the pans so very much," Clare said.

"I will forgive that dear lady for bilking you, only because she offered the information we needed."

"It is so very exciting, following after Lucas and Georgette this way. And you were quite right, which I knew you would be. Everyone talks to a tinker."

François frowned. "Nick and Ned have been gone too long. I do not trust them."

"What?" Clare gasped. "My dear François, how can you say that? They are honest young lads."

"Non. I know that they could be," François said. "But they lack intelligence, *n'est ce pas?"*

"But they try very hard, dear. " She smiled. "I think it a great compliment to you that they wish to become apprentice thieves now."

"I am honored." His shoulder twitched. "I should not have let them go alone this morning."

"They are only going to the village for bread and cheese. They shall be back soon, have no fear." Clare sipped from her cup and smiled in delight. "Then we shall have breakfast and be off after Lucas and Georgette. What a lovely day it shall be."

"Yes." François' face turned pensive.

"I believe that every year from now on, we should take a month off to be tinkers," Clare said dreamily. "Though we best not tell Bendford that is what we are going to do."

"Ma chérie." François reached for her hand. "I shall never meet your brother. I have told you. There can be no future for us."

"There will be though." Clare patted his hand. "I have been waiting for you, see? Have you not been, also?"

François looked at her with the saddest smile, withdrawing his hand. "I have. But you were not to be the sister of Lord Wrexton."

She giggled. "And you were not to be a thief."

He did laugh at that, picking up his cup. "I can see your point."

Clare bit her lip and then drew in a deep breath. She could not remain silent longer. "I have no doubt you are most excellent at anything you do, dear, and if you are not wealthy from thieving, it is no doubt because thieving is not supposed to be a successful occupation. The Almighty does not approve of it. Indeed, he comes the heavy on it. I learned 'come the heavy' from my nephew. So you must not take it too much to heart, my dear. You were rowing against the current as it were. A new occupation is all that you need."

François stared at her. His lips twitched. *"Mon ange. Mon amour.* I adore you."

"I am glad to hear that." Clare beamed. "For I fully adore you too."

A bewildered expression crossed his face. He shook his head. *"Non.* I should not have said that."

"But you should have," Clare said. "Why should you not?"

"Because even if I were not a thief, I am not rich enough for you."

"If you find the Silver Serpent before Lucas does, will that make you rich?" Clare asked hopefully. "Perhaps rich enough to help you change occupations?"

"What?" François dropped his tin cup. *"Ma chérie,* I—what . . ."

"It was very clear that you didn't wish to speak about it," Clare said. "And I have learned that there is rarely any use in attempting to make a man discuss matters that pertain to money if he is not willing to do so. I know you say it is because we women do no understand such weighty issues and we shouldn't worry our pretty little heads, though from what I can determine you simply do not wish for us to 'poke our nose into your business.' And I will try not to, but . . ." She flushed. "Only I cannot help but try and imagine just exactly what the Silver Serpent is. Is it a necklace? Or a painting?"

"No, *ma belle.*" François studied her. He sighed. "I cannot tell you everything. But I will tell you that the Silver Serpent is a very special dagger made for royalty. But that is all I will say to you. I do not wish for you to speak about this again. It must be kept a secret. And Nick and Ned must never be told."

"Most certainly," Clare said. "I am sure it is enough of a tangle with Lucas and Georgette chasing after it, though why they would make such a mistake is a mystery."

"It is one I keep considering myself," François said gravely.

"You may be certain that Lucas is confused about it." Clare soothed him. "He would never steal anything. He is in no need of money."

"I am glad to hear that, *ma chérie.*" François chuckled now. "I would not wish the young earl to steal a march on me."

"Oh, he wouldn't." Clare blushed. "But even if you never get the Silver Serpent, I do not care. Not a straw, dear. You will always be rich enough for me. As for Bendford, he is very testy, but I promise you, he shall come around. Though I don't wish for him to do so until after we elope."

"Elope!" François stared at her.

"Yes." Clare nodded. "I do think it the most romantic fashion to marry and if Bendford doesn't object, then we won't have a reason to elope."

"Clare." His heart in his eyes, François withdrew his hand.

"Yes, dear?" Clare said, flushing.

"I . . ." François stopped.

"What?"

He cocked his head. "Do you hear that? It sounds like a dog."

"Meow." Sir Percy sat up and licked his lips.

"It must be a dog," Clare said. "I hear him now. Do continue."

"Yes," François said. "I . . ."

"Meow!" Sir Percy flexed his muscles.

"Oh dear, that dog is coming our way." Clare sighed. "Quick, François. What were you about to say? Do you wish to elope? Or if you wish a large wedding we . . ."

"Clare. *Non,* I . . ." François gripped her hands tight. A crashing in the woods interrupted him.

"Hello!" Nick called as he and Ned appeared, riding up to them on the same horse.

"Look what we did?"

"We stole breakfast." Ned beamed.

Breakfast squealed its objection and wiggled its porky body. Ned clutched it all the tighter in pride.

"We wanted to show that we could steal." Nick nodded. "Going to be bang up to all the tricks."

"But not yet, I fear." François shook his head as he pointed behind them. A large shepherd dog charged through the thickets. He paused, and then charged at the horse, barking. The horse tried to rear. Laden down as it was with the two brothers and a pig, it didn't achieve much height. Indeed, it was more of a leap than anything else.

However, Nick and Ned weren't horsemen. They listed and then toppled off. Breakfast squealed, the horse neighed and the dog yapped. Nick and Ned only yelped.

"Mon Dieu, you stole an entire farm." François covered his ears to the din.

The shepherd dog continued to yap. It darted back and forth, nipping at ankles. From the mangle upon the ground, it finally unearthed the pig. Its intent was clear. Breakfast was to be herded back from whence it came.

"Gracious," Clare exclaimed in astonishment as the pig, with but one canine nip to its cloven hooves, waddled back toward the thicket. Except then Sir Percy sprang into action. He darted after the dog. "Sir Percy, do please leave that dog alone. He is only retrieving what is his."

"Quick, lads." François chuckled. "Your booty is escaping."

"Blast!" Nick scrambled up to run after the barnyard brawl. Ned was just behind him.

They both skittered to a halt, though, as a man appeared upon a horse. He carried an archaic-looking firearm.

"Oh no," Nick said, raising his hands. "Caught."

"It'll be Old Bailey." Ned sighed and raised his hands.

"You stole my pig." The farmer struggled with his weapon. "Blast it!"

"Pardon. You say these boys stole your pig? I do not see it anywhere here." François said it with an innocent face. Of course, the sound of pig, cat, and dog could still be heard off in the distance.

"They stole it!" The farmer said.

"There is no evidence of it." François frowned. "Me, I think your pig escaped all on its own. Your fine dog followed it to here and now herds it home. Nothing more." He frowned. "Though my lady's cat here has disappeared. Perhaps we should return to your farm and see if you have stolen it from us." He looked to Clare. *"Ma chère,* are you prepared to press charges against this villain."

"Here now!" The farmer ceased his struggles and gaped.

"Well, monsieur," François asked, "what do you think?"

"I'll tell you what I think. The world ain't right. Yesterday I have some hoity-toity lord with a cheeky halfing poaching on my land. And today I've got some

Frenchie telling me that my pig ain't been stolen! What next I ask you? What next?"

"Lucas and Georgie!" Clare exclaimed. She dashed up to the farmer. "Oh, sir, can you please tell me in what direction that hoity-toity lord and cheeky halfing went?"

François chuckled. "That is what is next, monsieur."

Nine

François tied the horse to a bush at the edge of the forest. He had left Clare and the two lads, informing them that he would scout ahead. His lips twisted. It hadn't required much scouting for him to determine that Montieth was making his way to Leatherman's farm.

He couldn't be certain what Montieth had actually discovered, but since it was Emherst who must have given him the information, François doubted that Montieth knew much at all. Emherst was a rank amateur and the weakest of links. He considered the fact that somehow Emherst had rendezvoused with Montieth rather than him. François smiled wryly. It was a farce.

He sobered. Unfortunately it wouldn't remain a farce for long if he failed to catch up with Montieth and deter him before he actually learned something and mucked up François' business. François withdrew a spyglass from his saddlebag. He strolled to the edge of the woods that sloped into a green valley. In its lowest point a small farmhouse nestled amid an unkempt clearing. The house read of neglect and solitude. He lifted the glass to his eye.

"Finally." François nodded. A coach stood before the dilapidated building. Now he could deal with Lucas and Miss Thompson posthaste. A movement from the corner of his eye froze him. He swung his glass a degree to the left.

"Pour l'amour de Dieu." His timing was not as perfect as he had thought. McGregor rode toward the farmhouse hellbent for leather. The man was nothing short of a scoundrel. He was a professional and far more intelligent than Emherst, but his methods could not be trusted. The Scotsman possessed a volatile temperament.

François narrowed his gaze in consideration. What would be the fastest way to intercept McGregor before he reached the farmhouse and Montieth? A shot rang out far off in the distance. Evidently someone else was pondering the same thing and had come to a conclusion.

"Mon Dieu." François needed McGregor alive. Prepared to spring into action, he stiffened. The nape of his neck burned. He never ignored that sensation. It had saved him many times within his life. A deadly calm settling over him, he turned.

His brows shot up. "Sir Percy."

"Meow!" Sir Percy sat watching him.

A chill raced through François. "What has happened? Is it Clare? Is she in danger?"

Sir Percy meowed. It was tinged with disgust, as if to say that surely Clare must be in danger, else Sir Percy would not have been there.

"Forgive me." François nodded. "This must be painful to you, to be forced to behave like a dog."

Sir Percy snarled with cat vigor. Turning, he stalked away. François glanced back to the valley. Another shot rang out. Sir Percy yowled.

François did something he had never done in his entire life. He turned his back upon a king's ransom.

Worse, he turned away from it at the demand of a scarred-up, orange marmalade cat.

"You moved, Lucas." Georgie lifted her gaze from the paper, her gray eyes condemning.

"Did I?" Lucas hid his smile. He had, of course. However, a man could only sit perfectly still for an hour at a time. "Perhaps you have chosen too much for your first sketch."

"No. You said I must prove to you that I can draw before you will teach me to paint." Georgie's full lip pouted out, but only for a moment. She immediately turned her attention back to her work.

"So you chose me as your subject to punish me?" Lucas drawled. He permitted his gaze alone to travel the room of the farmhouse. It had taken Georgie all of three hours to move comfortably into the shabby surroundings. She had seen no reason to live in the dusty shell without the comforts within the coach. Or the added "supplies" they had bought in the small village they had come upon before arriving.

Georgie then had the farmhouse completely dusted and scrubbed within the first day. Now they had settled down to sketching in the open common room. Trump dozed next to the blackened fireplace, in charge of watching the pot hanging above the crackling fire. The scene was very cozy. Except for Mr. Ferret's knife, which lay amidst the charcoal stubs upon Georgie's table. Lucas himself kept his own Manton close by, while the satchel remained hidden beneath his chair.

"Hm?" She rubbed at the paper. Her face showed as much charcoal as most likely the paper did, Lucas was sure.

"Never mind." A noise came to him. He frowned. "Was that a shot?"

"Don't move." Georgie frowned.

Lucas sat still. "That was a shot, Georgie."

"I didn't hear anything." Georgie worried her lip and studied her sketch. "Just one more minute, Lucas."

"Georgie . . ."

At that moment the flimsy wooden door to the house crashed open. A large, burly man somersaulted into the room, fluidly springing to his feet. Lucas jumped to his own feet, grabbing his Manton.

"Drat!" Georgie's charcoal flew in the air as she exchanged it for a knife.

Trump coughed to consciousness. "Gawd!" He dove immediately under the large table set before him.

A frozen pause transpired. The intruder's bright blue eyes scanned the room. He lifted a brow as he looked at Lucas. Then he studied Georgie. A grin crossed his face. "You've done wonders with the old place, lass."

"You . . . you know I'm a girl?" Georgie gasped.

"Any fool can see that, love."

Lucas sighed, shaking his head. "I am not insane then."

"I hope to God you're not." The man said, his gaze turning to the Manton. A look of envy flashed in his eyes. "That is a mighty fine piece you have there."

"Thank you." Lucas nodded.

The man sighed then, resignation in every tone. "The Comte couldn't make it? Is he still alive?"

"Sorry, old man, I wouldn't know," Lucas said.

McGregor looked at him assessingly and then bent to pick up the door. "You look like an English nobleman."

"I am. An earl to be exact."

"Pity. I'd rather have had the Comte. He's a great man to have in a fight."

"Saint Mary's night rail." Georgie gasped. Her expression of astonishment would have been priceless, if it hadn't occurred at this particular moment.

"What is it?" Lucas raised a brow.

A sheepish expression crossed her face. "Nothing. I—I will explain . . . later."

McGregor narrowed his gaze. "Who are you, mon? Friend or foe?"

"You must think me a friend," Lucas said. "Considering you are turning your back to me."

Which the large man did as he propped the door back into place. "I've got a bloody Serpent out there. I'll choose you over him any day."

"Serpent?" Trump jumped so hard he knocked the table. "Coor."

"Who is that maw-worm?" McGregor asked as he strode over to the window, and ignoring them all, shoved his pistol out of it.

"My coachman," Lucas said.

"Ah." The man squinted. "Could you cover the door?"

"Why should I?" Lucas asked mildly as he did just that.

The man shot out the window. "Damn. I missed him. I'll tell you, mon, if you're here for the information, you'll want to keep us alive. If you're not, which I'm wondering about now, you'd best help me. You picked a sorry spot to squat upon. Those Serpents are killers."

"I am here for the information," Lucas said. "I'm tired of all these games and ploys."

"You're telling me." The man laughed. "I'm fair fashed with them myself. I'm off to Scotland after this. I've done all I can. I've been uncovered and I'm of no use anymore."

"You'll receive no sympathy from me," Lucas said. "Where is the meeting and when?"

"Confound it, man," the man gritted. "Let us kill this Serpent first, heh?"

"I want the information about the abduction now, before I kill anyone on your word," Lucas said coolly.

"Abduction?" The man shook his head. "Faith and begorra, yer behind, mon. It's going to be an assassination."

"Oh no." Georgie paled.

Lucas clenched his teeth. "Why would you wish to assassinate Aunt Clare?"

The man stopped to stare. A shot rang out. He shook himself and returned to his watch. "New recruits, God save me from them. Why couldn't you be the Comte?"

"I asked you a question," Lucas said sternly. "Why would you wish to assassinate Aunt Clare?"

The man cast Lucas a pitying look. Lucas met his gaze levelly. He shook his head. Irritation transformed his face. "Bloody hell, you aren't using Aunt Clare as a code name, are you?"

"Code name?" Georgie's eyes widened.

"Code name for what?" Lucas asked.

A barrage of firing distracted them.

Cursing, McGregor turned, leveled his pistol, and shot. "Damn, I think I shot that small oak clean through. Very well, you asked. I will tell you. Do what you want with it. Those men out there are a clan; they follow the Silver Serpent. They are malcontents from everywhere. Men who have banded together to murder royalty."

"Royalty?" Georgie gulped.

"Anarchists?" Lucas asked.

"Men with vendettas. Men who have lost families and arms or legs because of whatever war, or whatever rule of a sovereign. They have formed together with the promise of helping each other kill their 'hated' ruler. Their leader is 'the Silver Serpent.' I think he chose that name because nobody can take it seriously. Except the bloody bedlamites who follow him that is. They have decided it is to be your fat prince first."

"Insanity," Lucas murmured.

"Yes." The man grinned. "That is why not a single official in power will lend an ear, let alone anything else. But these malcontents are ex-patriots, spies, assassins, and soldiers. They have what they need to succeed, but no one wants to believe it. Now, on the other hand, we have some talent, but unfortunately more goodwilled amateurs than what it takes, if you ken me. It's taken us six months just to find out who their first ruler was to be and what form of attack they would choose."

"Zeus," Georgie exclaimed. "When is this to happen?"

"Georgie, no." Lucas glared at McGregor. "Do not answer that."

The man chuckled and looked innocent. That he could do so as he let off another shot proved him to be a professional. "You asked for the information. I just gave it to you."

"That isn't the information I wanted," Lucas gritted. "I don't know how this transpired . . ."

Georgie coughed, flushing red. "I—I think I do, Lucas. I told you I thought that man's French was bad. But I fear mine was. I did not realize when he said 'the Comte' he meant a particular person with that moniker. I thought he meant 'earl.' "

Lucas stared at her. "Georgie."

She turned her gaze away from him and looked at McGregor. "How can we help you?"

"*We* are not going to help him." Lucas snarled.

McGregor smiled. "Thank you, lass, I can tell you are a loyal *Englishman*."

Georgie flushed. "When is the assassination supposed to happen?"

"We don't know. And I don't intend to find out. As I said, I'm going back to Scotland. I can't be too sad if it is your regent that takes the first shot."

"But we will be," Georgie said.

"Speak no more, McGregor," Lucas said. "We will be glad to help send you on your way but that is that."

"Do you not have any more information?" Georgie persisted.

"Thackery in Devonshire," McGregor said succinctly. "He is in the middle ranks of the Serpents. However, word has it that he could be turned. He likes his money. A fat merchant is he."

"All right," Georgie said. "We will go after him."

"No, we will not," Lucas said. "We will leave it to those who know how."

"Who knows how?" Georgie asked McGregor.

He rubbed his jaw with one hand while aiming the pistol with the other. "Our band is diminishing to tell you the truth. Let me see. I am leaving. There are three others, but I do not know where they are . . . or if they yet live."

"What about that Frenchman with the thick accent at the Hangman?"

"Emhurst," the man said. "A bloody nodcock. He'll be lucky to escape. I had hoped he had reached the Comte for me."

"Who is the Comte?" Georgie asked. She flushed again. "Since we are . . . er, taking his place."

McGregor grinned. "Don't exactly know, myself. Haven't met him face-to-face yet. I hear he is a spy for you English, and has been for most of his life. Can steal your purse right before your eyes. They call him the Comte because he dresses niffy-naffy . . . silks and lace."

"Truly?" Georgie asked, her face vivid with dreams. "How intriguing."

McGregor studied her. He cocked a brow at Lucas. "She's fey, isn't she?"

"Yes," Lucas said curtly.

"And the third one?" Georgette asked.

"The crazy Chinaman?" McGregor snorted. "Rumor has it that he was found floating in the Thames, but he's a bloody cat. He's had five lives already if I'm not mistaken. So I wouldn't count him dead yet."

"I will," Lucas said coolly. "Enough. I have no intention of listening to any more."

"Whist!" McGregor held up his hand. They all paused. Silence met their tension. McGregor smiled and withdrew his pistol from the window. "That's that then. I'll be leaving."

"You killed the Serpent?" Georgie asked.

"I would like to think so, lass." McGregor shrugged. "Most like he's gone back for his partners." He strode over to the table where Trump still shook. He lifted the table. "Move, mon." Trump obeyed swiftly. McGregor kicked the threadbare carpet back.

"A trapdoor!" Georgie exclaimed, clapping her hands together.

"Right." McGregor lifted the door up. "Now I'm going to leave this way. The tunnel will take me to the other side of the woods."

"We'll go with you," Lucas said firmly. Narrowing his gaze upon Georgie in warning, he picked up the satchel.

"Indeed, we shall," Georgie agreed. She snatched up her drawing and began folding it.

"Thought you might." McGregor nodded. "By then you can make up your minds which way you are going."

"Why, we will go after this Thackery man," Georgie

said, her gray eyes unwavering, the she-wolf unafraid. "We are loyal subjects, sir."

"What do you have to say to that, Earl?" McGregor asked, his tone a cross between sardonic and sympathetic.

Lucas shook his head, since he could neither shake Georgie nor kiss her. "What can I say?"

McGregor laughed. "I imagined you could say a lot, mon."

"We're going after Thackery." Georgie's look of gratitude and respect warmed Lucas against the chill of what he had just said. She could not know what she was considering, but he knew. He offered her a bow. "We are loyal subjects, as she said."

"Aunt Clare will understand." Georgie's eyes glistened. Lucas exhaled sharply. She knew. She knew exactly what she was considering. The cost of it was there within the hidden tears, but she wasn't about to count it.

"No, she won't." Trump's wail drifted up to them. "And I won't!"

McGregor surveyed them. A confusion of emotions battled over his face and his large chest heaved. "Right then. A change of plans. The Serpent don't know who you are any more than I know who you are. Me, I don't have much to lose trusting you. Besides, I go by what my blood tells me. You are loyal subjects and God help you. Though the way you've stumbled into all this, I'm thinking He can't be smiling upon you." He waved his hand. "Bosh, what I'm saying is that you're new to this, completely new." A smile won over his seriousness. "By the saints, you have as good a chance as any of us. You two take the tunnel. When you're gone I'll cover and hide it. Then I'll take that coach of yours outside. That should help confuse them. If they aren't watching, I'll be able to be clean gone.

If they see me leave in it, I'll lead them away and then loose them." He shrugged. "That is all I'm willing to do."

Lucas nodded. "It is more than enough."

"Yes it is," Georgie said solemnly. "More than enough. We will not fail."

François clenched his teeth as he peered through the branches. How had his sweet Clare become entangled with Bull? Bull was a loutish fellow who sold weapons and secrets to any party with the best price. He had disappeared after one traitorous deal too many. The world now thought him dead.

"Honest, Burt," Nick stammered from where he sat, hands tied behind him. "N—no need to cut our gizzards out."

"Couldn't double-cross you," Ned said, leaning against his brother and similarly tied. "Don't know how."

François' brows shot up. Bull was Burt, Nick and Ned's stepbrother? He silently cursed. Nick and Ned had not lied when they said their stepbrother Burt was a "rum one." He must have retired to the Boar's Head. No, not retired. The lads had said that Burt had very important things to do. He was still running some kind of skulduggery from the inn, but under the name of Burt.

François smiled evilly. Ah, the puzzle pieces fell into place. That was why Bull knew of Little Ike and the Hangman. He and Little Ike had often been cohorts and had often worked out of the Hangman, just like François did. There was such a pool of talent to draw from there. But Bull made a grave misstep in coming out of hiding merely to ransom his sweet Clare. Of that, François would make certain.

"Truly, Mr. Simmons," Clare said from her tied position, close to the lads. "They are not double-crossing you. They would never try and give you the slip."

"That ain't what Little Ike told me when I found him."

"But Little Ike wasn't . . . er privy to our plans. He was quite unconscious at the time. We in fact are going after dear Lucas and Georgette, who took off in a completely wrong direction I fear. Once we find them, the boys can follow your plan. They truly weren't double-crossing you."

"No?" Bull rumbled as he sharpened his knife and eyed his two stepbrothers with a cold stare. "Then who's this François fellow who knocked Little Ike out, heh?"

François shrugged. Clearly this should be his entrance. Alas, he could not make it grand. Cocking his pistol, he aimed at Bull. He hesitated. *Non,* he could never do such a deed in front of his dear lady.

He peered about, judged his position, and then rustled the branches. Burt responded correctly by lifting his hand and warning all to shut their yappers. François snapped and crackled the leaves and stepped softly behind the tree.

Bull, true to his name, limped into the thicket as boldly as you please, knife in hand. François waited until the lumbering man had stepped past his hiding place. He slipped out and employed the butt of his pistol with great force to Bull's skull.

Bull groaned and stiffened. That was all. He didn't fall. Rather, he growled and spun. His growl turned feral when he saw François. Apparently he recognized François from the time that François almost sent him to the nubbin cheat. "You!"

"Yes." François forced a smile. Bull's knife would

be faster than his pistol. "Forgive me for missing your funeral, monsieur."

Bull paused to swear. That one pause saved François. Sir Percy chose that moment to spring, garnering a most excruciating purchase upon Burt. Such was the particular spot that Bull bent over in roaring agony.

"Merci, Monsieur Percy." François employed the butt of his pistol once more.

This time it did the trick. Bull fell like a great oak tree. Sir Percy was caught beneath one beefy leg.

"Forgive me, Monsieur Percy," François offered.

Sir Percy scrabbled from beneath, brrred his displeasure, and stalked away.

Chuckling, François grabbed up Bull's arms and dragged him into the clearing.

"François!" Clare struggled up. "I knew you would come."

"Meow," Sir Percy said.

"Yes, dear, I am so very grateful that you found him for me. Thank you." Clare hastened to François.

She was beautiful as she walked toward him. She wore the flimsiest pink confection that the bonds upon her wrists could not detract from. Her eyes were as bright as the stars and shone with adoration for only him. François gritted his teeth. How he wished to take her into his arms.

Such he could not do. He clasped up her offered hands, tied though they were. Bowing, he kissed them reverently. *"Ma belle.* You are all right?"

"Oh yes, now that you are here." Clare blushed sweetly. "I—I wasn't too frightened, I assure you."

"I was," Ned said.

"I still am." Nick swallowed hard.

"Yes, of course." François released Clare's hands and swiftly unbound them. With those ropes he turned and bound the unconscious Bull's hands. He forced himself back to the issues at hand. "We must hurry. I have found your Lucas and Georgie."

"How wonderful. Then we most certainly must hurry."

They hurried. Indeed, they hurried so fast that within minutes they were upon the trail, François driving with Clare seated safely beside him. Nick and Ned were in the back of the cart, their duty to watch the trussed-up Bull, who lay crammed amongst pots and pans. Lifting his large body up to the cart had taken much of the time.

"Where are dear Lucas and Georgie?" Aunt Clare asked as the cart rocked and jerked from its spanking pace.

"At a farmhouse in the valley." François frowned. There would be no telling what they would discover after this delay.

"A farmhouse?" Clare frowned.

"Though they might have left by now." François spoke his best wish.

"Oh dear, I hope not." Clare's voice was filled with anxiety.

François changed the pace from spanking to bone-jarring. A sharp yell came from behind.

"Is everything all right?" he called back, refusing to halt.

"Yes," Nick yelped.

"Er. Yes," Ned called.

"Don't stop," Nick said.

"No need to stop," Ned said.

"Must hurry," Nick said.

"Must hurry," Ned concurred.

François slowed as they came to the edge of the woods overlooking the valley and Leatherman's farm. François alighted and then went to assist Clare down.

"They are down there?" Aunt Clare lifted her hand to her eyes and peered down. "Why, it looks quite romantic. How charming."

"Yes, *ma chère.*" François drew out his spyglass and trained it upon the house. Tensing, he scanned the rest of the valley. "Ah ha!"

"What is it, dear?" Clare asked.

"What is it?" Nick's voice asked from behind.

"What is it?" Ned asked.

"Their coach, I see it! It is just leaving by the old road."

"Old road?" Clare asked.

"It looks very old," François said. His sheer relief to see the coach leaving had made him unwise. Another alarm rang in his mind. He spun, glaring at Nick and Ned. "Why do you stand here? You are supposed to watch Bull, I mean Burt."

"Oh yes." Nick shuffled his feet.

"Don't need to," Ned said. "Not really."

"What?" François frowned.

"He fell off," Nick said.

"Didn't expect it," Ned said solemnly. "It was that big bump."

François stared. Then he howled with laughter. *"Bien.* Let us go."

"But we can't leave Nasty Burt in the middle of the road." Aunt Clare frowned.

"We cannot wait, *mon ange,*" François said, subsiding to chuckles. "Your Lucas and Georgie leave far across the valley. We must circle around it."

"Can't we just go down into it?" Aunt Clare asked.

François sucked in his breath. He didn't know what had happened to McGregor, and suddenly he didn't intend to find out. Reuniting Clare with Lucas and Georgie and insuring that all of them were far away from his business had superseded anything. *"Non.* I take a shortcut, but even then, we cannot wait."

"Knew it!" Nick said.

"We are in a hurry!" Ned nodded.

Bull limped toward the farmhouse. He had heard François say that Lucas and Georgette were there. Rage shot through him. He'd had enough. He was going to kill the lot of them, hang the money.

He made it to the door. He prepared himself to ram it open, only to discover that it was only propped. He shoved it open and walked into the house. He stomped through it, blood lust thrumming through him. He checked the downstairs. It was empty. He checked the upstairs. It was empty. It was clear that he would be bulked of the satisfaction of murdering them.

He limped downstairs. He stopped. Three men burst through the open door, pistols in hand. Bull smiled. Ah, someone for him to fight. It was second best, but it must suffice.

Ten

"That, madame, is a foul tale," Thackery said gravely. He eased back into his chair to watch the little woman before him. She had appeared from nowhere while he was working late in his shop.

Dressed in full mourning in a dress of frightful design, she clutched a reticule that appeared to be a black gunnysack. She had begged an audience with him, declaring she was in need of placing a hasty order for drapes. A lone woman without an escort of any kind or the accompaniment of a servant might have deterred another man. Indeed, a different man would have turned her away directly, thinking it all too odd.

Thackery knew better. He enjoyed nothing better than a woman in mourning. They were always unstable, desperate creatures perfect for the taking. Just perfect. The truth was showing itself now. She had just placed a large order for drapes from a material he could not have sold in two years. She was merely staying in town for a week before continuing on her journey.

"Yes, very foul." Georgie dabbed roughly at her red eyes. It was far more effective than onion and did not leave such a telling odor. She clenched her hands together, two fingers crossed. "How, how I detest the Regent. My father and brother were killed because of his war-mongering. My mother died from a broken heart. How I wish I could kill him!"

Thackery stiffened, a thrill passing through him. He understood that feeling. How he understood that feeling. He loved money the most. Next to that was his desire to see the portly regent die. Only then could a man really make money, as he should. The widow's gasp drew his attention back to her. Her eyes were wide upon him.

Georgie affected fear. "Forgive me. I—that is treason."

"No. Do not fear. I understand how distraught you are." He smiled indulgently.

"Yes, yes I am. Thank heaven it is only me and you." She sniffled and gave him a soulful look. "I—I do not know why, but I feel I can trust you."

"You can, madame. You most certainly can."

"You said you needed to be paid for the drapes now?"

"Yes." Thackery nodded quickly. "You must understand that I would not wish to make drapes and then have you decide against them."

"Never would I do that. You, sir, can trust me. But I quite understand. Indeed, I—I am departing this country forever. I intend to make a new life in America. Since I—I have no one, but no one in the world now to care about me. But I will not go unprepared, I must have drapes." Georgie let out a great wail. She saw Thackery's eyes glaze over. She was overdoing it. She opened her black gunnysack to draw back his attention. "N—now how much do I owe you?"

Thackery thought quickly. He doubled his sum and told her.

Outrageous, Georgie thought. She smiled, for she would be more outrageous. "Yes." She promptly pulled out a wad of notes and let a few more fall to the floor.

She dithered and played with the money until she gave him his outrageous demand precisely. The display showed him that the amount for the draperies did not halfway match what she still held in her hands. What was left in the bag she left to his imagination.

"Madame." Thackery forced a frown, though his mouth actually watered. It always did when he was in the presence of money. "You—you carry an inordinate amount of money."

"Yes, I have sold everything that I have. I will leave this terrible country and that monster governing her. If I were not a weak, frail woman, I vow . . ." She quickly put her balled hand to her mouth. Then she stared at Thackery. Here was the greatest risk. Would he choose to take her money by force? Or would he act the way Lucas determined he would. "What I would not give to . . ."

"Madame"—Thackery could not help himself— "just . . . just how much money do you possess?"

"Ten thousand." Georgie sobbed. And sobbed. And sobbed. He must make the move. Lucas had been firm about that. However, he merely sat mumchance. Georgie sprang up, more from nerves than anything else. Yet the sack gaped open and spilled out all the money. "Oh dear."

"Madame!" Perspiration broke out on Thackery's forehead. "How . . . how would you like to support a cause that . . . that might just er, bring the Regent down."

Georgie plopped back down. "What?"

"I cannot tell you all the details." Thackery licked his lips. If he did this right, the money would be his, and his alone. After all, it did not come from a valid source, and if the lady did leave the country, who was to know that he had taken the funds from her? "But . . . but there is a—plan which needs funding . . ."

"Truly?" Georgie leaned forward. "Tell me. Oh, please tell me."

"I—I could not tell you much," Thackery said. "Y—you would need to merely give me your money and know that it will go to the cause."

"No." Georgie looked wild, which was easy. "I must know, know for certain if I have given up my future for this. Tell me! Tell me that when I leave this country, I know the Regent will be a dead man because of me. I will gladly be a pauper for the rest of my life if I c—could know I had contributed to his downfall!"

Georgie paced in the small clearing, exhilarated. She had succeeded. Now she could only hope that Lucas had succeeded. Her heart suddenly galloped away with fear. What if he did not succeed? Worse, what if he were hurt. Or killed?

Georgie halted. Faint, she walked to a log and sat down upon it. That wouldn't happen. Couldn't happen. Lucas was the smartest, most amazing man. Over the past week she had discovered that.

The first afternoon they had walked, but not for long. Lucas, regardless of his swell clothes, had accepted a ride from a farmer. Georgie had lived in dread, since all they had was a satchel of money. Lucas told her not to concern herself. The man was honest.

At the first town he actually had bought them tickets upon the common stage. By then he had bought himself a fine old set of clothes, along with a long, swirling coat, into whose lining she had sewn the money.

Georgie sighed and rested her hand on her chin. He looked positively dashing in that attire. And his humor amongst squalling babies and rough farm wives and rotund merchants had actually been patient and kind. Whereas hers had not been. It taxed her not to be able to talk to him openly about the upcoming events. She was in fidgets to endure such forced inactivity.

She smiled. She knew directly how impatient her mood was when at the next stop he had acquired a book from the innkeeper for her to read. The stop after that, he had replenished her paper and charcoal.

When they arrived in town, Lucas then showed himself to be a master of human perception. His patient study of the man Thackery over three days had been wondrous to watch. His plan to bamboozle the information out of Thackery, Georgie thought magnificent.

Her heart twisted. At least, she hoped it was still magnificent. If anything happened to Lucas, she would be lost.

Georgie started at the thought, her chin slipping off her hand. She blushed a fiery red and peeked about in embarrassment, though she knew she was alone. Such a thought was dangerous. She was an independent female and she mustn't forget it. Her heart attempted to argue with her, but Georgie ruthlessly squelched it, causing an empty feeling in the pit of her stomach.

At that moment she heard a rustle in the woods. She gasped as a masked man slipped from admist the trees. Then her heart leapt.

"Lucas! It is you!" She ran to him and flung herself into his arms before the independent female realized what she had done.

"Yes, it is." Lucas lifted her up to swing her about once. He then set her down, his sherry eyes teasing. "Who did you think it would be, Miss Thompson?"

She flushed and stepped back. "You startled me, that is all."

"I see." The way his lips twitched, it was clear that

he did. "It is nice to know you were concerned for me."

"I knew you would pull it off." Georgie stepped back another step.

"And that you do not greet just any masked man that way," Lucas said smoothly.

She refused to look him in the eyes. "Were you able to steal the dibs back?"

"Ah, now to the nitty-gritty of it all." In the most natural of manners, Lucas took her hand and tucked it into the crook of his arm. "I shall let you make the decision."

He drew her along and she let him, as if it were natural as well. She refused to think how her hand tingled.

"By your signal, I am under the impression that you yourself were successful."

"Jupiter, but I was," Georgie said breathlessly. She laughed. "He was a ball of wax within my hands."

"Such modesty, my little dodger."

"He responded precisely as you told me he would."

"I knew it!" Lucas nodded.

"Such modesty, Sir Machiavelli." Georgie grinned roguishly at him.

"Touché!"

"No, I was roasting you. It was famous." She forgot her worries of before. She couldn't contain her delight. "Personally, I believe this has been our best adventure to date, Lucas."

"Georgie, you are incorrigible."

"And you, my lord, are devious. Very devious."

Lucas's eyes gleamed, deep amber in sunlight. "We are a pair it seems."

Georgie missed a step, her heart wrenching. They were a pair, and she loved it. She loved him.

"What is it?" Lucas asked.

"Nothing." Georgie shook her head. She was suffering from too much excitement. She couldn't be in love with Lucas. "I cannot wait for you to tell me your news. And for me to tell you *my* news."

"Very well." Chuckling, he stopped. "Tell me your news now. I do not wish for mine to be put in the shade by yours."

Georgie drew in her breath. "The Silver Serpent intends to assassinate the Prince at the Coventry Gardens Theater within a fortnight."

"Bold, very bold. And too often tried and failed. The man possesses a strong conceit." Lucas frowned. "Thackery did not tell you the exact night?"

"Unfortunately not. He said that only the Silver Serpent himself knew that. Which is ridiculous, for it would also depend upon when the Prince wishes to attend the theater, does it not?"

"Indeed. He did not disclose the Silver Serpent's name?"

"He doesn't know it. I believe him."

Lucas laughed. "Ten thousand pounds does not buy much these days."

"It bought us more than we had before," Georgie said, indignant.

"As well as being our best adventure to date." His smile erased her pique immediately. "Now, on to our next adventure."

He pulled her from the trees into the road. Georgie halted with a gasp. A slow grin crossed her face. A coach awaited them; Trump sat as proud as a peacock upon the box. He had a right to be puffed up in his consequence. The equipage was up to the nines in every way. The team before it was fresh and frolicsome. "You certainly got the ready and rhino back."

"I am heartily tired of the stage. If anyone chooses to trail us now, they will need be fast about it," Lucas drawled as they advanced to the coach. "Do not get down, Trump, I shall assist Georgie."

"Yes, my lord." Trump's face was filled with awe. "I pinched myself, Miss Georgie, and I ain't dreaming. Ain't it a beauty?"

"Fine as five pence." Georgie nodded.

"My lady." Lucas bowed and offered Georgie a hand up into the coach.

She settled into the plushest of cushions.

"Take us to London, Trump," Lucas ordered before he joined her.

"Yes, my lord." Trump all but sang his acquiescence.

"Ah, London." Lucas's lips curved. "I believe I will be happy for a spot of civilization."

"I wonder if I shouldn't pinch myself," Georgie said, easing back with a sigh. "No, I feel too comfortable to do that."

"I shall be able to dress as a gentleman again. And you may remain dressed as a girl."

Georgie cast him an impish grin. "I might have to still be a lad."

"Categorically no," Lucas said. "You will dress as a female and that will be that."

"Perhaps." She thought a moment. "We must infiltrate the theater. That should be exciting."

"We must gain assistance from the higher echelon as well."

"Will you go to the Prince with this?" Georgie asked in excitement.

"Not yet. There is not enough information and proof. I'll not have Prinny laugh in my face. No, I shall try a better source. A source that I trust completely."

"What source?" Georgie couldn't help it. She wiggled upon the cushion. It felt divine.

"Georgie!" Lucas said, sounding choked.

"What?" She forced herself to pay attention.

"Nothing." Lucas looked away.

"What source are you going to?" Georgie asked. She could well grow accustomed to this *spot* of civilization.

"Isabelle," Lucas said, his voice soft. "She will believe me. I can trust her."

"Yes, of course. That is an excellent notion." A pain knifed its way across Georgie's heart and into her very soul. That alone told her what she had been trying to ignore. She loved Lucas, loved him like she never ever should have. "Why didn't I think of her?"

Clare drew out her basket from the cart. François with Nick and Ned had roamed a distance away, gathering wood for a fire. Sir Percy sat by her skirts. He offered a loud meow.

"Yes, dear, isn't it lovely? Teatime is also a picnic. Though it would be so much more pleasant if Georgette and Lucas were with us. I do not understand why they will not stop for us."

They had been chasing Georgette and Lucas for two days. However, Georgette's coachman was driving as if the very devil were after him. She had never expected Trump to have such skill and spirit. Things could have been settled if one of them were to take a horse and scout ahead. However, François would not permit it. He vowed he'd not leave them to be caught by Burt once more. Nor would he send Nick or Ned ahead. He didn't trust them not to attempt some want-witted thing and come back with it.

"Ah, teatime!" a voice with a brogue said, quite out of the blue. "Might you have scones?"

Sir Percy crouched and burred.

"Gracious!" Clare jumped and spun.

"May I join you?" A tall, redheaded Scotsman stood grinning down at her. He held a pistol in his hand.

"We have no scones," Clare said, blinking in confusion.

"Do you have cream and sugar?"

"Yes." Clare frowned. "Pardon, I do not wish to be inhospitable, nor do I know the etiquette when one is traveling upon the road, but may I ask who you are, sir?"

"Nay, rather who are *you?*" The man lifted the pistol. "Why have you been following me."

"I haven't been following you." The man looked at Clare with a sardonic brow. "Have I?"

"You have, love," he concurred. "I've done my best to shake you."

Clare sighed. "Oh dear, I don't want *you* at all."

He barked a laugh. "You wound me to my heart. I've always though myself a lady's man."

A shout arose. First Nick lumbered from the woods. Then Ned did. François remained absent. The man hauled Clare to him and placed the pistol to her side.

"Oh my," Clare exclaimed. Sir Percy growled. "No, dear, please do not attack."

"Come no closer or the lady will be in danger," The man called out. "Put your hands in the air, lads."

Nick and Ned, their expressions matched bookends of fear, obeyed readily.

"Do not worry, dears," Clare soothed them. "This gentleman has come for tea, and I do think it might be a good thing."

"Has he?" Nick broke into relieved grin. "Sorry. Thought he wanted to abduct you. Everyone wants to abduct you."

Ned frowned. "If he's come to tea why is he holding a pistol? And why must we keep our hands in the air?"

"He thinks we are following him," Clare said.

"Which I do hope we are not, but this can be discussed over a cup of tea. Now, sir, you really should release me, or our tea will be quite ruined. I own it is one of my favorite times of the day." She frowned. "And I do think the boys are right, it must be bad form to bring a pistol to tea, even if it is alfresco."

"We can't drink tea with our hands in the air," Nick added with consideration.

"Can't even eat our biscuits." Ned frowned darkly.

"Biscuits?" The man's voice shook. "My mouth is watering. You did not tell me you had biscuits."

"I do." Clare worried her lip. "But you will destroy it all if you don't put down your pistol. François I know will take exception."

The man chuckled. "Why do you think I won't release you. You best tell your François to come out with his hands up high."

"McGregor!" François stepped from out of the woods with his hands up. "What the devil are you doing?"

McGregor squinted. "Comte, is that you?"

"That's François," Ned said. "Not Comte."

"Not Comte," Ned said. "That's François."

"It is." François called and approached. "Unhand my lady."

McGregor lowered his pistol. "Your lady?"

"Yes, my lady," François said stiffly as he came to a stand.

"Forgive me, madame." McGregor grinned.

"That is quite all right. You were confused." Clare sighed. "Or we were confused. I know I still am."

François surveyed the man. His face turned grim. "You are driving the coach, are you not?"

McGregor grinned. "That I am. I thought you were a serpent sent after me."

"Serpent!" Clare gasped. "The Silver Serpent?"

"Are Lucas and Georgette with you?" François asked, his tone cautious.

"You mean the earl and the lass who's dressed like a boy."

"Georgette is masquerading as a boy?" Clare asked. "Why what fun she must be having."

"She's going by the name Georgie now." McGregor's blue eyes lit. "Are you her mother?"

"No, I'm not. Georgie?" Clare said it experimentally. She smiled. "I think that a charming name for her. Georgie is an orphan. I am her Aunt Clare."

"You just said she . . ." McGregor halted. His eyes widened and he whistled. "You're the Aunt Clare they were after!"

"Where are they, McGregor?" François paced up to him. His blue eyes turned to midnight with anger.

"Dearest, what is?" Clare asked. "Oh dear!"

McGregor lifted his pistol and cocked it. His eyes flashed. "Dinna come any closer."

"Tell me."

"Very well." McGregor shrugged. "I thought Emherst had sent them and I told them everything."

Mon Dieu." François' gaze shot fire. He studied McGregor a moment. *"Non.* You knew Emherst didn't send them on purpose."

"I was pressed, mon," McGregor said, his tone fierce. "I've been uncovered and I'm off to Scotland."

"Where are they?"

"They are off to find Thackery in Devonshire." McGregor's gaze shifted.

"Why?" It was as if François were the one who held the pistol.

"He should have more information about the Silver Serpent."

"There's that fellow again." Nick shook his head.

"Who is he?" Ned frowned. "Don't think I will like him."

"You told them everything and Lucas and Georgette . . . I mean, Georgie, are still going after the Silver Serpent?" Clare frowned. "I own I am surprised. No matter how expensive a dagger is, I did not think they would consider stealing it."

McGregor frowned at her. He looked at François. "What is she talking about?"

"Oh dear." Clare gasped. She looked at François with regret. "I am sorry, dear. I know I wasn't supposed to say anything."

"She thinks the Silver Serpent is a dagger? Gads, she better not say anything." A rumble of mirth came from McGregor as he cast François a sardonic look. "Now I see why you want to kill me for my honesty, Comte."

"You let two innocents go after the Silver Serpent," Comte said quietly.

"Now, mon, that Lucas isn't an innocent," McGregor said. "You're no judge of character if you think so."

"He is an amateur then," François gritted out.

"I thought you dead. Emherst is useless. The Chinaman dead. And I'm off to Scottland. That earl has as good a chance as any of us."

"Chance for what?" Clare asked, her heart pulsing the worst kind of pain throughout her. Never before had she felt so bereft, but then again, never had her beloved lied to her. If he had, he surely must have had a very good reason, she told herself. Oh let it be a strong reason and not something small to break her heart with.

"Don't think you should ask," Nick whispered.

"Don't think we want to know," Ned added his whisper.

"Should I tell the lady?" McGregor said softly.

"No. I will." François turned the saddest gaze upon her. "Forgive me, *ma belle*. I did not tell you the truth."

"That's an understatement," McGregor said. "A dagger? That is rich."

"A dagger meant for royalty," François said directly to Clare.

McGregor stopped laughing. His brow rose and respect crossed his face. "That is good. Very good."

"The Silver Serpent is a leader of a group of men who wish to kill the royalty of each country," François said.

"Make that the Prince Regent of England," McGregor said. "By assassination."

"Oh my!" Clare swayed.

"Ma chère." François moved swiftly, catching her to him. He glared at McGregor. "Be silent."

"No." Clare teared up and she broke into a smile. "Oh, my dear, that was a most wonderful reason for you to lie to me."

"What?" François blinked.

"What?" McGregor's mouth fell open.

"I was afraid that you lied to me for no reason," Clare said. "That would have broken my heart. But you had a wonderful reason. And you didn't really lie. You told me the truth."

"Ma belle." François' gaze shone with joy.

"You were not honest with me though. But I have that failing myself." She sighed. "I never know if telling the truth is more important, or being honest is."

"Faith and begorra." McGregor exhaled. "She *is* your lady, Comte. But do you deserve her?"

"Non. I do not deserve her," François said, his tone reverential.

"He does deserve me." Clare dashed away her tears.

"And if Lucas and Georgie are going after the Silver Serpent, so shall we."

"You do deserve her." McGregor chuckled. He uncocked his pistol. "Now, how about a cup of tea. And biscuits! What kind of biscuits do you have, love?"

Eleven

"*You* are the Miss Thompson that Sarah Chalmers has been gossiping about." Isabelle, her violet eyes wide, studied Georgie.

"She did?" Lucas lifted a brow. Georgie sat upon the chair, as mum as an oyster, to use her own phrase. He had warned her to let him do most of the talking, but he hadn't expected her to take him so much to heart. She rarely did. In this regard, she hadn't said a word to Isabelle past the first hello. Rather, she sat in her faded gray dress looking more like a statue than his Georgie.

Isabelle turned a speaking look to Lucas. He lost himself in the depth of that gaze. Dressed in a delicate apple-blossom silk, its folds gracefully gathered and draping along her delightful curves; her shining, golden hair cascading from a wide white satin ribbon to artfully fall in playful curls and ringlets, she was more beautiful than he had ever seen her. A ruff of white lace circled her neck and from its folds descended a stunning pearl necklace, each pearl perfectly matched of a nacre pale gold in color and generous in size. Pearl drops, a broach, and a six-strand cuff completed her ensemble. Respect filled Lucas. She had risen above all obstacles and had made a life for herself as duchess. "Fie, Lucas, did you truly think she wouldn't brute it about with all its embellishments. She was making certain I would hear of it."

"I am sorry," Lucas said.

"I realize now how much she wishes to hurt me." She smiled, her gaze filled with longing. "But why should it? You must have your own life."

"Do not let it hurt you." Lucas's voice turned rough with anger.

"No, I won't." Isabelle smiled, the sadness erased. "I knew . . ." She halted and the frown returned. She looked at Georgie. "Sarah said the boy's name was Georgie."

Lucas groaned. He had warned Georgie not to talk because he didn't wish for them to be caught out in their story. Now he had walked directly into a trap. He had determined not to let anyone know, including Isabelle, that he had traveled alone with Georgie at any time. What had seemed improper before, now, sitting with Isabelle, seemed lurid. The world would never understand how with Georgie, everything was innocent.

"It is." Georgie finally spoke. "His name is George. My name is Georgette."

"Really?" Isabelle's gaze narrowed.

"Our entire family is enamored with the name," Georgie said. "And neither of us like it, so we have both chosen Georgie." She grinned, finally a spark of her spirit showing. "Which works out nicely. As long as we are not in the same room, or town for that matter."

"George—Georgie has been returned to his school," Lucas said. "After some strong disciplinary measures. He will not be seen again, shall he, Georgette?"

"He will not," Georgie said. "He will not be a problem to you again, I promise you."

Lucas frowned. Georgie's response, subdued, held a tinge of something indefinable in it. Concern filled Lucas. She had behaved strangely ever since their arrival in London. Granted, at this moment, she was no doubt overwhelmed by the sheer opulence of the duke's home, but Lucas couldn't help but wonder if there wasn't another hidden reason for her reticence. "He was not such a problem as all that."

"Lady Wrexton introduced you to Lucas?" Isabelle asked.

Georgie looked to Lucas with a question in her gaze.

"Yes, she did." Lucas shook himself. Here was another entire portion of facts he had decided not to tell Isabelle. Aunt Clare's abduction was not something Isabelle needed to concern herself with. Certainly worrying over the Regent's assassination would be enough. "I thank you for your offer to assist us, Isabelle."

"I am glad you did not forget me," Isabelle said softly. It was a soft, plaintiff voice that in the past was capable of tormenting him, bringing him to jump to action to bring back joy in her words.

"I could never forget you," Lucas returned, his voice strong and true. Only, now, he didn't feel the torment.

Isabelle drew in a breath. It sounded shaky. "I am sorry to say, however, that His Grace is out of town. He is at his hunting lodge. I will send a messenger posthaste bidding his return, but until then, you do not have him, you have me." Her gaze became warm.

"We are honored, I assure you," Lucas said. Why didn't he feel the torment?

Isabelle nodded. That flirtatious look, the one that drove him crazy, entered her eyes. But he didn't feel crazy. "Thank heaven. I would not wish to be put into the shade by my husband."

"That could never happen." Lucas laughed. Why didn't he feel crazy?

Isabelle's smooth brow wrinkled. Her violet eyes deepened to almost purple. "I promise you, Lucas, I shall be at your disposal day and night to untangle this plot. I am already thinking of the people we should see." She turned to look at Georgie. "And you, Miss Thompson, you say that you will er . . . infiltrate Coventry Gardens?"

Georgie's chin tilted up. "Yes, I will."

"As a seamstress," Lucas said firmly. Georgie still thought she should take on her breeches. Lucas had only won his way after much debate. It didn't matter to him that she had successfully fooled everyone else. It drove him crazy when she wore them, and he'd not have it anymore.

That was when he looked at Georgie. Really looked at her. Truly looked at her. No wonder Isabelle didn't torment him or drive him crazy. How had it happened? When had it happened? He was in love with Georgie. Plain and simple. Yet, he felt no torment when he looked at Georgie either. Only when she dressed as a boy did it drive him crazy.

He looked back at Isabelle. Her gaze was steady upon him, an arrested expression on her face. She knew. He looked at Georgie. Confusion crossed her face, nothing more. She didn't know. It was a damnable position for him. Lucas winced. Worse, it was he who had put himself there.

He straightened. He was a complete fool. Why, why did he continue to fall in love with women who would never be his? Isabelle's father had forced her into wedlock with another. As for Georgie, no one would ever be able to force her into wedlock, including him. He could only imagine what she would say if he proposed.

* * *

Georgie stood to the side of the curtain, watching the group of actors and actresses that milled about, both upon the stage and in the pit. She tried not to sigh. Three days had passed and her role as third assistant dresser to the dresser had proven excessively dull.

She grimaced. It wasn't truly dull. It could have been intriguing, if her heart weren't as laden as a stone monument. For instance, she was watching the beginnings of what would be auditions for the next show. That should be interesting.

Yet all she could do was think of Lucas and miss him. Her notion to infiltrate the theater kept her tied to it, though it was only running for this and fetching that. While Lucas's efforts to circulate in the higher orders kept him going to routs and balls and wherever else Isabelle suggested.

How Georgie wished the duke would return to town. What manner of man would ignore a missive that involved the safety of his sovereign? Impatient, Lucas had finally decided to go to the officials. Isabelle had declared to know exactly which man to apply to and had requested an interview with him. To date the man had not responded. Another one who took the safety of his sovereign lightly. At this pace, Lucas would be tied to Isabelle for the next hundred years. Georgie bit her lip. "Ouch!"

"You hurt?" Jeb, a stagehand who enjoyed loitering, asked from behind her.

"No," Georgie whispered. Indeed, she wasn't hurt. She refused to be hurt. She could and would live without Lucas. She had plenty of dreams and none of them had included Lucas. Before. Unfortunately, now her mind and heart played very unkind tricks on her. Dreams arose within her, fresh and new. All of them included Lucas. That cottage by the sea looked frightfully dull, unless Lucas was there. Learning to paint without him now seemed a melancholy enterprise. Worse, who was she to discuss all her thoughts with once she had read every book in the world?

Georgie forced her mind away from such thoughts. She reminded herself of how Aunt Clare had made a wonderful life without marriage. However, that thought depressed her as well. Where was Aunt Clare? Somehow, in her deepest of feelings, Georgie knew she was all right. That feeling might be just a defense against a hard reality she didn't want to face; still Georgie couldn't lose it.

"A sorry lot today, if you ask me." Jeb snorted from behind.

Georgie blinked. She scanned the clutch of aspiring thespians. They did look a sorry lot. After only three days, she had learned what actors and actresses were supposed to look like. Not how they were supposed to act, of course, but how they *looked*. That was very important. For the ladies, that look not only included beautiful, but fast and loose.

"Look at the shoulders upon that one." Jeb laughed.

Georgie nodded and studied the lady he had pointed toward. The lady did indeed possess shoulders that appeared as if she could toss heavy weights about. Her other features, however, were appealing. Her black hair was long and flowing. Her brown eyes had an exotic slant. Georgie frowned, fascinated by the lady's eyes.

She started. "The crazy Chinaman."

"What?" Jeb asked.

"Nothing." Georgie shook her head. "I just thought of someone. Er, that she should meet. I play matchmaker once in a while."

"Poor bloke." Jeb chuckled. "He better be blind."

"I think she is very pretty. Other than her shoulders, of course," Georgie said. Her heart raced. She wasn't wrong. She knew it. If she had never masqueraded as a boy, the thought would never have crossed her mind. However, she knew that the notion wasn't as far-fetched as the rest of the world would think. In fact, it was just perfect.

She studied him a few more minutes. Yes, just perfect. "Pardon me."

"You ain't serious?" Jeb hissed as Georgette walked toward the actresses.

She turned. "Indeed I am."

He shook his head. "Yer a daft one."

She grinned. "I know."

"Forgive me, but if I take this to the Prince he will laugh at me, and then demote me." Lord Darrimple promptly tossed the small sheaf of paper back across his shining mahogany desk. "It is not even signed. Where did you get it?"

"I stole it from a draper in Devonshire," François said softly, refusing to shift in his chair, or take the paper. "It has noted the assignation and the Coventry Theater."

Lord Darrimple laughed. "That is all it notes. It says nothing about the Prince."

"If the man McGregor says that it will be the Prince Regent to be assassinated, it will be him."

"I do not know this McGregor, do I?"

"He is a Scottish mercenary."

"Who has now conveniently disappeared, hasn't he?"

"My lord, how long have I worked for you?" François voice was soft.

Lord Darrimple paused. "Faith, I cannot remember how long."

"I do." François knew to the day when he had joined

England against his country, the country that had mur-
dered his family. "You must not overlook this. The
Silver Serpent is real, very real."

Lord Darrimple waved a hand. "I will increase the
guards about his Royal Highness tonight, but I will
not . . ."

"Tonight?" François sucked in his breath. "He will
attend the theater tonight?"

Lord Darrimple sighed. He raised his gaze and studied François. "If you had a name for me François,
other than that of 'the Silver Serpent,' I would take
you more seriously."

François narrowed his gaze. *"Non,* that is not what
stops you. It is something else. Tell me."

Lord Darrimple's gaze narrowed in return. "You retired from this department over a year ago. Now you
appear here in my office with this Banberry tale. Just
now, before tonight."

"You have had other operatives tell you about the
Silver Serpent, I know," François said angrily. "Why
do you think I came out of retirement? Thomas told
me about it just before he disappeared."

"Thomas turned out to be a traitor," Lord Darrimple
said curtly.

"You do not know that. He was killed before you
brought him to trial. Do you not ask yourself why?
Alors"—François stood—"you could be responsible
for the death of His Highness."

"That or I could be made a fool by you," Lord Darrimple said, his lips twitching. "The Regent will be
with a very important envoy of diplomats tonight."

"What diplomats?" François asked.

"One of which is Lord Wrexton." Lord Darrimple
said it as if it were of grave importance.

François stared. "Impossible!"

"You are attempting to make it so."

François broke into laughter. *"Non.* It . . . it is too ridiculous. Too . . . never could it be."

"You are amused?" Lord Darrimple lifted a brow. "You were not when Lord Wrexton took you off the Treemont assignment because of your incompetence."

"True. I was not. For I was not incompetent. His lordship was too quick to jump to the wrong conclusion," François said. "But that was five years ago, my lord. It is in the past. For you to think that I would come to you with this story merely to ruin Lord Wrexton's assignment? Do not be an imbecile!"

Lord Darrimple stiffened. "You may leave, François."

François raised his gaze to heaven. *"Mon Dieu.* Your humor, it is not *amusant."*

"Do not blaspheme before me as well. I said, you may leave."

François turned his gaze back to Lord Darrimple. "At least increase the guard. Please. And tell His Highness this story. Tell him it as a joke if you must, but tell him, my lord." Standing, he offered Lord Darrimple a perfect leg and left the man.

He walked out of the office. Then he walked out of Whitehall. He walked to the corner of the street where Clare and Nick and Ned awaited him. Sir Percy announced his appearance with a meow.

"What did he say, dear?" Clare rushed up to him. "I do wish you had permitted me to join you."

François gazed down at his true love. God, the thought could weaken the knees of the strongest man. "No, *ma chérie.* I told you it would not be necessary."

"It wasn't?" Clare sighed.

"Non." François would never have met Clare if her brother Lord Wrexton hadn't departed to go on a diplomatic mission and unwisely left her to her own dis-

astrous devices. So in a sense the man had brought
them together. Now he would tear them apart.

Of course, François had told Clare that they could
never be together. Though he had never told her all of
the reasons. Indeed, over the past few days he had almost forgotten them. He had actually begun to believe
that there might be a chance for them against all odds.
He forced a smile and took up her hand. *"Mon petit
chou,* all is well. Lord Darrimple will take care of it.
The prince is saved."

"How famous." Clare sighed. She gazed at him and
her brow puckered. "What is the matter, dear?"

"Nothing, *ma chérie,"* François said. "Nothing at
all."

"That is good." Clare's look grew distracted. "Now
we must have tea. A very special tea in celebration.
You may tell us everything then."

"Yes." François smiled. Actually smiled. How he
loved his lady. He had not fooled her one whit. Still,
she would wait until tea at least.

Her breath rasping through her painfully, Georgie
ran blindly down the alley. The small leather case she
clutched was wet with her perspiration. She halted,
looking back. The alley was empty.

"Thank you, God." A shiver wracked Georgie.
Had the Chinaman taken a fatal shot for her? "Don't
think."

She buried the casing into her deepest pocket.
Straightening, she proceeded down the alley at a normal pace, as if but taking a stroll through the dark
access. She came out upon another street. The bustle
of people and vehicles warmed her, steadying her ach-
ing legs. She waved down a hack. "Take me to the

Earl of Kelsey's . . . no, take me to the Duke of Rochester's house."

She climbed into the hack. Leaning back against the cushions she closed her eyes. Her fears attacked. She opened then. "Please let Lucas be all right. Please."

What had she done? She had set up a meeting between the Chinaman and herself. Since it was to be within two hours from after the auditions, Georgie had agreed to the assignation and then had sent a messenger to Lucas requesting his presence. The messenger had returned saying that he had been sent to the duke's house and had delivered it there.

Georgie cringed. Had she lured Lucas into a trap? Had they taken him out first? She drew in a deep breath. "You don't know that." She only knew that he hadn't appeared. She had met with the Chinaman alone. He had shaken her hand and she had been surprised to receive the leather case. Then bullets zinged about them. He had taken one to the shoulder, it tearing into his blue dress.

Georgie had stood stunned, until he had cried out for her to run. He had lifted up his skirts and did just that, his agility and speed astounding her. Georgie had followed suit, picking up her skirts and taking off in a different direction.

The hack stopped and Georgie looked out the window. The duke's house. She swallowed. It was such a grand establishment, even grander than Lucas's. Both made her feel like the meanest trespasser. Adams had said that one could become accustomed to wealth and power. She doubted it. The hack driver opened the door and Georgie alighted, her stomach striving to supplant her chest. She paid the driver and walked up the steps, taking the last ones much more quickly. She must know Lucas was safe. She pounded on the door.

It opened. Isabelle's butler stared down at her with proper disdain. "Yes, miss?"

Georgie self-consciously smoothed down the skirts of her dull brown round dress and cream apron. She started. There was a singed hole in them, bullet-sized to be exact. She covered it and forced a smile. "Is . . . please tell me . . . is Lucas, I mean, the Earl of Kelsey here?"

"Miss?" He lifted a brow.

"I am Miss Thompson," Georgie said quickly. "I have been here before. Please, tell me if the earl is here!"

"He is, miss." He nodded.

"Thank God." Relief flooded her. "You . . . you are positive. You aren't just saying that to be kind?"

"No, miss." He frowned repressively. "He is closeted with Her Grace this very moment."

"Thank God." Georgie flushed. She could tell the butler was considering her as a zany. She straightened. "May I please see him?"

"I am sorry, miss. Her Grace gave strict orders that they were not to be disturbed."

"Please. I must know that Lucas is safe."

"Miss?" He frowned.

"I . . . it is a very long story, but I must see Lord Montieth."

Something akin to pity passed through his gaze. No doubt she appeared a desperate bedlamite. Which she was, but it wasn't pleasant to know that he knew. "I am sorry, miss."

"May I wait for him then?" Isabelle's butler possessed a rather large frame. Forcing her way past him didn't seem advisable. "It is very important."

His eye twitched. "Very well, miss." He turned and

permitted her to follow him into the large entrance hall. Her directed her to a very uncomfortable high-backed chair of ornate design.

"Thank you." Georgie sat down upon it and offered him the demurest smile she could muster. "I'll just wait here."

"Yes, miss." He nodded. "Once they are . . . er, finished, I shall let you know." He turned and left.

Georgie rose immediately. Her spirits soared. Lucas was alive and well. Somehow, things had become confused. She had scribbled her note in haste. He must have read it wrong. Nor had she questioned the messenger well enough either. He must have failed to relay Lucas's answer correctly.

She walked softly toward the door of the salon where Isabelle had entertained them before. She'd rather not walk into the wrong room or come across the servants if possible. She looked about before cracking the door open and peering into the room.

Gerogie's stomach heaved. Isabelle reclined upon Lucas's lap, her graceful arms wrapped tightly about his as they kissed. She slowly closed the door. In a daze she walked away from the salon. She struggled with the feeling of betrayal that rose within her. She had no right to it. Lucas hadn't betrayed her. Not really.

She walked out of the hall. Lucas had never hidden his love for Isabelle. Though Georgie had thought him a man of honor. Yet he had said he had stayed away from Isabelle because of his feelings. Clearly, they had overwhelmed his good intentions.

She walked out of the duke's house, closing the door quietly. And Isabelle was in love with him. What woman wouldn't be? She hadn't given her hand to the duke upon her own will. She couldn't resist Lucas. What woman could?

She wandered down the street, determined to keep the pain at bay, determined to keep the vision away. She knew she would never forget it though. She had been right. Falling in love with a man who had given his heart to another was abysmal.

Twelve

"Isabelle. We cannot do this." Lucas turned his lips away from her. He felt addled saying it, since she was already on his lap and within his arms. She had moved so quickly that she had surprised him. No, not surprised. "Discombobulated," as Georgie would say. One moment they had been discussing the Silver Serpent, and the next she had leapt over and descended upon him.

"Why not?" Isabelle pouted her lips, a flame of raw desire within her eyes. Her heavy perfume enveloped him. "You said you loved me."

"Yes," Lucas said. "And I respect you."

"Please do not deny me." Isabelle's eyes glistened with instant tears. "Rochester has turned away from me."

"No!" Lucas's heart filled with sympathy. Not jealousy, but sympathy. He had started to harbor suspicions these past three days, but he had cast them aside. "I find that impossible to believe."

"He does not love me." Isabelle kissed his face, pressing her body against him with an inciting slide. She was a matron now. Of course she wasn't the innocent he had known.

"I am sorry, Isabelle," Lucas breathed out. "Truly sorry."

Isabelle drew back. "Why? You need not be sorry. I am free. I have married Rochester. I am Her Grace. Now I may do what I wish."

Surprise crossed Lucas's face. Then he hid it. Isabelle had been forced into a marriage of convenience and that was the norm within a marriage of convenience. Lucas had always found it distasteful. Marriage vows were sacred and no man or woman had the right to put them aside for gain. "I cannot."

"Cannot or will not?"

"Both."

"It is because of that drab little Georgie, isn't it?" Isabelle's expression hardened. "You have fallen in love with her."

"Yes." Lucas couldn't lie. He owed that to Isabelle.

"You fool. She has duped you. She is the Silver Serpent, can't you see?"

"What?" Lucas stared at her. "Georgie is no traitor."

"Of course not. She is a desperate but very cunning hussy who has created the entire bag of moonshine to draw you into her clutches."

Lucas clenched his teeth. He laughed, though bitterly. "I only wish she had."

Isabelle snorted. "I am glad I snagged Rochester before that little tart arrived in town. Sarah Chalmers was a greenhorn compared to your little Georgie."

"What?" Lucas stiffened.

Isabelle paused. Her gaze turned pleading. "You said you loved me, Lucas. And I love you. I do. I've done everything to protect you. No one knows you've fallen for her lies. I didn't send a message to anyone. Not to Rochester. Or Darrimple. No one will know you were gulled by Baron Nobody's daughter."

"Isabelle!"

"Be my lover," Isabelle whispered. "I've dreamed about it, Lucas. I married Rochester for his title, but it is you I fantasize about." She laughed lowly. "Even when I'm with Rochester I'm thinking of you."

"Isabelle." Lucas drew in his breath. Holding her close, he stood.

"We will be so good together."

Lucas turned slightly. "No. We won't."

He dropped Isabelle to the settee and drew in his first breath of clean air. The weight was lifted. He had dropped all the baggage of the past.

"What?" Isabelle shrilled. The flabbergasted expression on her perfect features was a sight to see. No doubt she was as flabbergasted by his rejection as he had been by her seduction.

"Irrevocably no. Never." Offering her a slight bow, and a slighter smile, he turned his back upon her. Amazingly, it felt wonderful. He had been a fool, but no longer.

"You are leaving me to go after that little bitch!" Isabelle cried out. "Well I hope that there truly is a Silver Serpent and that he's killed her by now."

"What?" Lucas came to a standstill. He turned slowly, his muscles tensing. "What are you talking about?"

"She sent you a message saying that she was meeting a crazy Chinaman. Ha! She is imaginative if nothing else. She knew I had almost won you back and sent that letter. You are so very chivalrous she could count upon you to come charging to her side." Her gaze turned venomous. "And away from mine."

"Where was I to meet her?" Fear ripped through Lucas. Isabelle lifted a shoulder pettishly. He stalked over to her. "Where, Isabelle?"

"I don't remember."

"Tell me." Lucas reached down, grabbed her by the shoulders, and shook her. He couldn't waste time with her games.

"I don't remember!" Isabelle gasped. "Truly I don't. I didn't look. I—I was busy dressing . . . for you!" Spite filled her violet eyes. "The note said she would meet him well over half an hour ago. You will be too late for *her* seduction."

Lucas jerked his hands away from her as if he had clasped something rotten. He didn't waste one more word on her. He didn't need to do so. He needed to find Georgie.

"Georgie!" Lucas's voice called out as the door shook from his pounding. "Georgie. Are you there?"

Georgie closed her eyes tight. She lay huddled upon her small bed in the small room that she had rented for her life as third assistant to the dresser. She didn't want to answer. She wanted to pretend that he wasn't there. If only she could pretend that the entire day hadn't happened. "Go away, please."

"Georgie? Thank God." A pause ensued. His voice changed. "Georgie. Are you all right?"

"No," she whispered. Tears welled up. She thought that she had cried the very last one possible. Her pillow was pitifully wet. She cleared her throat and raised her voice. "I am fine. Just fine!"

"Georgie please, open the door." Lucas rapped upon the door. "I did not receive your message. I vow I didn't."

"I know." Georgie sighed. She also knew what he was doing while she was being shot at. It wasn't his fault but it hurt like the very devil. "I mean, I gathered that. I understand."

"Isabelle didn't tell me." Lucas's voice was deep with agony. "Open the door. Please!"

"Very well." She couldn't deny him. It wasn't his fault. She forced herself to uncurl and roll from the bed. She dashed away her last tear and went to unlock the door. Lucas stood, his red hair windswept, his sherry-colored eyes dark with fear.

He looked so wonderful. Georgie broke into fresh sobs. She loved him so.

"You *are* hurt!" Lucas stepped into the room, slammed the door, and hauled Georgie into his arms. "Tell me, darling."

"No," Georgie gurgled into his lapel. She couldn't let him know. She couldn't! She lifted her head and sniffed. "My skirt has a bullet hole in it. That's all."

"God!" Lucas kissed her, enfolding her in such a fierce hold as to bend her slighter frame back.

Georgie flowed molten to his will, kissing him with a pent-up savagery that should have shocked her. Should have shocked Lucas. Yet it didn't. She needed him. Loved him. It should have mattered that he had just come from kissing another, and it would, but not at the moment. She felt safe again. She felt whole again. She drew from his passionate kiss the very strength she would need to take with her when she never saw him again.

Lucas lifted his head. He laughed. It was husky. "When Isabelle told me, I was frightened, Georgie."

"Yes." Georgie swallowed hard. She attempted to step from his arms.

Lucas held her close, resting his cheek on her head. "I never want to let you go again, Georgie."

His arms were both haven and heaven. Georgie longed to settle within them. However, the wildest sensations began bubbling through her blood. She had no right to them. She forced a laugh. "Y—you must."

"Marry me," Lucas said.

"What?" The bubbles popped promptly.

"Marry me." The softest and most hesitant of expressions crossed his chiseled features. "Then you will never need to leave my arms again."

"I do not understand," Georgie whispered, actually frightened to speak her question. "Wh—what about Isabelle?"

Lucas sobered. "I cannot speak of her. Honor will not permit me to do so."

"I see." Lucas had turned away from Isabelle out of honor. Georgie might love him for that, but she could not marry him. Not knowing that she would never possess his love. She had already lived with a man who didn't care about her. Her heart chilled. Her father had lost any ability to love after her mother had passed on to her rewards. Would Lucas take that course, no matter what any other woman did? She drew in her breath. "I cannot marry you, Lucas."

Lucas smiled sadly, though he refused to release her. "I was afraid you might say that. Indeed, I know I shouldn't have proposed at this moment. I hadn't planned to do so. Only . . ."

"Only?" Georgie asked.

"I was so damned frightened for you," Lucas admitted, his voice hollow.

"I understand." Could anything be worse? Lucas loved another woman and had proposed to Georgie on the spur of the moment merely because he had been frightened. If her resolve was already slipping, that lowering thought bolstered it.

"Georgie, I love you," Lucas said softly.

Georgie gasped. She looked up. Lucas's gaze was warm upon her. His eyes actually looked as if they held love within them. Her heart wrenched. She knew better. "You do not have to say that, Lucas."

Lucas's brow rose. "What do you mean I do not? I love you and I want you to know it."

Georgie struggled from out of his arms. Cold immediately, she wrapped her arms about herself. "I will not marry you, Lucas. There is no reason for you to . . . to try and use all the proper words."

"Proper words?" Lucas frowned. "I am not trying to use proper words. Nor did I think that kiss was very proper." He stepped toward her. "I love you, Georgie, and . . ."

"Stop saying that!" Georgie snapped. His words were indeed magic. Regardless of all she knew, her determination was melting away. If he said another word she'd be lost. She spun away from him. "I do not love you!"

A silence passed. Georgie refused to turn around. If Lucas saw her face he would know she had lied.

His voice came soft. "I see. Then there is no reason for me to persist."

"No, there isn't." Georgie busied herself with reaching into her pocket. "I have discovered the real name of the Silver Serpent by the by."

"Have you?" Lucas's voice was subdued.

"His name is Leonard Desard. The Chinaman gave me it before we were interrupted. Do you know the Chinaman was dressed as a female?"

"Was he?" Lucas's voice became more natural.

Georgie breathed a slight sigh. He was going to permit her to change the subject. "Now we need to only discover which night the assassination is to take place. Which should be simple. It will be whenever the Prince Regent attends the play. Isabelle can . . ."

"No. Isabelle cannot. She hasn't believed us, Georgie. She never wrote her husband. Or contacted the authorities."

"What?" Georgie spun, staring at him in astonishment.

"I misjudged her." Lucas shrugged. "It will just have to be you and me to capture the Silver Serpent."

"Yes." Georgie hated herself as her spirit jumped with joy. She had a purpose and excuse to remain with Lucas.

"François is late," Clare said. A strange feeling overcame her, a dark and sad feeling. She blinked. Only one other time had she experienced such. "Oh dear. I have had a premonition."

"A what?" Nick gazed longingly at the tea setting and special biscuits.

"A premonition." She shivered. "That is when something is wrong."

"Don't have sugar?" Ned frowned.

"No, dear, we have sugar." Clare had paid particular attention to every detail. Even down to tidying the small private room of the queer little inn to which François had delivered them. He had said he must perform an errand or two before tea. "I meant to say that something bad is going to happen."

"Oh." Nick turned pale. "Don't like that. Was happy."

"It's teatime." Ned nodded.

"Meow," Sir Percy said from his own chair.

A knock sounded at the parlor's door at that precise moment.

"Don't open it," Nick said. "It's her premonition."

"No, dear." Clare shook off her feelings. "It is François." She hurried to the door and opened it. Her feelings returned doublefold. Two unknown men stood before her. They both were armed. The one bowed. "Miss Wrexton?"

"Yes?" Clare asked, butterflies winging hard against her chest. Nick and Ned came to stand behind her.

The man looked at them closely. "Are you Nick and Ned?"

"Am." Nick nodded. "How did you know?"

"He had a premonition too?" Ned frowned.

The second man nodded. "That's them, Jules."

Jules reached into his vest and drew out a letter. "This is for you."

Clare, her hand shaking, took the missive. She opened it.

Mon Ange,
   I love you. Remember that always.

                                        Farewell,
                                        François

Clare stared at it. She looked at the gentlemen. "Is . . . is that all?"

Jules turned red. "Thomas and I are here to er . . . guard you."

"Guard us?" Nick yelped.

"Guard us?" Ned moaned.

"Guard us." Clare winced as pain coursed through her. "Did he say for how long you were to . . . er, guard us?"

"No, Miss Wrexton," Thomas said. "He will send word to us when all is safe. But it shouldn't be but for tonight."

"Safe?" Nick asked.

"That's good?" Ned asked hesitantly.

"Thank you," Clare said, blinking back tears. "W—would you two gentlemen care for s—some tea? We were just going to . . ." Both men shifted, their faces embarrassed. "Oh dear, what am I thinking? I am such a scatterbrain. You came to guard us, not to sit down to tea. Thank you." Numb, Clare closed the door on the two men.

"I don't understand," Nick said.

"Bumfuddled." Ned nodded.

"What does the letter say?" Nick asked.

"Here, dear." Clare handed him the missive. She walked slowly to the settee and sat down. Coldness invaded her bones and even her blood. Sir Percy jumped down and paced over to jump on her lap. She absently ran her fingers through his fur.

"Meow!" Sir Percy's meow was sharp.

"I am sorry, dear." She hadn't realized her force. "François has given us the slip. He is going after the Silver Serpent, but he doesn't want us with him."

Nick opened the letter. His lips pursed and worked as he studied the missive. He shook his head. "Doesn't say that." He offered it to Ned. "Does it?"

Ned took the paper over and perused it with equal pain. "No. Don't see that. It says . . ." He looked up, frowning. "Farewell. That's all. Where'd you see the rest?"

"I didn't really read it." Clare sniffed. "I know it."

"That's something," Nick said.

"Noticed that," Ned said. "Always seeing things we don't."

"I will never see my François again." Clare burst into tears.

"Here now!" Nick hopped back as if Clare had drawn a sword.

"Don't c—cry," Ned stammered. "Don't know what to do."

"You'll see him again." Nick gulped. "He's a knowing one. Even if he's going after the Silver Serpent. He'll trounce the fellow."

"Yes, but I will never see him again." Clare sobbed. "He doesn't want me. It is useless."

"Don't say that," Nick said. "Not useless."

"He wants you," Ned said. "Must believe it."

"Must believe in love," Nick yelped. "That's what you always say."

"Yes. And I do." Aunt Clare sighed. "But I fear, I truly do fear that it is for everyone else but me."

"No." Nick shook his head. "François loves you."

"I will never see him again." Clare straightened her spine. She dashed her tears away. "It is for the best. He is right. We do not belong together. I—I am merely a bubbleheaded widgeon. And he . . . he is very important. He saves countries and kings."

"You're important," Nick said. "Very important."

"You help people," Ned said solemnly.

"Help them find love," Nick said.

"As good as saving a country," Ned said.

"Countries don't need love," Nick said.

"People do." Ned nodded.

"François does," Nick said. "No flies on him. He loves you. You love him. Just have to make a push." He smiled with eagerness. "That's all."

"He's right." Ned scratched his head. "Don't know why. But he's right."

"I know why," Nick said. "Been watching you. Been watching François. Been learning."

"That's why." Ned smiled in relief.

Nick's expression turned earnest. "You could have left us."

"Would have been in the suds," Ned said.

"Would have been dead," Nick said, more to the point.

"Yes," Ned said. "A bad dead."

"You are good," Nick said.

"We love you." Ned flushed.

"Don't want to be bad anymore," Nick said.

"Dearest, you never were bad," Aunt Clare said

through her tears. Her heart was breaking, and these two were angels of mercy.

"But weren't good," Nick said.

"Weren't anything." Ned blinked, clearly moving toward an epiphany.

"But we are going to be good." Nick's chest puffed out.

"Like it," Ned said.

"Going to fight for you," Nick said.

"Going to get her François?" Ned asked.

"Yes." Nick nodded.

"Thank you, but there is no need to do that, dears." Clare sniffed. "I have decided. I do not wish to see François ever again, not if he doesn't wish to see me."

"What?" Nick stared.

"What?" Ned said.

A reviving spark flared within her. Alas, she was a Wrexton. That noble, if defiant, blood welled up within her, possibly for the first time in her life. "I was very wrong about him. H—he lied to me. And now he has left. He is not my true love." Pain like she had never felt wracked her. "I do not want him for my true love."

Nick goggled. Ned gaped.

Nick recovered and jabbed Ned in the ribs. He leaned into him and whispered. "That's bad."

"Yes." Ned nodded. "Better go find François."

"He will know what to do." Nick nodded.

"We cannot." Clare sobbed. "That is why the guards are outside. They are there to stop us from going after him."

"No!" Nick gasped.

"Thought they were here to protect us." Ned frowned.

"You have it wrong," Nick said in a positive tone. He went to open the door. It wouldn't open. He sighed. "You have it right."

"How does she do that?" Ned sighed. "She always knows."

"She's in love." Ned frowned.

"I am not," Clare said. "I refuse to be in love with François. He—he has put me under guard. Even Bendford wouldn't do that!"

"Must think." Ned began to pace back and forth across the room.

"Yes." Ned paced forth and back across the room.

Clare might have become dizzy from it, only she was too disheartened.

"Have it!" Nick halted. He waved frantically at Ned. "We escape."

"That's it!" Ned halted. "By Jove. That's it!"

"We go find François." Nick added his second step to the plan.

"Good. Good." Ned frowned. "How?"

"Must think." Nick resumed his pacing to and fro.

"Yes." Ned continued his pacing fro and to.

"He will be at the theater tonight," Clare said, fresh tears welling in her eyes.

"What?" Nick asked.

"Why?" Ned added.

"The guard said it will be for tonight only. François must have learned that the assassination is tonight."

"Just have to believe her." Nick looked to Ned.

"Let's pick the lock." Ned brightened. "Check for the guards."

The two boys rushed over to the door. Nick knelt and peeked through the hole. "Can't see them."

"They left?" Ned asked, his voice hopeful.

"Oh oh. Got what she's got." Nick scrabbled back.

"What?" Ned asked.

"Got a premonition." Nick yelped as the door burst open. He swallowed. "Hello, Burt."

"Burt?" Ned's mouth dropped open. "That you?"

"Burt?" Clare asked as Sir Percy *burred* in his throat. Drawn for her depression, she looked up. "My goodness!"

Burt stood in the doorway. His one arm was in a sling and his one eye sported a giant plaster patch held in place by a white bandage wrapping his forehead. He leaned against a crutch. Only his smile looked strong. And evil. "Got you now!"

"What happened to you?" Nick gulped.

"You look bellows to mend." Ned nodded.

"Oh dear. We shouldn't have left him in the middle of the road," Clare observed, pity entering her heart. "Did a carriage run over you?"

"No." Burt glared. "I followed you to the bloody farm."

"What farm?" Nick frowned.

"Didn't go to the farm." Ned cocked his head. "Did we?"

"I know, you bloody idiot," Burt shouted, his face turning purple. "If you had, you would have met up with three men who would have killed you."

"Oh."

"That's what happened to my arm." Burt growled. "But they are dead for it. Then I follow you to that draper's house. Almost had you."

"Never saw you." Nick frowned.

"Not a bit." Ned gulped.

"The fool thought I was there to rob him." Burt snarled. "Got the eye and the cracked knee there. Left him barely living."

"That was nice of you," Clare said.

Burt glared at her with reddened eyes. "I was saving my strength."

"For what?" Nick asked.

"Er. Yes?" Ned asked.

"For killing her!" Burt pointed a shaking finger at Clare. "That's what!"

"Can't let you do that." Nick straightened.

"Can't." Ned balled his fists.

Burt grinned evilly. "You damn puling little cravens think you can stop me?"

Nick eyed him. He broke into a huge grin. "Know we can."

"Yes." Ned nodded vehemently. "Learned a trick or two. Will polish you off. What?"

Thirteen

Georgie peeked out from the side of the curtain. Actors and actresses swarmed about her. From wing to wing, the place was abuzz. So excited were the players that they didn't notice that the third assistant dresser to the dresser was slacking in her duties. Tonight, the Prince Regent had made a surprise appearance. They could not help but be flattered.

Georgie could not help but be frightened. Tonight could very well be the night of his assassination. It was a surprise visit. Did that mean it was a surprise to Leonard Desard, the Silver Serpent? Frustration roiled with her fear. To know the name of the assassin but not the face of him was a torment.

If that weren't enough of a taxing burden, another surprise of an unkind nature had occurred. The Prince was hosting a contingency of diplomats tonight. One of them was none other than Lord Bendford Wrexton. Whatever were they going to say to him? That they no longer knew where his abducted sister was, but were presently on the trail of the Silver Serpent?

Georgie bit her lip. She had forgotten. She wouldn't have to say anything to Lord Wrexton. There was no such thing as a "we" between her and Lucas. In the sight of the *ton,* she had never been associated with him. Only Georgie, her fortunate cousin, had been.

And that was just dandy with her. She must start thinking of it in that same fashion. None of this had happened. She was not in love with Lucas. He had never asked her to marry him out of whatever sympathy or pity he harbored for her. Or worse, a terrible notion had risen in Georgie. He had offered for her because he knew he had flown too close to the flame of Her Grace and would need some form of defense or distraction from her.

Georgie's gaze turned to the box where Lucas had said he would be situated. He had not arrived as yet. Georgie swung her gaze to the right, where Isabelle had just entered the duke's box. A distinguished-looking lord accompanied her tonight. She appeared royalty herself in a purple crepe dress over a golden sarsenet underskirt, trimmed with amber beads. Over her gown she wore a light short jacket in amaranth styled with two separate folds, each trimmed with the same amber beading. She gracefully sank into one of the velvet chairs.

Georgie bit her lip. To her recollection, she couldn't remember one time when she had ever glided like that. Isabelle disdainfully flipped open her Brisé fan with the air of a queen. Indeed, she sported a king's ransom in jewels. A stunning collar of diamonds and amethysts circled her neck. More diamonds dripped from her ears, nestled amidst her golden curls, and sparkled about her wrists. They outshined the theater's huge chandeliers in brilliance.

If only the duchess had believed Lucas. Why she hadn't, Georgie couldn't fathom. Lucas was the most levelheaded and honorable of men. If he said he had discovered evidence that the moon was going to fall from the sky, then one could expect the moon was going to fall unless there was an intervention.

Even more discombobulating was the fact that Isabelle had lied to Lucas. Lucas's face had shown such a reserve that Georgie had known better than to question him more upon that head. In truth, what would be the purpose? Railing at the man about the woman he loved would be futile. One could not help whom he loved. Look at her.

Georgie realized she was glaring at the duchess, who waved a fan and laughed to her companion, as if she hadn't committed the gravest of sins. She had abused an honorable man's heart. Oh yes, and might very well have endangered her sovereign.

Georgie forced her fuming attention away and scanned the theater once more. The production would soon begin. She looked back to Lucas's box, which was on the left. Her heart caught. He was just entering. Alone. How must he feel when he looked over toward the duchess?

Georgie's heart whispered traitorous words to her. Marry Lucas. Marry Lucas and grab hold of whatever small portion of the man that you can garner. Her spirit cried out at that, however, knowing it would die living once again under the rule of a man who did not love her.

She forced her thoughts back to the matter at hand. Lucas would surely see for himself the unfortunate circumstance of Lord Wrexton's presence within the prince's party. The Regent's box was angled to be in full sight of his. Either Lord Wrexton's missive that he was in town had not reached Lucas, or Lord Wrexton hadn't seen fit to write one. From what she gathered from afternoon teas and Aunt Clare's ramblings, in all probability he had not taken the time to write one.

The theater darkened. A rustle of anticipation ran

through the theater. Then a clunk and bump and what sounded like a howl arose from a box to the far left. Georgie's attention was drawn to the latecomers.

Georgie gasped, her world reeling. Could it be? The lady entering the box looked like Aunt Clare. Two young men, who appeared to be tripping over the chairs rather than sitting in them, escorted her. So enthralled was Georgie, she didn't even notice as the curtain boy shoved her to the side, hissed that they were opening them, and did just that. Only when the actresses shoved past her to take the stage did Georgie bolt. It had to be Aunt Clare. No other lady would take a long, trailing paisley shawl off to reveal that she had brought an orange marmalade cat to the theater.

Georgie, panting, stopped before the velvet curtain to the box, which she hoped was Aunt Clare's. Her studying the theater and its layout had already paid off. Lucas had warned her that she better not think she would be involved single-handedly in catching the Silver Serpent. Indeed, after tonight he would make sure that the proper authorities were notified.

Still, there was tonight. A thrill ran through Georgie. How had the abducted Aunt Clare made her way to the theater? She would soon know. Georgie grabbed hold of the curtain to the box and drew it back. "Aunt Clare?"

Two male yelps arose as the men turned at Georgie's entrance. One lifted a pistol in a menacing gesture.

"St. Mary's night rail!" Georgie gasped. These were Aunt Clare's abductors and she without the money.

"Georgette!" Aunt Clare cried as she looked away from the opening scene. Hisses from the two boxes beside them arose. Aunt Clare whispered. "I mean, Georgie, isn't it now?"

"How did you know?" Tears welled up in Georgie's eyes. A large knot lodged in her throat. Aunt Clare *was* alive. She was the dearest sight in the world. "I . . . I have been so worried for you."

"I am sorry, dear. Things did get quite muddled. Do pray have a seat." Aunt Clare waved to a chair. "This is Nick and Ned, dear. Do you know that the Silver Serpent is going to try and kill the prince tonight?"

"Tonight?" Georgie forgot the pistol in the lad's hand. She forgot all the other questions, too. Such as who were Nick and Ned? She entered the crowded box. Sir Percy meowed as she stepped on his tail. "Forgive me, Sir Percy." She forged her way to the front and leaned over to look over at Lucas's box. He had his glasses trained upon them. She waved at him. Cupping her hands and lifting them to her mouth she whispered. "It is tonight."

This drew censure from the five boxes between them. Georgie broke into a relieved smile as Lucas nodded and stood. He offered her a bow and a sardonic grin, and he departed.

"Where is he going?" Nick asked.

"I am not sure." Georgie felt better already. "But he understood."

"Dear me, I wish we had a better view of the stage than this." Aunt Clare sighed.

"Why?" Georgie asked in concern. "Do you think Desard will shoot from there? Shall I return to backstage?"

"No, I just thought the boys would enjoy the play better," Aunt Clare said. She frowned. "Who is Desard, dear?"

"He is the Silver Serpent. Leonard Desard." Georgie repeated it, mulling over it for the hundredth time. "Whoever he might be."

"You discovered his name?" Aunt Clare beamed at Georgie. "How very smart of you, dear."

"There he is!" Nick hissed and pointed a finger down into the pit.

"The Silver Serpent?" Georgie leaned over and studied the man he pointed toward. She blinked. She had seen the silver-haired man with his lace before. "Why, he's the barkeep from the Hangman Inn."

"He's François," Nick said.

"He's a barkeep, thief, *and* spy." Ned nodded. "No flies on him."

"Except he locked us up." Nick frowned.

"And he made Aunt Clare cry," Ned added.

"What?" Georgie exclaimed.

"I see him, boys." Aunt Clare stood and this time she leaned over the box. Her whispered voice rang out nicely to the tenor who spoke from the stage. "Yohooe, François! Up here!"

François, the barkeep-thief-spy, stiffened. He looked toward them. So did half of the audience in the pit. He didn't appear to be overly pleased to see Aunt Clare flagging him.

"Yoicks!" Nick swung his divining finger to the far right of the pit. "Burt's here."

"Bad." Ned shook his head. "Escaped again."

"Burt?" Georgie narrowed her eyes to see the man thumping ruthlessly through the crowd, his gaze trained upon them as he knocked about all and sundry with a crutch. His features were rather rearranged with plaster and bruises, but Georgie recognized him. "He's from the Boar's Head Inn! Gracious, what has happened to him?"

"Keeps following us," Nick said darkly.

"Bad. Bad." Ned nodded.

"Leonard Desard, dear!" Aunt Clare called out in a higher pitch. A booming baritone was striving to deliver his lines over Aunt Clare. He failed and she won. The man François' face lit with knowledge. He stood. Aunt Clare rather sang, "Watch out for Burt, dear!"

Georgie blinked and looked back to the innkeeper, who evidently wanted to go after the barkeeper. Only, the innkeeper was no longer moving, which should have pleased those about him. Except for the slight man who appeared to have his foot underneath the large, frozen man.

"Clare!" A new voice was heard, a full rumble over the leading lady's less-than-strong mezzo-soprano. It came from the Prince Regent's box. Georgie looked over. Lord Wrexton had stood up, his hand shielding his eyes. "What the devil?"

Clare lifted her hand to peer back. "Bendford is here. Oh dear, why is he here?"

"He is with the diplomatic group that the Prince is hosting tonight," Georgie murmured.

"My Georgie, you are aware of everything . . . bang up to the mark." Aunt Clare waved to her brother. Considering the thunderous expression on his face, it was fortunate he was across the theater from them.

"Your friend is waving to you," Georgie said, still fascinated with those in the pit. Lord Wrexton was generally in a thunderous mood after all.

"What?" Aunt Clare looked back. François didn't only wave at her, but he blew her a kiss and offered a courtly leg, to the displeasure of all those about him.

"Gracious," Georgie said.

"He—he understands," Aunt Clare said, a brilliant blush rising to her cheeks. Even in the dimness it was apparent. "And he's pleased, I believe."

"Watch the boxes," François sang back in quite a nice tenor. Then he weaved his way through the crowd.

"Where's he going?" Nick asked.

"Running from Burt?" Ned said.

"No." Georgie frowned. The frozen Burt at last came to life to the relief of the small man whose foot had been pinned beneath the walloping big boot of the innkeeper. He whirled and pushed his way through the crowd. "It's Burt that is running away."

"Why he is," Aunt Clare exclaimed. "How queer."

"Odd." Nick said.

"Rum," Ned said. "Very rum."

"Do you think your François is going to the Prince?" Georgie asked. She had a suspicion that that would be Lucas's destination.

"Perhaps." Aunt Clare stood. "We must watch the boxes, Georgie."

"Oh yes." Georgie dutifully turned her gaze to them. She was surprised to discover that most playgoers in the boxes were watching each other rather than devoting their attention to the play. Her gaze roamed past one of the few empty boxes and then turned back as the curtain to it moved. She started as Jeb, the stagehand, entered the box. "What *is* he doing?"

"Who, dear?" Aunt Clare asked.

Georgie pointed. "Jeb. He won't have enough time to get back to the wings. He has to bring the curtain down for the close of the act." She sucked in a shocked breath. "Oh dear, I think he means to bring something else down." Jeb quietly withdrew a pistol from behind the curtain. "He's Desard."

"So he is," Aunt Clare said, her voice excited. "You were right, Nick. That pistol will come in handy."

"Yoicks! Bad notion." Nick shoved the pistol over to Ned. "You do it."

"Can't," Ned said.

"Oh dear!" Georgie watched in horror as Leonard Desard lifted his pistol and aimed. "Stop!"

Jeb, *née* Leonard Desard, didn't seem to listen. He

aimed, even while others about them gasped and shouted.

"Saint Mary's night rail!" Georgie grabbed the pistol away from Ned. She aimed it. How she wished she had Lucas's arms about her. That fleeting thought traced through her mind just before she fired the pistol. Her bullet went wide and plowed into the plaster to the side of Jeb's box. He started. People turned and pointed at him, shrieking. He lowered his own pistol and darted back through the box's curtain.

"Missed him!" Nick said. Quite unnecessarily in Georgie's opinion.

"By a mile." Ned nodded.

"But the prince is safe." Aunt Clare beamed. "How famous!" Amidst the shrieks and cries, Georgie turned her gaze toward the Prince's box. Frightful to admit it, but it wasn't in concern for the Prince. She needed to see Lucas. Her heart failed her. He wasn't among the gesturing group in the box.

"Unless that fellow nips around," Nick said then.

"Something Burt would do," Ned admitted.

The four of them departed their box before another shriek from the audience arose.

Lucas slowed as he approached the Prince's box. Another man advanced from the other direction.

"My lord, we must proceed with caution," the man called out softly.

Lucas halted and frowned. "Do I know you?"

The man nodded. "I am François. Or 'the Comte,' if you will."

"You!" Lucas frowned.

"Yes, me." He shrugged. "I see you are not happy to see me. But then again, I was not happy with you before this either. But enough. We must work together."

"Must we?" Lucas asked dryly.

"Desard will be amongst the party in there," François said. "I have not seen him for many years, but this I know."

"And how do you know that?"

"Desard uses the knife. He must always be close to his victim, *n'est ce pas?* His brother Leonard assassinates with the gun." François frowned. "I do not like Clare to be in the audience."

"God. Georgie is too."

"Alors." He forced a grin. "Let us say we will pity Leonard and not our ladies. Now, how to proceed. Desard most always waits for his chance after Leonard takes his. Between the two of them, they do not fail. Me, I think Desard will not kill within the box. His escape would be . . ."

A roar of noise came from behind the curtain to the prince's box.

"Bien, we do not need to decide," François observed before the curtain to the box was flung wide. The diplomatic cortege spewed out.

Lucas couldn't move fast enough. Lord Wrexton plowed into him.

"Heh?" Lord Wrexton stared at him. "There you are, boy. What the devil is going on?" The Prince Regent, surrounded by his guard, came from the box. "Where is Clare?"

"Him, monsieur!" François immediately dove for a particular diplomat. The man sprang back. In a flash he had a knife within his hands.

The stunned guards began to merge upon the two.

"Stay where you are," Lucas ordered.

"Listen to him, dolts!" Bendford Wrexton ordered.

"Yes, men," Prinny said. It was delivered more as a

royal sanction than anything else. The guards had drawn to attention at Lord Wrexton's bellow.

Guards and diplomats all stepped back, permitting François and Desard to circle each other.

"Desard." François smiled. "I suppose you wouldn't wish to surrender?"

"You will go to hell with me, Comte," the man answered.

"Blast and damn," Lord Wrexton said, peering at them. "Is that you, Count?"

"Yes, Lord Wrexton," François said. He darted forward, feinted to the left suddenly, and grabbed Desard's wrist as he swung by the angry man. The knife went flying.

"Good move," Prinny said. "Place a monkey on your count, Bendford."

"Ain't my count," Bendford muttered. "Though I won't take it. Desard's a slow top. Knew it from the beginning."

"Mon Dieu!" Desard gasped. "I hate the English!"

"Non," François returned, twisting the man's arm from behind. "They are *fort amusant.* Better than French peasants."

"François!" Aunt Clare's voice called from down the hall. "Oh, François!"

"Mon ange!" François said, his voice desperate. Desard, just as desperate, but for another reason, broke from François at that moment.

"Lucas!" Georgie's voice called.

"Georgie!" Lucas dove for Desard and brought him down. He shied a bruising blow to the man's chin, knocking him out cold.

"Unsporting, old man." Prinny frowned.

"The ladies come, Your Highness," François returned.

"A shame." Prinny waved to his guards. "Do take

care of the fellow. Clear him away. We do have the frailer sex to consider."

The guards converged upon the fallen Desard. Lucas rolled from him and stood upright. Georgie and Aunt Clare, followed by two young men, raced down the hall. Lucas suddenly recognized the two in tow. They were the two from the Hangman Inn.

"François dear!" Aunt Clare dashed up to the count. She flung herself into his arms and he willingly held her close.

"Ma chérie!" François breathed it with open adoration. He kissed her reverently.

"Clare!" Lord Wrexton roared. "What in blazes are you doing?"

"Oh, dear." Aunt Clare pulled away from François. Reproach filled her eyes. "I forgot. You are no longer 'my dear'!"

"Then who is he?" Georgie entered directly into the question. She merely looked at Lucas, flushing. So much for a hero's welcome from her. Lucas forced himself not to draw her into his arms and kiss her wildly.

"I'll tell you who he is," Lord Wrexton said. "He's a man you are to have nothing to do with, Clare Wrexton. Do you hear? I'll not have it. And get out of his arms, blast it. You are too old to be acting like Haymarket fare."

"Do not poke at age, Wrexton," Prinny said. "We like it in a lady."

"Yoicks. The Prince," Nick observed then. He promptly bowed to the ground.

"Alive too." Ned bowed just as low.

Lucas grinned as Aunt Clare and Georgie took due note and curtsied their lowest. Sir Percy meowed and lowered his ears, obsequious for him, to be sure.

Prinny frowned. "Cats should not attend the theater."

"Forgive me, Your Highness," Aunt Clare said. "But I could not leave Sir Percy unattended. He falls into scrapes when I do."

"Sir Percy? We are sure we have not knighted a cat. Not even in our cups."

"He saved my life, Your Highness," Aunt Clare said solemnly. "He is a very valiant and noble cat. I did not think you would mind very much."

"Very well. But he must not attend the theater again. Nor will he be listed in the peerage." Prinny laughed at his own cleverness and waved his hand. "Now we want the original question answered, Count. Who are you?"

François gently released Clare. He offered his own courtly leg. "I am François Gerard, Comte De Chevalier, Your Highness."

"François," Clare cried. "You lied to me about that too."

"He's a fool, Clare," Lord Wrexton cried.

"He saved our life," Prinny said. "He can't be a fool for that."

"Ah, my Juliet," François said softly, his eyes bright and longing.

"She's Aunt Clare." Nick frowned.

"Thought you knew that," Ned said.

"No. She's my 'Juliet.' " François smiled. "Yes, *mon amour,* I lied about that too. Your brother, he does not care for me. And me, I do not care for him. You see, the families feud."

"But you could have told me that," Aunt Clare said. "You could have told me you were a count. You lied."

"*Non.*" François shook his head. "I never once said I was too lowborn to wed you, *ma chère.* I told you I was too poor."

Aunt Clare blinked. "You are right." She stepped back from him. "It does not matter. You were truthful, yes. But not honest. A true love should be both."

"That's it. Send the cad packing," Lord Wrexton said, with approval. "You're a widgeon, but not that much of one. Don't have a thing to do with him."

"I won't." Clare teared. "He is no longer my true love."

"Ma chérie." François' voice pleaded.

Clare sniffed. "You went away and put guards at my door."

"Did he?" Lucas laughed. Georgie frowned at him.

"For your own protection, *mon petit chou,"* François said. "I was wrong. I did need your help tonight. You were marvelous."

". . . If that nasty Burt hadn't knocked them out." Aunt Clare continued as if she hadn't heard. "And if Nick and Ned hadn't been so very brave and then knocked him out . . ."

"Did you?" François asked Nick and Ned. "Well done, boys. Bravo."

"Who is this nasty Burt? We demand to know," Prinny asked.

"Our stepbrother," Nick said.

"Very bad man." Ned nodded.

"Wonder where he went." Nick frowned and started peering about. "Best be careful."

"Might circle around." Ned nodded.

"Gracious. Just like Leonard Desard." Georgie flushed. "We forgot about him."

"You mean Leonard." Lucas laughed as Georgie's eyes widened. He pointed to the limp man that the guards were hauling up. "That is Desard."

"Gracious." Aunt Clare blinked.

"They are brothers, *ma chère."* François nodded solemnly. "Leonard prefers the pistol. Desard . . . the knife."

"I shot at Leonard," Georgie said.

"She did, Lucas. It was famous," Aunt Clare said proudly. "He was aiming a pistol and she shot at him."

"You did?" Lucas exclaimed. Pride and fear washed over him.

Georgie nodded. "I think I'd rather learn to paint."

"Truly?" Lucas chuckled.

"We are becoming more confused," Prinny said with a cheerful tone. "Who are you, pray tell?"

"I am Miss Georgie Thompson." Georgie flushed. "I am the late Baron Theodopholus Thompson's daughter. You would not know him. Or me, Your Highness."

"We do not." He smiled. A rose blush covered Georgie's cheeks, and her gaze turned starry-eyed. Jealousy shot through Lucas. No matter his girth, the Prince Regent still possessed the charm of his earlier days when he was known as handsome Prince Florizel. He also still possessed an eye for beautiful women of any age. "You saved us then, our loyal and lovely subject."

"Your Highness!" Another voice called out. Lucas froze. Isabelle rushed from down the other hall. She curtsied low. "You are safe, thank God."

"Yes?" He lifted his brow.

Isabelle rose from her curtsy. "Lucas . . . I mean the earl and I have been working steadily these past few days to uncover this dreadful plot." She cast Lucas a warm glance as if the last scene they had played out had never happened.

"Another beautiful and loyal subject," Prinny drawled. "We admire all our loyal subjects' efforts, but why were we not warned of this before tonight. Not only might we have been killed, which we would have disliked excessively, but a performance of one of our favorite plays has been ruined."

Lucas tensed, studying Isabelle. She gazed at him, lifting her chin. She was clearly daring him.

"Forgive us, Your Highness." It was Georgie who spoke very softly. "We did not have enough proof until a few hours ago. And we did not know it was to be tonight."

"I did approach Lord Darrimple," François said. "However, he did not believe me. He thought I created a story in order to ruin Lord Wrexton's mission."

"You said Darrimple did believe you," Aunt Clare cried. "Oh, François. I knew something was wrong . . ."

"Premonition." Nick nodded.

"That's it." Ned nodded.

"But I didn't know you had lied to me so completely." She sucked in her breath, her eyes widening. "Gracious. I never knew a heart could break so many times in a few hours."

"Mon ange. Forgive me," François said. "I was a fool. I wished to protect you."

"I'll at least give that to you, Chevalier," Lord Wrexton said. "Looks like you tried to keep a rein on Clare. Don't know what's gotten into her, but it's going to have to stop or my name isn't Bendford Wrexton. Ever since . . ." He halted and harrumphed. "Well, won't go into that. But she's kicked over the traces one too many times. Always gallivanting about, going where she oughtn't." He looked sternly at his sister. "This mission has been botched. I'll be remaining in town, Clare. You and your cats can move back to the house tonight. But I warn you, it is time for you to stop your totty-headed transports and bubbleheaded schemes."

"Yes, Bendford." Clare nodded. Her tone dutiful, she would not look at anyone. "I am sorry . . ."

"*Non!*" François stiffened. "You are not sorry, *ma belle*. Do not say that to him."

"I . . ." Clare looked at him, a sad defeat in every feature.

"*Non.* Marry me!"

"What?" Lord Bendford cried. "Hear now!"

"Marry me. I left you to save you from a life I thought not good enough for you. Still, life with me must be better. No man shall treat you like that. I am poor . . ."

"Ha. See he admits it. You cannot marry him," Lord Wrexton said. "I forbid it. He's a landless Frenchie, Clare."

"He saved our life, Wrexton," Prinny said. "We shall honor him with a title and lands."

"Your Highness! What?" Lord Wrexton exclaimed. "That . . ." He halted, turning blue in the face.

"Marry me, sweet Juliet," François said. "I shall be truthful and honest forevermore."

"Oh, my Romeo." Clare smiled. "Yes. I will marry you."

"Clare. You can't," Lord Wrexton tried again.

"Wrexton, don't be a clunch," Prinny said. "We shall give them our permission and our blessing."

"Thank you, Your Highness, but I would prefer if you did not." Clare beamed at him and curtsied.

"Madame?" Prinny's brow rose.

"Mademoiselle means that she shall wait for her brother's change of heart first," François said, his lips twitching. He reached for her hand. "Is that not what you mean, sweet Juliet?"

"Oh yes." Clare nodded and put her hands in his with the sweetest of expressions. "That is what I meant."

"Don't look like the type." Nick eyed Lord Wrexton up and down. "Won't have a change of heart."

"Crusty." Ned nodded.

The Prince said. "We agree."

"What?" Lord Wrexton exclaimed.

"Wrexton, don't bellow at us." The Prince laughed. "You are indispensable to us, but you are crusty."

"Needs love," Nick said, his eyes widening.

"That's the ticket!" Ned nodded.

François placed a kiss on Clare's hand. *"Ma chérie,* you teach us all. Our united love is still denied, but we shall be brave. *Oui?* Come, we take too much of His Royal Highness's time."

"No, no." Prinny waved it away good-naturedly. "We missed the play. We wish for entertainment."

"In that case"—Georgie drew in her breath—"please, Your Highness?"

"Yes?" Prinny looked at her. "Miss Thompson, is it?"

"If Lucas . . . I mean the earl st—still wishes to m—marry me, I—I would like to marry him, with your permission."

"Georgie!" Lucas looked at her. She offered him the most hesitant of smiles. "Would you?"

"No!" Isabelle's eyes blazed. "You cannot!"

"Why can we not give our permission? Do you question this?" Prinny asked.

Isabelle glared first at Lucas. Then at Georgie. She lowered her gaze. "Forgive me, Your Highness. I spoke out of turn."

"That you did." Prinny nodded, turning cold and haughty. He looked at Georgie. "Continue, Miss Thompson."

Lucas tensed. Georgie nodded. "I know he is above my touch . . . very far above my touch, Your Highness."

"We agree."

"And he could marry someone far m—more prominent."

"We know this."

Georgie peeked at him. "I did shoot at Leonard, Your Highness."

"She missed," Nick said.

"By a mile," Ned said.

The Prince quizzed, "What do you have to say to that, Miss Thompson?"

Georgie chewed upon her lip. "I need more practice?"

Prinny barked a laugh. "Beware, Montieth. She is a fire-eater."

"Indeed, Your Highness." Lucas smiled, rather bemused.

"I know I am." Georgie dragged in her breath, clearly taking that as an insult. "But Lucas . . . Lucas vowed he'd not marry anyone. That wouldn't do either, Your Highness. He would turn into . . . well, it would simply not do."

"True. He might become as crusty as old Wrexton here." The Prince's eyes twinkled. "However, you have shot wide of your mark again, Miss Thompson."

"Your Highness?'

"We were going to give you permission before. But now you have reminded us."

"Of what, Your Highness?" Lucas tensed.

"We have not seen you in society this past year." Prinny frowned. "We have not seen you take your seat in the House of Lords." He looked at Georgie. "If we give permission to this marriage, Miss Thompson, we will expect you to insure that Montieth enters society once more."

Georgie bit her lip. Lucas knew that look. He lowered his voice. "This is no time to pound deal, Georgie."

"I know." She hissed back. "But the *ton* will not care for me."

"We approve of you, Miss Thompson." Prinny lifted his brow.

She finally smiled. "Very well. Adams says that one can become accustomed to wealth and power if one must."

"Who is Adams?" the Regent asked.

"Lucas's butler," Georgie said.

That brought laughter from him. *"Pon rep,* now we must give approval. The butler has sanctioned it." The Prince looked at Lucas. "We have come into agreement with Montieth and the Fire-Eater. What have you to say?"

"I would not wish to disappoint my butler, Your Highness," Lucas said solemnly. He smiled. "I also love the Fire-Eater with all my heart."

"We approve." The Prince laughed. "You shall raise valiant and loyal subjects for us, we expect."

"Oh, François," Aunt Clare said. "Isn't it wonderful? My last boy is going to be married. I have made restitution to them all now."

"Faith, you and your infernal boys, Clare." Lord Bendford growled. "That's what started this all, be damn."

"No, Bendford dear," Aunt Clare's gaze was upon François. "Love is what started it all, dear."

Georgie giggled and tucked her hand in Lucas's. "And love will finish it."

Fourteen

"Enough." Lucas chuckled, turning his lips away. "You, Madame Wife, must move to the other seat."

"No. I shall behave." Georgie cast Lucas a teasing glance from under her lashes. She snuggled into his arms, enjoying his warm embrace and the lull of the rocking coach. Memories took her back to the first time they had kissed in a coach. She giggled. She had thought Lucas didn't *want* to kiss her. Now as an experienced matron of a month, she knew much better. She sighed in delight. "Though it will be difficult."

"Prinny was right. You are a fire-eater." Lucas nuzzled her ear, no doubt to take the sting out of his words. "I would love you no matter what, dear Georgie, for all your other fine qualities. I admit, however, that I am glad that you love this as much as you do all other things."

"Mm. I do." Georgie kissed him, that famous feeling of breathless excitement welling within her. "I am ever so glad for your instruction, Lucas."

"You are not behaving as you promised, madame." Lucas groaned.

"But I will," Georgie murmured. "You distracted me."

His eyes lit up with amusement and love. "Hie thee

to the other seat. I'll lay you odds that your toes are curling at this very moment."

"Lucas!" Georgie blushed. They were indeed curling. Embarrassed, she scrambled to the other side of the coach.

They both looked at each other and broke out into laughter.

Lucas's sherry-colored eyes turned golden amber with emotion. It was something Georgie had discovered within her new husband and particularly enjoyed. "I shall be forever grateful, Georgie, that you decided to ask Prinny for my hand. Eternally grateful. Though it still astonishes me."

"I think I astonished myself too. Only, the duchess appeared so very conniving at that moment. I couldn't see you loving her for the rest of your life."

"She was far more conniving than you would ever imagine. You spiked her guns without even knowing it."

Georgie refrained from comment. Lucas had told her one evening about what had truly transpired between him and Isabelle that afternoon. He had spoken of it of his own free will. Georgie had still not confessed that she had seen part of it, and had misinterpreted it. Perhaps after twenty more years she would confess. "Yes."

His gaze turned serious. "Will you mind giving up that cottage by the sea?"

"No. I had realized that it would be frightfully dull without you long before that night."

"Did you?" Lucas grinned. "I promise you, Georgie, I will do all that I can to make life within my paltry establishment exciting, so that you never hanker after that cottage. I know what you have given up for me."

"You are roasting me." Georgie drew in her breath.

"I must thank you for this month. I never thought to see Italy and Spain, Lucas."

"Every true artist should," Lucas said, his tone grave. His smile twisted. "You are frightened of returning here to England and entering society like you promised the Prince."

"I am not!" Georgie objected.

"Of course not." Lucas nodded. "Come here."

Georgie gladly obeyed. Once she had settled into his arms again, she sighed. "Very well. I am." His eyes laughed at her. "Just slightly."

"Do not be." Lucas hugged her close. "I promise it will be our best adventure ever."

"Yes." Everything eased within Georgie. She knew then that he was right. She had been looking at it entirely wrong. "I do believe it will be."

"The first thing we shall do when we arrive, though," Lucas said, "is to settle the impasse between Lord Wrexton and Aunt Clare."

"I still do not understand why Aunt Clare and François did not apply to the Prince that evening."

"I do not know." Lucas frowned. "But I am sure that Aunt Clare had a scheme in mind. She always does. But if not, we will manage to bring it about. It would only be right. After all, she brought us together."

"Hm, yes." Georgie kissed him. Lucas returned the kiss with new fire. Every time, a kiss shared between them was different, expanding, wondrous.

A shot rang out and the coach jerked to a halt. Georgie, if not anchored in Lucas's arms so firmly, would have toppled to the coach floor. As it was, they merely hit their teeth against each other.

"Ouch!" Georgie gasped.

"Confound it," Lucas muttered.

"Stand and deliver!" a voice shouted from outside

the coach. "You, coachman, get down from there with yer hands up!"

"What?" Georgie blinked and stared at Lucas.

"Trump is developing a backbone it seems." Lucas raised his brow. "This tour has been good for him."

Georgie smiled. "Did you do this, Lucas?"

"No, I own I wish I had. I imagine Aunt Clare did. Shall we, dear?"

"Of course." Georgie scrabbled off him, and quite by habit, she permitted Lucas to descend from the coach before her. His eyes sparkled as he assisted her out. When she looked at the highwayman who had demanded them to stand and deliver, she knew why. "Mr. Ferret!"

"Hello there, Countess." Mr. Ferret grinned from ear to ear. Gone was his odious large freeze coat. He flaunted the flashiest of black satin outfits. Golden lace dripped from his cuffs. He leveled a magnificent and very ornate pistol upon them. "Yer coachman piked off, you know."

"He does that in times of danger." Lucas nodded.

"He shouldn't be working fer you then, gov," Mr. Ferret said.

"I keep him for sentimental reasons." Lucas took hold of Georgie's hand. "May I ask why you are holding us up, Mr. Ferret. Are you not out of your er, ken? Or lay?"

"It's both, my lord." Mr. Ferret grinned. "This here is just a friendly welcome back ter England."

"Aunt Clare must have sent you." Georgie smiled. "How sweet of her."

"Ain't yer Aunt Clare. She and the Chevalier are off traveling the countryside pretending to be tinkers. Don't know when those two will appear." He pulled a face. "Or what they'll be playing at next."

"Really?" Georgie asked.

"It's all above board." Mr. Ferret nodded. "I'm supposed to let yer know. Leg-shackled, they is. Tied the knot right and proper."

"Have they?" Lucas exclaimed. "We were just thinking about how to get them married."

"Ain't as knowing as ye ought ter be, Earl. She and the count was only waiting fer you two te get shackled properlike. Then they ran off to Gretna Green just like she always wanted ter. Heard from Nick and Ned that the ceremony was spanking."

"Oh my!" Georgie gasped.

"That is why she didn't want the Prince's approval." Lucas chuckled. "He would never have accepted a runaway marriage."

"They are traveling about now in . . . er . . . cognito. All those noble blokes of hers are going ter work on the Prince so he ain't miffed." He grinned. "Now there's a job fer you, gov."

"Certainly," Lucas said. "Georgie and I will do all we can."

"And ye better set yer mind to a proper wedding gift fer them, I'm warning you. Or you'll be put in the shade. Truth, I think that's why the Prince has his nose out of joint anyhow. He only gave the Chevalier a manor, a pile'a bricks mind ye, and a baronetcy. Whilst that Earl of Raleigh and his countess gave them a castle with a ghost in it. It's suppose ter have hidden passages, too. That's what I call downright handy."

"Faith, we must strive to do better than that." Lucas laughed.

"That's the ticket, gov." He waved his pistol. "Now, hand over the dibs."

"You are not truly going to rob us, are you?" Georgie asked indignantly. "I thought you said Nick and Ned sent you."

Mr. Ferret grimaced. "Yer right. Only reforming

ain't that easy as ye would think. Now Nick and Ned have taken ter it like ducks ter water. And I appreciate working for them much better than I did fer old Burt. I just thought if'n you had some ready you didn't need it'd be good fer fixin' up the True Love Inn."

"True Love Inn?" Georgie blinked.

Mr. Ferret's bony chest puffed out. "That's what Nick and Ned have named it, now that old Burt stuck his spoon in the wall and the Prince gave them the inn. The Prince said since Burt killed that Leonard bloke, even though that Leonard bloke killed him back, that Nick and Ned could keep the inn as next of kin."

"Very fitting." Lucas nodded.

"Bet old Burt is spinning in his grave. As he should, the old blighter." Mr. Ferret shrugged. "Least he did one good thing in his life. Killed that traitor. 'Course it's only cause he'd double-crossed the traitor. Ha, traitor to a traitor. Queer how they came across each other like that. Guess it was er . . . what do you calls it?"

"Poetic justice?" Lucas asked.

"That's it." Mr. Ferret nodded. "You wait tills you see the inn. Nick and Ned are taking over Aunt Clare's matchmaking business, you know. Or leastways, they are going ter be her apprentices."

"You don't say." Lucas chuckled.

"Why that is famous," Georgie said with approval.

"Guess who they want ter go to work on first?" Mr. Ferret asked.

"I cannot imagine," Lucas said.

Georgie frowned. "Neither can I."

"That crusty old Lord Wrexton. That's who!" Mr. Ferret hooted his enjoyment.

His hoot was cut short, however, as another shot rang out. The three looked up as another man rode down upon them. His horse was mangy, his attire soiled, and his face young and angry. "Halt! Stand and deliver!"

"Wait ho. I just did that, young cawker." Mr. Ferret frowned. "What do you mean by horning in on me? Who hired you?"

"No one hired me. I work for meself." The lad cocked his pistol. "This is my stretch of the highway. And them, by rights, should be my victims."

Mr. Ferret shook his head. "Bejesus, if this here popper was real I would have blown yer head orf, you young fool." He looked to Georgie and Lucas. "You don't have my favorite equipment with you, do ye?"

"No." Georgie shook her head. "I am sorry."

"Very well." Mr. Ferret sighed. He narrowed a squinty look upon the irate would-be highwayman. "You and me should have a talk then, lad. What's yer name?"

Lucas wrapped his arm about Georgie. He cocked a brow. "Do you feel better about returning to England now, dear?"

"Oh yes." Georgie laughed. She lifted her arms up to him. "Our adventures are just beginning, are they not?"

"That's the ticket. The dandy. Or whatever you will, dear Georgie." Lucas lowered his lips to hers. He proceeded to kiss her with an utter lack of propriety.

Georgie's knees weakened and she clung to him. Those marvelous sensations whirled through her. Through the glorious heat of them, she heard Mr. Ferret's voice.

"Stop gawking at them, boy. They're still on their honeymoon. You can try and steal the dibs from them later. Though I warn ye, those two are a dangerous pair, they are. You might want ter throw in yer hand with me. My partners and I have a new lay."

More Zebra Regency Romances

__A Taste for Love__ by Donna Bell　　　　　$4.99US/$6.50CAN
　　0-8217-6104-8

__An Unlikely Father__ by Lynn Collum　　　　$4.99US/$6.99CAN
　　0-8217-6418-7

__An Unexpected Husband__ by Jo Ann Ferguson　$4.99US/$6.99CAN
　　0-8217-6481-0

__Wedding Ghost__ by Cindy Holbrook　　　　　$4.99US/$6.50CAN
　　0-8217-6217-6

__Lady Diana's Darlings__ by Kate Huntington　$4.99US/$6.99CAN
　　0-8217-6655-4

__A London Flirtation__ by Valerie King　　　$4.99US/$6.99CAN
　　0-8217-6535-3

__Lord Langdon's Tutor__ by Laura Paquet　　$4.99US/$6.99CAN
　　0-8217-6675-9

__Lord Mumford's Minx__ by Debbie Raleigh　　$4.99US/$6.99CAN
　　0-8217-6673-2

__Lady Serena's Surrender__ by Jeanne Savery　$4.99US/$6.99CAN
　　0-8217-6607-4

__A Dangerous Dalliance__ by Regina Scott　　$4.99US/$6.99CAN
　　0-8217-6609-0

__Lady May's Folly__ by Donna Simpson　　　　$4.99US/$6.99CAN
　　0-8217-6805-0

Call toll free **1-888-345-BOOK** to order by phone or use this coupon to order by mail.

Name_____

Address_____

City_____ State_____ Zip_____

Please send me the books I have checked above.

I am enclosing $_____

Plus postage and handling* $_____

Sales tax (in New York and Tennessee only) $_____

Total amount enclosed $_____

*Add $2.50 for the first book and $.50 for each additional book.

Send check or money order (no cash or CODs) to:

Kensington Publishing Corp., 850 Third Avenue, New York, NY 10022

Prices and numbers subject to change without notice.

All orders subject to availability.

Check out our website at **www.kensingtonbooks.com.**

The Queen of Romance

Cassie Edwards

Celebrate Romance with one of Today's Hotest Authors
Meagan McKinney

I think the author was trying to grand finale to her trilogy, but over did it.

Discover The Magic of Romance With

Jo Goodman